Praise for #1 *New York Times* bestselling author

LAURELL K. HAMILTON

"What *The Da Vinci Code* did for the religious thriller, the Anita Blake series has done for the vampire novel." —*USA Today*

"Hamilton remains one of the most inventive and exciting writers in the paranormal field."
—Charlaine Harris, *New York Times* bestselling author

Praise for *New York Times* bestselling author

YASMINE GALENORN

"A powerhouse author; a master of the craft who is taking the industry by storm, and for good reason!"
—Maggie Shayne, *New York Times* bestselling author

"Galenorn's kick-butt fae ramp up the action in a wyrd world gone awry!" —Patricia Rice, author of *Mystic Guardian*

Praise for *New York Times* bestselling author

MARJORIE M. LIU

"Readers of early Laurell K. Hamilton [and] Charlaine Harris . . . should try Liu now and catch a rising star." —*Publishers Weekly*

"The boundlessness of Liu's imagination never ceases to amaze."
—*Booklist*

Praise for national bestselling author

SHARON SHINN

"Shinn is a master." —Mary Jo Putney

"Sharon Shinn's books have been on my comfort shelf ever since *Archangel* came out." —Anne McCaffrey

NEVER AFTER

LAURELL K. HAMILTON
YASMINE GALENORN
MARJORIE M. LIU
SHARON SHINN

BERKLEY BOOKS, NEW YORK

THE BERKLEY PUBLISHING GROUP
Published by the Penguin Group
Penguin Group (USA) Inc.
375 Hudson Street, New York, New York 10014, USA
Penguin Group (Canada), 90 Eglinton Avenue East, Suite 700, Toronto, Ontario M4P 2Y3, Canada
(a division of Pearson Penguin Canada Inc.)
Penguin Books Ltd., 80 Strand, London WC2R 0RL, England
Penguin Group Ireland, 25 St. Stephen's Green, Dublin 2, Ireland (a division of Penguin Books Ltd.)
Penguin Group (Australia), 250 Camberwell Road, Camberwell, Victoria 3124, Australia
(a division of Pearson Australia Group Pty. Ltd.)
Penguin Books India Pvt. Ltd., 11 Community Centre, Panchsheel Park, New Delhi—110 017, India
Penguin Group (NZ), 67 Apollo Drive, Rosedale, North Shore 0632, New Zealand
(a division of Pearson New Zealand Ltd.)
Penguin Books (South Africa) (Pty.) Ltd., 24 Sturdee Avenue, Rosebank, Johannesburg 2196, South Africa

Penguin Books Ltd., Registered Offices: 80 Strand, London WC2R 0RL, England

Cover art by Don Sipley.
Cover design by Annette Fiore Defex.

PRINTING HISTORY
Jove premium edition / November 2009
Berkley trade paperback edition / October 2010

Library of Congress Cataloging-in-Publication Data

Never after / Laurell K. Hamilton . . . [et al.].—Berkley trade pbk. ed.
p. cm.
ISBN 978-0-425-23832-5
1. Fantasy fiction, American. 2. Man-woman relationships—Fiction. 3. Betrothal—Fiction. 4. Princesses—Fiction. 5. Magic—Fiction. I. Hamilton, Laurell K.
PS648.F3N48 2010
813'.0876608—dc22

2010014354

PRINTED IN THE UNITED STATES OF AMERICA

10 9 8 7 6 5 4 3 2 1

CONTENTS

Can He Bake a Cherry Pie?

LAURELL K. HAMILTON

The Earl of Chillswoth was a pervert, and everyone knew it. Elinore knew it, and the sensation of his age-spotted hand over her pale young one frightened her more than anything had ever frightened her before, because the earl, though a known abuser of every kind of vice, was wealthy and well connected at court. Her father was neither of these things, because of the small matter of a disagreement with the current king's father about a war. The war was long over, the king's father long dead, but Elinore's father longed to regain his standing at court. It wasn't just for himself, he reasoned, but for his two sons. The fact that the price of saving the family reputation was his only daughter's health, happiness, and body didn't seem to bother her father. Elinore found that . . . disappointing.

He'd never been particularly affectionate, except in that absent way that fathers have, but she had thought, truly, that he loved her as a daughter. The fact that he had already agreed to marry her to the aging earl, with his hungry eyes and wet lips and overly familiar hands, without so much as, *I'm sorry, Elinore*, had made her realize that to her father, she was not real. She was not a son, and thus was only something to negotiate with, to use as a bribe, like land, or a fine horse. She was property. Legally, she knew she was, but she hadn't realized that her own father believed it.

Her mother had been deaf to her pleas, and even now sat smiling at the other end of the huge banquet table. It was the celebration for midsummer. It was a time of games, dancing, bright colors, and looking the other way when some of the young girls and men went off by themselves. Many a hurried marriage followed midsummer. Elinore had always been a good girl. She had refused all those handsome young men. She had been dutiful, and pure, and everything a daughter should be. She had her mother's long yellow hair; skin like milk that had never known a hard day in the sun. Her eyes were the color of cornflowers—by far her best feature, so her mother told her. She had her grandmother's eyes—again, so she was told. Her grandmother had been a great beauty in her day, but sadly stubborn. Elinore was even named after that lost ancestress. She'd always been very unlike the dead grandmother. She had been pliable, and look where all that good behavior had gotten her.

The Earl of Chillswoth—"Call me Donald"—leered down the table at her. He was sitting by her father, not because he had the highest rank, but because he was the highest in favor at the distant court of the king. She did not wish to call him Donald, and she did not wish to have her father announce to all that she would be the earl's fourth wife. Or was it fifth? Two of them had been as young as Elinore, and they had not lived to see twenty-five. One had died in childbirth, but no one wanted to talk about what happened to the last one. She'd heard whispers that the old man was becoming unable to perform, and so his desire of the flesh had turned to harder things. She did not understand everything that was meant by that sentence, but she understood enough to know that she did not want to be the earl's fourth, or fifth, wife.

Elinore would rather have lived as an old maid, done her sewing, overseen the cooking, and done what a good wife does. Their keep was small enough, and the time hard enough, that she could actually cook, and sew, and do all the things that made a woman's world. Many noble girls were fairly useless. Elinore liked to be busy, and because her desires were all women's work, no one had ever objected.

She herself had helped arrange the tails on the peacocks, stuffed and cooked and brought lifelike to the table. The head cook had said, "Begging the miss's pardon, but you have a fine eye and hand for the kitchen."

Elinore had taken that for the high praise it was, and not been insulted in the least. She loved the big kitchen, and would have spent more time there if her parents had allowed. She'd been mostly forgotten until she was too old to be mistaken for a little girl. Then, suddenly, it was time to find a husband.

If only she had gone with Bernie Woodstock last midsummer. He had asked her first, but she'd refused, and now he was married to Lucy of Aberly, and they had their first child. Bernie was heir to a fine estate, not as fine as their own, but he and

Lucy seemed happy enough, though the baby cried every time she visited. As Elinore watched her father call for silence, and begin to stand, how she wished, she *so* wished, she had gone off with Bernie last year. Once her father announced her engagement officially, it could not be undone without causing great disgrace to her family.

Elinore rose faster than her father, with his one bad knee from the long-ago war. She stood in the silence, and her father said, "Elinore, it is not necessary for you to stand."

"I wish to make an announcement, Father, a traditional announcement for midsummer." She spoke hurriedly, afraid her nerve would fail her.

Her father smiled indulgently at her, probably thinking she would do the traditional maiden's toast for this time of year, for she was still a maiden in every sense of the word.

"I will go rescue Prince True." It was an old saying now, older than the war that had gotten her father in trouble. It was more fairy tale now than truth to most people, for it had been more than fifty years since he vanished. But once, Prince True had been heir to the whole kingdom. Yet as often happens in fairy stories, he had been arrogant and unkind to women. He had declared that women's work was worthless, and only men, and their work, had value. One day, so the story went, a witch overheard him and challenged him to come to her cave. She told him she would prove to him that a woman was stronger than a man. He laughed at her. She accused him of cowardice, and, being a foolish prince, he went to accept her challenge. He was never seen again.

Many men tried to rescue him, but finally a body came back

with a note that read, "Only a woman's art can win the prince his freedom." For many years after that, noble houses that had two daughters, or more, would make one or two of them learn to be a man. They learned weapons, and riding, and hunting, and all the things that make a hero a hero. They would ride off in their armor, and never be seen alive again. You could go to the edge of the first moat and gaze down upon the armored skeletons, complete with horses, that had been dashed to their deaths on the rocks below.

No one had tried to rescue the prince in a long time, because his father was now dead, his brother on the throne, and there was an idea that even if a rescue worked, the current king might not welcome his eldest brother's return. But the idea that Prince True was held captive, young forever, tortured by the witch, would occasionally make some brave soul go out, and die.

Elinore had gazed upon the broken bodies once, with her brothers. She'd had nightmares for a week. But she knew the moment the earl cupped her breast with his horrible hand that she would rather die. She knew she could not run away, because her father would find her wherever she went, and anyone who helped her would be hurt. She'd learned that lesson from her cousin Matilda, who ran away once, and bore the scars on her back to this day. Matilda was married and the mother of three, but what had haunted Elinore was not the scars from the beating, but the death of the shepherd boy who had helped her cousin.

No, Elinore would endanger no one but herself, and a true suicide would mar her family's name. But if she went to rescue the prince, then she could die, not marry the earl, and not disgrace her family. It seemed a perfect plan, or as perfect as she could come up with on the spur of the moment.

"Elinore, sit down," her father said, in a tone that had quailed her since childhood. But that tone had lost its ability to frighten her. She had the earl to look at, and nothing her father could do was worse than that.

"I will rescue Prince True, or die in the effort, so I swear by my maid, mother, and crone. May the moon take me, if I lie, and the lightning of God strike any who try to prevent me from this most solemn duty." She said the last looking directly at her father, and for the first time ever, the look of her dead grandmother was on her face, and in the set of her shoulders. Elinore the Younger had found her backbone at last.

Elinore was not brave, but she was not stupid either. She turned from the banquet table and went for the door. She knew that if she did not go now, in front of all these witnesses, her father would stop her. He did not believe in the lightning of God striking the evil. If it did, or could, the earl would have died long ago. She would go now, tonight. It was high summer; the sun was still up, and would not set for hours. She would call for her horse, and she could be there by twilight, and be dead before dark. It was a plan, and it was the only plan she had, so she stuck to it. The trick about such plans is to keep moving, and not think too hard, because if she thought too hard, she might decide that life with the horrible earl would be preferable to death.

It became a parade. Other young nobles joined her on their horses, and in carriages. Her mother tried to dissuade her once, but Elinore gave her such a look that her mother dropped her hand away. Her mother had grown up with that look, out of those eyes, and knew that when the grandmother had that look, nothing could move her from her course. Elinore mounted her white horse, with its sidesaddle, and her mother began to plan the funeral of her only daughter.

Elinore rode at the head of the parade. They sang behind her, the old songs about the other princesses and noble princes who had died trying to rescue the true prince. There was the Lament of Prince Yosphier, very dirgelike. There was the bawdy drinking song of Princess Jasmine. That one always implied she'd run away and joined a circus, Elinore thought, though as she grew older she wasn't entirely sure that Jasmine was performing in a circus, after all. Then there was her favorite, Yellen's hymn to the prince. Yellen was a minor noble daughter, but she had gotten the farthest and pronounced the prince handsome and still young as the day he vanished.

Elinore listened to the musicians and the singing, and hoped they wrote something pretty for her. She made sure she sat the horse well, and let her long yellow hair free of its ribbons so that it flew out behind her, with her horse's white skin, and her pale yellow cloak that she had dyed herself. If she could not be brave, she hoped she made a pretty picture.

They came upon the bridge that crossed the first moat just as the sky was darkening, just at the beginning of twilight, as she had hoped. Elinore had always been a good judge of distances on horseback. If it had been more ladylike, she would've ridden more. Now she wished she had. She wished she had ridden her lovely white mare out in the sun, until her pale skin tanned like a peasant's, and men like the earl would have seen her as headstrong and not worth looking at. Oh, she had so many regrets as she dismounted her white horse at the edge of the bridge. She did not think it possible to have accumulated so many regrets in but seventeen short years, but she had assumed there would be time, so much more time than this.

Servants began to bring up torches to sit at the edge of the drop, and she could see the skeletons far below, by the light of the dying sun, and the coming torches. She actually had turned from the sight of it, her nerve failing. Surely, life was better than this.

Then her father was there, whispering, "You have disgraced me, Elinore, before the earl. If you go to him tonight, before the wedding, then he will forgive all. He will marry you and our family will rise at court."

"You once told me, Father, that to rescue Prince True was another way of saying you would rather die. Well I would rather rescue Prince True than go to the bed of the earl tonight."

He struck her then, laid her low in front of them all. She tasted blood in her mouth, and the world swam for a moment. When she could see clearly again, she looked up at her father, and called out, in a loud ringing voice, "I will rescue Prince True or die in the effort."

"You are a selfish, foolish girl," he said.

"Yes, Father, I am all those things." She got to her feet, a little shakily, for she had never been struck in the face. Whippings, yes, but never this. She straightened her cloak, settled her skirt, resisted the urge to touch the blood she could feel trickling from the corner of her mouth, and said, "Good-bye, Father."

She turned with no other word, and went straight for the bridge. She did not look down from the dizzying height to where her body would soon be lying. She did not look at the skeletons and their skeleton horses on the razor-sharp rocks below. She kept her eyes front, her back straight, as a well-bred woman should.

Her father called, "Elinore!"

She did not answer, for she had said her good-byes. She was strangely calm, calmer than she had ever been outside of the kitchens. The bridge was wooden, and had no rails, but it was solid and wide enough to drive a large carriage across. She got halfway, when she felt the bridge move. She was already looking at the far end of the bridge, and the small watchtower that marked the end of this moat and the beginning of the second. She did not have time to look up, or look down, or be surprised. She saw the giant step out of thin air, and come striding toward her. He held a huge club the size of the great oak back home. It was just like the songs and stories. The first danger was a giant with a club, and when you fought him, he would smash you to the rocks below.

The bridge swayed and pitched, and she knelt, not out of fear of the coming giant, but because she did not want to fall off the bridge. It seemed important somehow that she should die by the giant's club and not some silly fall. If this were to be the last thing she ever did, she would die well, and, if possible, in such a way to make her father regret his actions. Yes, seeing her fall would be horrible, but seeing her beaten to death by a giant, that well served her father right.

The giant thundered toward her, bellowing. He raised his great club, and at the last moment Elinore closed her eyes. She closed them for a long time, it seemed. She opened them, cautiously, and found herself staring at the giant's ankles. They were very big ankles, big as barrels. She looked up from the ankles and found the giant looking down at her. His club was at his side.

They stared at each other for a moment or two, the girl and the giant. Elinore noticed that the giant's eyes were brown, and the size of serving platters, but they were not unkind, those eyes. They were certainly kinder than the eyes of the earl.

"What is your name?" the giant asked, in a voice like thunder.

She swallowed hard, and then spoke up, so that the nobles watching could hear she'd died bravely. "I am Elinore the Younger."

She got to her feet, carefully, making sure she did not trip on the hem of her skirt. There were still no rails on the bridge, and the giant was taking up a lot of room. She eased past him, holding her skirts up, delicately, wishing she had thought to change out of her dancing slippers and into something more serviceable. Dancing slippers were fine for quick deaths, but if it was to be slow, and there was to be a challenge, then there were other shoes she would have chosen.

When she was on the other side of the giant, and had more room to maneuver, she dropped him a perfect curtsy. "Thank you, giant."

He pointed with a finger the size of a young tree. "Go there, Elinore the Younger. Go there and meet my cousin. Your death at my hands would have been quick. If you fail the next trial, your death will be slow and fulsome."

She curtsied again. "I would rather die quickly, if it's all the same to you, giant of the kind eyes. Could you not kill me now, and save me a slow and fulsome death?"

"No, I cannot, because you have passed my test. Now go, Elinore; go to my cousin, and remember kindness may get you further than anger."

She curtsied again, frowning. "My mother says that it is easier to be kind to begin with, than to apologize later."

"Your mother is wise. Now go, while I keep the crowd occupied."

Elinore looked back where he motioned, and saw that some of the young men, growing brave, had started on the bridge. They were armed with sword and shield. Apparently they had decided the giant could not be as fierce as first thought, if Elinore could pass it so easily.

Elinore went to the other side of the bridge, and the wooden door in the gate. The moment she was off the bridge, the giant charged the noble young men, screaming and sweeping them to their deaths with his great club.

Elinore knocked upon the huge wooden door in the stone gate, to the sound of screams and fighting. She could not fight a giant, or save anyone foolish enough to try. She could only go on.

The door opened, silently, on well-oiled hinges. At first she saw nothing but a stony passageway. Then there was movement at the far end of the hallway. Something shifted in the shadows. She would have said something huge, but she had just seen the giant, and so the ogre seemed almost small.

"Where's your sword, girl?" the ogre cried with his mouth full of sharp fangs, tusks like the boar's head that hung on her father's study wall.

"I have no sword," she said.

"Then where's your ax?"

She frowned at the ogre. "I have no weapon."

"Then it will be easy to kill you."

She nodded. "I suppose it will be."

The ogre ran at her, with an ax that was bright and looked sharp enough to cut stone. Elinore didn't wait, but closed her eyes immediately. Somehow dying from a fall, or a club, had seemed less awful than being chopped about by an ax. She did not want to see it, and tried desperately not to wonder how much it would hurt.

She had her eyes closed for a very long time, but no ax came. She opened her eyes, and found herself staring into the hairy, warty chest of the ogre. His great, gleaming ax was limp by his side. He was staring at her, intently, out of eyes that were almost as blue as her own.

"Are you not afraid of me, girl?"

"Yes, I am," she said.

"Then why do you not fight me, or scream?"

"I am no fighter, and if I am to die this day, I will die without screaming."

He leaned forward with his tusks and teeth, and growled, "I can make you scream."

"Yes, you can. I'm sure you can."

"You say you are afraid, girl, but you do not act it."

"I am Elinore the Younger, and I have come to rescue Prince True or die in the effort."

The ogre gave a harsh snuff, and his breath was not pleasant, as if he'd eaten too much garlic for dinner, but it was not the breath of a monster, just of a very large man. His eyes were not as kind as the giant's, but they were not cruel either.

"You may pass me, Elinore the Younger. My aunt waits for you in the next room. I would have cut you up and eaten you for supper tomorrow. My aunt will eat you while you are still alive." And he leaned in close to add menace to the threat.

Elinore felt her pulse in her throat, because being eaten alive sounded even more awful than being cut up by an ax and cooked later, or knocked off a bridge by a giant, but she couldn't go back. She had to go forward. Surely, eventually, someone would kill her and it would be done.

She curtsied to the ogre. "Thank you, ogre. I hope you have a pleasant supper tomorrow, but I am glad it will not be me."

"You will not be glad," he called after her, "once you see my aunt."

Elinore went to the end of the stone corridor, and found a much smaller door. She hesitated with her hand above the curved metal of the door handle. She really did not want to be eaten alive. That seemed a worse fate than marrying the Earl of Chillswoth; didn't it?

She stood there so long that the ogre came at her back, and asked, "Why do you hesitate, girl?"

"I am afraid," she answered simply; "I do not want to be eaten alive."

"You can go back," the ogre said. "As you passed me and my cousin the first time, you may pass the other way."

She turned and looked at him, and she could not see that her eyes were very blue and very wide, and full of a trust that was rare in one her age. The ogre saw.

"I may truly leave, and you will not harm me?"

"I have said before, you have passed our tests. My cousin and I will not harm you now."

"But your aunt, behind this door, may eat me alive," Elinore said, and she did not try to keep the fear out of her voice.

The ogre nodded. "She will if you fail her test." He touched her yellow cloak with one dirty finger. "Who dyed this cloth for you?"

"I dyed it myself, with the help of servants, but I gathered the herbs for the dye."

Elinore wasn't certain, but she thought the ogre smiled around his mouth full of tusks. "Go forward, girl, if you have the courage. Go back, if you have not, but whatever brought you to us is still waiting for you on the other side of the bridge."

She nodded. "The Earl of Chillswoth," she said.

"I do not know that name."

"If I fail your aunt's test, will she really, truly eat me alive?"

The ogre nodded. "She will. She has. She likes her meat fresh and wriggling."

Elinore shuddered, and swallowed hard enough that it hurt her throat. Was marriage to the earl truly a fate worse than that?

She remembered his hands on her. The moment in the dance when he had not just brushed her breast, but held it, caressed it. Her father would have had any of the young nobles beaten for such liberties, or at least thrown out of the banquet. She remembered how her skin had crawled, and her very being had shrunk from the touch, and the look in his eyes. Was it a fate worse than death? Perhaps not, but Elinore had come to die rather than marry the earl. She would do it. Even if the death were horrible, it would last only moments, and then she would be free. Marriage to that man could last years. She shuddered again, but not from fear of what lay behind the door.

She wrapped her hand around the handle, and said, "Thank you, ogre. You have been kinder than I would have ever dreamed."

"You are welcome, Elinore the Younger."

She let go the door long enough to give him a curtsy; then she opened the door, and found herself in an empty stone room, where the only light was a great fireplace against the far wall.

She hesitated only a moment, then stepped through in her impractical dancing slippers. She closed the door firmly behind her, and faced the empty firelit room. Her moment of fear was past. She was calm again.

"Your nephew the ogre has sent me," she said to the emptiness. "I await your test."

"You sound very brave," said a woman's voice from the shadows.

Elinore swallowed hard again, and could not keep her pulse from racing, but she answered firm enough. She would die bravely for the song they would write about her. It would be a shame to have them write a laughing ballad like they had for the one princess who died screaming.

"I am not certain I am brave, but I am here for your test." She peered into the shadows, trying to see the woman, or ogre, for there was no room for a giant.

There was a shape in the dimness, but it was not a woman's shape. Elinore's eyes could not make sense of it, at first; then the voice's owner stepped into the firelight, and Elinore did scream. She clapped her hand over her mouth to hold in the sound, but never had she dreamt of anything like what stood before her. It was worth a scream, or two.

It was a great predatory cat, the color of ripe wheat, glowing and golden in the light. It padded toward her on huge cat feet. But it wasn't a lion, or even a cat, for the upper part of the animal had breasts and arms, and a woman's face with long, wavy brown hair. Her eyes were the yellow slits of a cat's, but if you hadn't seen the lower part, you'd say she was beautiful.

Elinore stood, her hand to her mouth, and watched the woman-cat pad toward her, in a graceful walk that reminded her of the kitchen cats.

"Do you know what I am?" she asked.

Elinore shook her head, and finally forced herself to move her hand from her mouth. She tried to stand like a lady, and not a frightened child.

"I am a sphinx, and my kind loves to ask riddles and questions. I will ask you three questions, and if you fail to answer correctly, I will kill you."

Elinore's voice came out, breathy and afraid, but she could

not help it. "Your nephew, the ogre, said you would eat me alive. Is that true?"

The sphinx smiled, and though a lady's mouth did the smiling, it was the smile a cat would have, if it could. Elinore knew the answer, and it was not good.

"I am part cat, and we like our meat fresh."

Elinore nodded again. "Ask your question, and when I fail, I would ask only that you kill me before you start eating me. Surely, I will be freshly dead, and that is fresh enough. I ask this one thing, dear sphinx."

"I am not your dear anything, girl, but I will think upon your request." She sat back on her curved haunches, so that her human upper body was very visible. "Here is my first question to you. Get it wrong, and I will kill you. Answer correctly, and you will have two more chances to die."

"Or to live," Elinore said, in a voice that sounded squeaky as a mouse, even to her.

The sphinx laughed, head back, face sparkling with joy. "Only two in fifty years have gotten past me, and I do not think it will be three before the calendar doth turn again."

Elinore nodded. "You are quite right. I am not bright enough to answer questions from such as you. But ask, sphinx; ask and let me die."

The sphinx turned her head to one side, the way a cat will when it's trying to judge a thing. "I thought you were here to rescue Prince True and become queen of all."

"That is supposed to be the goal, yes, but in all honesty, I came to die, rather than marry the Earl of Chillswoth. If I commit suicide, then my family is disgraced, but if I die trying to rescue the prince, then I am dead, and my family can go on."

"Is the earl such an odious man?"

"Yes, I believe he is, or I would not be here."

The sphinx looked at her. "What is your name?"

"I am called Elinore the Younger."

"Who is the elder?"

"My grandmother."

"Does she yet live?"

"No."

"Ah, then they will soon need another Elinore." The sphinx began to pace around her. She tried to hold still, but finally began to turn to keep the monster in sight. She could not fight it off, but at least she could see it coming. It was the best she could think to do.

"What was used to make the dye of your cloak, Elinore the Soon to be Dead?"

Elinore frowned at her. This couldn't be the first question, because it was too easy. Was it a trap? "Is this the first question?"

"Yes, unless you want a different one."

"No, this is a lovely question. Yarrow. Yarrow made the dye."

"Hmm," said the sphinx, gliding around and around her. "The ingredients for gingerbread, what are they?"

Gingerbread was a rare treat, very expensive, but Elinore's family had money enough for such luxuries. "Butter and sugar, spices and flour, eggs and molasses and milk."

"Did you supervise the baking at your home?"

"No, I would never dream of supervising our head cook; she would not tolerate it, not from me."

"Then how did you learn to make such a delicacy?"

"She allowed me to make it last Winter's Moon." Elinore almost reached out and touched the sphinx, then dropped her hand. "You must not tell Mother, for Cook would get in trouble for risking such expensive ingredients with me, but Cook says I have a good hand and eye for the kitchen."

"Indeed," said the sphinx. She looked Elinore up and down, and then said, "Let me see your shoes."

Elinore did as she was asked, because she was certain that now there would be some question of history or mathematics that would be too hard to answer, though she could not fathom what her slippers had to do with mathematics.

She raised her party dress and showed her dancing slippers with their jeweled embroidery. "Did you think dancing slippers were the thing to wear to fight monsters?" the sphinx asked.

Elinore hesitated, and then said, "No, ma'am, I did not."

"Then why did you wear them?"

Elinore almost pointed out that wasn't that a fourth question, but it seemed impolite to say that to someone who could gut you and eat you alive.

"I had to leave as soon as I announced I would rescue Prince True. If I had waited, even to change my slippers, my father would have found a way to detain me. Also, in truth, I wanted to be pretty when I died, so they would sing of it."

"Is it better to be pretty or brave, Elinore the Younger?"

A fifth question. Should she point it out, that she'd answered four already? "It is better to be brave, but since I am not, I thought I would be pretty for the bards and musicians, and jeweled slippers are prettier than muck boots."

"You own a pair of muck boots?" the sphinx asked.

"Well, yes; you can't wear dancing slippers to gather herbs and things for dyes. Also, how do you know the kitchen boy is giving you the best vegetables unless you go out into the fields for yourself?"

"Do you garden, then?"

Finally, Elinore braved the question, "That is the sixth question you've asked me, ma'am. Have I passed your test?"

The sphinx waved a careless hand. "Yes, yes, you pass. Go through the door by the fireplace and you have but one more task to complete."

"Only one more?" Elinore asked.

The sphinx nodded.

"Then I will live?"

"We shall see."

"I never really expected to succeed."

"Perhaps that is why you are doing so well." The sphinx walked back into the shadows and vanished.

Elinore was left with another door, and another challenge, and no hint what lay ahead, but she had survived, and only one more task lay before her. She might actually rescue Prince True. All the stories made him out to be a womanizing bounder, and a scoundrel. Had Elinore run from one bad marriage into another? They never tell you in fairy tales that sometimes the prize may not be worth the effort. But she went for the last door, because what else could she do?

It was a throne room, bigger than the king's room. The throne at the end of that long walk gleamed silver, and was studded with pearls and soft, gleaming jewels. A beautiful woman sat in the chair. Her long yellow hair lay in heavy, straight folds, like a second cloak to decorate the black dress she wore. The underdress was silver thread, and as Elinore got closer, she saw embroidery at the sleeves and collar. The bright colors contrasted with the silver and black starkness of the rest of the dress.

She kept expecting there to be guards, or servants, or someone, but the woman sat alone on the throne. This had to be the sorceress, didn't it?

When she was almost touching the steps that led upward to the throne, Elinore dropped a curtsy as low as any she'd given at the courts of the king.

"You may rise," the woman said in a deep, pleasant voice, as if she would sing low, but well.

Elinore stood, hands clasped in front of her. "Are you the sorceress?"

"I am she."

"I have come to rescue Prince True."

"Why?" the sorceress asked.

Elinore frowned at her, and then answered truthfully. She told of her father trying to marry her to the earl, and her decision.

"So, in truth, Elinore the Younger, you do not wish to rescue the prince at all. You merely wish to die in such a way as to free yourself from the earl, and not disgrace your family."

"That is true, but I have come so far through all your

challenges, it has made me wonder if perhaps I might live, after all."

"So you do wish to try to rescue the prince?

"If that is the only way to free myself, yes."

"I will give you three choices, Elinore. I can offer you a quick and painless death. Does that please you?"

"You said there were three choices. I would like to hear the other two, if it's all right. A quick and painless death is not a bad choice, especially since at one point today I thought I would be eaten alive, but I would like to know my options, please."

"You are most polite, child."

"My mother would be pleased that you say so."

The sorceress smiled, a small smile, and then continued. "The second choice is to show you a secret way out of my lair. You may go forth and never see your father or the earl again. You can make your way in the world, Elinore."

"I suppose I could do that, but I have never been out in the world. I'm not certain I would know how to make my way. What is the third choice?"

"That you try to rescue the prince."

"What happens if I fail?"

The sorceress clapped her hands, and two young women walked out, one from each side of the room. There must have been doors there that Elinore couldn't see, or was it the same kind of magic that had made the sphinx able to vanish and appear?

The women took up their posts on either side of the throne.

One held a bowl of fruit, the other a jug of wine, and a goblet. The sorceress took the wine but did not touch the fruit.

"This is Princess Meriwether"—she pointed at the tall one with wavy brown hair—"and this is the Baroness Vanessa," she said of the raven-haired one.

Elinore gaped at them. "The Princess Meriwether and the Vanessa from the songs?"

"The very same," the sorceress said.

"The songs say they died valiantly."

"No. They failed to save Prince True, and as punishment they have served me these long years."

"So if I fail, then I will become your servant?"

"Yes."

Elinore thought about her options, and then asked, "Could I meet the prince before I decide?"

The sorceress smiled, and waved the two failed rescuers to posts at either side of her throne. "That is a wise question, Elinore. You wish to see if he is worth the risk, eh?"

Elinore nodded. "I do."

The sorceress drew a silver chain out of her bosom. There was a silver whistle on the chain. She blew it, one clear, birdlike note.

A man walked out of the wall just behind the throne. Were there no normal doors in this room or were they all bewitched so that Elinore could not see them?

The prince, for he still looked like his portrait in the great hall at court, knelt before the throne. "My mistress calls and I must answer."

"You have another rescuer, but she wished to see you first."

The prince looked over his shoulder, still kneeling, but definitely looking at Elinore. His brown hair was cut short, but still had tiny curls in it. His eyes were a blue as deep as her own. The brows that curved above those eyes were graceful and a little darker than his hair. He was pale of skin, though in the portrait he was tanned. But then, he had not been outside of this place for more than fifty years. He had grown pale in his long years of captivity. But beyond that, he looked as if he had just ridden through the doors. As with the two women who had come and failed, they had not aged a day.

"Stand up; let her see you better."

The prince came to his feet and faced Elinore. His face was arrogant, defiant, and almost angry.

Normally, she would have lowered her eyes from such a stare, but this was too important to look away. She studied his face, and found him handsome enough, and his spirit was not broken. So many years, yet he still stared out like that. This was a strong man, not just of arm, but of character, as her grandmother had said.

"May I ask the prince a question?"

"You may, though whether he will answer is another question."

"Your highness, are you worth the risk of my freedom, and maybe my life?"

The arrogance faltered, and she watched him have a thought. She wasn't sure what that thought was, but she saw it. "In all these long years no one has asked that. If you win my freedom, then you will be my wife, and queen of all. Isn't that worth risking your freedom?"

"Your brother has been king for over twenty years, longer than I have been alive. Do you truly think he will simply give up his throne to you and your queen, just like that?"

"Of course he will. I am the heir to the throne. I am his older brother."

"Prince True, your younger brother is as old as your father was when you vanished. He has two sons and two daughters of his own now."

"I am the heir, and our laws will force him to give up the throne to me."

Elinore studied the handsome, but oh, so arrogant face. She turned to the sorceress. "What would the challenge be, if I took it?"

"You would either face the prince in combat, or cook a dinner. Combat is simple: defeat the prince, and you win his hand. The meal is more complicated: you will prepare your best food, and it is my taste you must please. I have yet to taste anyone's pies that can rival Prince True's."

Elinore knew she would not choose combat, but she was confident of her pies. Cook said she was good enough to cook at the palace, and Cook would not lie.

"If the prince had pretended to be bested at combat, would you have let him go?"

"If he had been willing to allow himself to lose, then he would have learned his lesson, and earned his freedom."

"But he bested them all?" Elinore asked.

"He killed them all," the sorceress said, and she watched Elinore as she said it.

"They came to save him, and he slew them?"

"He did."

"And if he put salt in the pie instead of sugar, then one of the other women would have won the contest and he could have been free, yes?"

"Yes, but he still cannot bear to lose, not at anything, and definitely not to a woman."

Elinore folded her hands along the soft edge of the cloak she had woven and dyed. "I think I could best him at cooking, because our head cook praises me. Never in front of my parents, for they would not understand that her approval meant more to me than theirs."

"Your head cook is a servant," the prince said, "and she has to tell you that you are good at something."

"So you will take the challenge?" the sorceress asked.

"No, I will not," Elinore said.

The prince stared at her. "What?"

"I have seen and talked to you and I do not think your freedom is worth mine."

"But I am Prince True, heir to the kingdom."

"You are Prince True, but I think your brother, or his children, would find a way to deny you the throne. They could say your years with the sorceress had driven you mad and lock you up in a tower."

"They would not dare!"

"Sorceress, you said there was a secret way out."

"I did, but what will you do, Elinore the Younger, by yourself, in the wide world?"

"I can sew and cook, and garden. I know my herbs and their uses."

"So does every peasant woman," the prince said.

"I bake the finest pies in our lands."

"I bake a finer pie than you, girl."

"I propose a different challenge," the sorceress said. "I propose that the two of you bake me a pie. If Elinore makes the best pie, then I will give her a dowry so she may set herself up in business, or wed a baker, or a weaver. If the prince is best, then Elinore may leave empty-handed, but she may go with my blessing."

"And what do I win?" the prince asked.

"A lesson in humility, I hope."

The kitchen was large and airy, and made Elinore wish she could give Cook such a kitchen back home. The moment she thought "home," her chest tightened, and her throat closed around something hard and hurtful. She would never see home again, unless she won the prince his freedom and went back to be queen. But Elinore had been to court, though only once, with the other fifteen-year-old noble daughters. She had been introduced to the king and his queen. She had danced with their sons, tried to talk to their daughters. She didn't think they would so easily give up their throne to a long-lost brother and uncle.

She would not miss her father, but would miss her mother, and some of the servants, and she did have a friend or two, that it would matter to her if she never once spoke to them again.

She thought that she and the prince were the only ones in the kitchen, until something she could not see picked up an apron and offered it to her. She was startled for a moment, but then allowed the invisible hands to help her cover her dress and tie the bow in the back. She had laid her cloak on a bench to the side of the room out of the way of flour and ingredients.

She asked the air for a ribbon to tie back her hair and one floated to her. Things she could not see bound her hair back from her face.

Prince True in his own apron busied himself around the kitchen. His hands were strong and sure of themselves. He rolled his dough with sure, hard strokes, but not too hard. If you pressed too hard, you tore the dough.

Elinore realized she was spending too much time watching the prince, and not enough doing her own cooking. She formed her own dough, and began to roll it out carefully on her section of floured counter. She was not as quick as the prince, but she was careful, and thoughtful. There was no need to rush, because there was no time limit. Best to do it right, if there was no need to hurry.

Elinore thought about having enough money of her own to start a business, buy her own house. It was a frightening idea. It was an idea so new that her hands began to shake as she rolled out her dough.

"Why are you afraid, girl?" the prince asked.

Elinore folded her hands back against the apron. "I am not afraid, your highness; I am excited."

He stood a little taller. "Are you having second thoughts about trying to rescue me?"

"I was thinking that your rescue was the only way I could ever see my family and friends again."

He smiled, and it was such an arrogant look that Elinore

knew there was no going back. There would be no living with this man, even if his brother didn't execute them both.

"You will not best me at cooking, girl. I have mastered it as I have mastered everything I have ever tried to do in my life."

She nodded. "As you say, Prince True, you are master of many things, but you are not mistress."

He frowned. "What does that mean?"

"It means cook your pie, and I will cook mine, and we will see." It was high summer, so there were berries on the table, in glazed bowls of many colors. Elinore tasted the berries to make certain they were as ripe as they appeared, because she had learned when making pies and jellies that a pretty fruit was not always the sweetest.

The prince was done long before Elinore. But she let nothing rush her, not even his taunts. For he did taunt, like all bullies. She ignored him, and as she shaped her top crust so that the edges formed that perfect waved edge that Cook had been teaching her since she was old enough to reach the counter on a stool, she was pleased. She knew she had done her best. She cut out a design of the crescent moon in the center, for it represented the maiden form of the Goddess, and Elinore was still a maiden in every sense. She prayed as she baked, for the other meaning for maiden, virgin, was a woman whole and of herself. A woman who depended on no one. She wished to be such a woman.

They carried their pies to a banquet hall, as rich and marbled as the throne room had been. The king himself had no room so fine. The sorceress was at the table, but so were the giant, and the ogre, and the sphinx. Elinore could not hide her surprise.

The giant said, "You did not expect to see the monsters sitting down to the table, did you, Elinore the Brave?"

"I did not, kind giant, and I am still Elinore the Younger."

"No," said the ogre. "Elinore the Brave, we name you, and a name given by the monsters you defeat is a telling name."

"Yes," said the sphinx, who crouched closest to the sorceress, "I approve of such a name."

"As do I," said the sorceress.

"You have not given me such a name," the prince said.

"No," she said, "we have not."

He scowled, and put his pie before her with a little more force than needed. The edge of the crust broke, and fell upon the table.

Elinore placed her perfectly browned and unbroken pie before the sorceress.

"Elinore the Brave is the winner," she said.

"But you have not tasted the pies," the prince said.

"But hers is the prettiest, and appearances count."

"Taste them," he ordered.

She sighed. "It has been over fifty years, and though a good cook you have become, you have learned little else." Everyone took a fork and tasted the pies. The vote was unanimous; Elinore's pie was the sweetest.

"No," said the prince. "I did not lose."

"You did, but you lost to someone who was not bidding for your freedom."

"Will you give me enough money to set up a shop of my own?" Elinore asked.

"A fine shop, but what shall you sell?"

"I think I will bake."

The sorceress conjured a bag from thin air and the weight of it almost made Elinore drop the bag. "Our aunt the sphinx will show you the way out, Elinore the Brave."

"But she has beaten me. She will be my queen, and I will be free."

"She does not wish to be your queen," the sorceress said.

He looked at Elinore, and he was finally perplexed. "How can you not want to be my queen?"

"You are not kind enough to marry."

"Kind? A man is not kind. A man is strong."

"It was gentleness that made the crust of that pie. It was too much strength that broke its crust. I want a husband who can bake a pie without breaking it in anger."

"That makes no sense, girl."

"My name is Elinore the Younger, named Elinore the Brave by a giant, and an ogre, and a sphinx."

"Free me, Elinore." A look passed his face, a look of pain at last. "Please, let me go."

She looked at him, studied his fine blue eyes. She looked at the sorceress. "I have won the contest fairly, have I not?"

"You have; do you want him to husband now?"

"No, but could he be freed, and tell the story of how I died bravely in the attempt?"

"Why would you free him, Elinore the Brave?"

"Because he said 'please.' "

The sorceress seemed to think about that, and then nodded. "Very well, it will be done."

And it was; the prince rode free, and told a heart-wrenching story of how Elinore was madly in love with him, but died tragically before he could bring her out as his queen. He made himself save her from the giant, the ogre, and the sphinx, but even in his version, she was Elinore the Brave.

A few months after his triumphant return, when the balls and banquets that his brother threw were done, the prince fell ill. He died soon after, of a stomach complaint. On his deathbed he kept repeating, "It was in the pie. It was in the pie." Funny, the things people rave about when they know they've been poisoned.

Elinore passed herself off as the bastard daughter of a noble. He had given her enough money to set herself up in business, but wanted no more of her. She bought into a family business of bakers where the elderly couple, though having raised a large brood, had none who wanted to be bakers. Elinore learned the business from them, and they found a child who loved their business as much as they did. In the years to come Elinore would meet and marry a baker. Her pies were the talk of the kingdom, but if anyone ever thought she looked like the dead Elinore, well, she was the bastard daughter of a noble. People winked and nodded, and believed.

Elinore's husband was as gentle and firm as he needed to be with his dough, and his family. He could never equal Elinore's pies, but she could never quite get the bread to crust as he could. But they didn't see that as a bad thing, for they understood that life wasn't about being the best; it was about being happy. And at that Elinore, her husband, and their children were very good, indeed.

The Shadow of Mist

AN OTHERWORLD NOVELLA

YASMINE GALENORN

An áit a bhuil do chroí is ann a thabharfas do chosa thú.

Your feet will bring you to where your heart is.

—CELTIC SAYING

The sea gives and the sea takes away.

—GRANDFATHER TO FIONA CONNEELY

FROM

THE SECRET OF ROAN INISH

1

I stared out over the water as the call of the waves sang to me. They raced in my blood, enticing me to shed my humanity and dive deep, to return to the Mother's core. The Ocean Mother's presence was strong here, and she was a part of me now, a part of my life like she'd never been on the distant shores of my old home. I'd lived long enough on the western coast of Washington State to realize that my old life was slowly receding into the past for good.

Oh, I was a lot older than the one hundred and one years that had passed since I first set foot on Ellis Island, claiming the United States as my new home, but my past was retreating, and I wasn't sorry to see the memories fade, like aging photographs. Over the intervening years, life had shifted and changed drastically, and so had I. But now . . . now I felt ready to settle in as my true self. To fully adopt this land as my home, this life as my fate.

And even more, I was ready to step out of the closet and tell my neighbors, my employer, and the world who I really was. For the first time in my life since I fled under the cover of night to the waiting boat, I was ready to step out and say, *I'm Siobhan Morgan, and I'm a selkie, a wereseal if you will. I'm part of the Supe Community and I'm not going to hide anymore.*

Life in this country had treated me well. Oh, there had been setbacks and downfalls, but now . . . I patted the rounded curve of my belly, which up until the last few months had always been flat and toned. Now there was life within me, and I had everything I ever wanted.

"Little daughter," I whispered to the presence within. "I've waited a long, long time for you. I just wish I could bring you into a world that wasn't so hostile and angry."

As if in reply, a faint kick from a tiny foot answered back. Or was it a flipper? Mitch and I would have to talk to the midwife before long to get clear on everything that would happen to me—and the child—during the birthing. I knew I would have her in the water, with the mothers of the Pod surrounding me. But beyond that, I wasn't sure. Mitch and I had tried for so long to get pregnant, our hopes dashed time and again. And now, it was really happening, thanks to the elfin medics that my friends—the D'Artigo sisters—had hooked me up with.

As I blinked against the gray clouds that were threatening a downpour during the autumn afternoon, my cell phone rang. I flipped it open, expecting to hear Mitch's voice—he was the only one who knew where I was right now—but to my surprise, a deeper voice answered.

"Siobhan? Siobhan Morgan?"

Crap. I let out a cry and dropped the phone, staring at the glowing screen. Should I pick it up again? Could I be wrong? Could it be someone else? Praying I'd made a mistake, I cautiously retrieved the phone from the ground and slowly raised it to my ear.

"Who's speaking, please?"

"You know damned well who I am. Don't play dumb." His accent had faded, as had my own, but it was the same rough tone I'd run away from all those years ago.

"Terry? Is that you?"

"Yeah, it's Terrance. And before you hang up—because I know you're thinking about it—let me leave you with this thought: I've been tracking you down, girl. For a hundred years, I've searched for you. And now that I've found you, I'm going to make sure you live up to your end of the bargain."

I caught my breath. It couldn't be him. Not after a hundred years. I'd crossed the ocean to get away from him, and then crossed the continent. I'd run so far, so fast, leaving everything behind, that I could barely remember the days before I landed in New York.

What the hell was I going to do?

"It wasn't my bargain, Terry. I didn't make the arrangements, and I didn't agree to them. In fact, if you'll recall, I wanted you prosecuted by the Tribunal. But so much for justice. I claim my freedom. I claim injury by what you did to me that night. So you might as well turn around and go back home to Cobh, because I'll never set foot on her shores again."

"Babe, I left Ireland to find you, and I swore I'd make it happen, no matter how long it took. I've been home a few times, but I've spent most of the years combing this land. And now I know where you are. You can dance around the issue all you like, but the facts are simple. Even though you ran away and signed up with another Pod, your parents struck a contract with my parents, and you're honor-bound to fulfill it. Siobhan Morgan, you're going to marry me. You belong to me, and I'm coming to get you. So resign yourself to your fate, because you'll not get away from me this time. I'll track you down no matter where you go."

With that, the line went dead. I pressed my knuckles to my lips. I'd spent the past century moving from place to place, lying about who I was, darting glances over my shoulder to make sure Terry hadn't followed me.

After twenty-five years, I felt a glimmer of hope.

After fifty years, I began to believe I'd managed to escape and went back to using my own name.

And after ninety, I relaxed, and that was when I met Mitch and fell in love. For most of the intervening years, technology had been in its youth, and until recently, tracking down someone who didn't want to be found had been a whole lot harder. Until the Internet, I thought. That must be how he found me.

I flipped the phone shut and shoved it in my pocket as a drizzle began to splash to the ground, trickling down my cheeks like tears. The taste of acid rain burnt my tongue as I caught one of the fat drops and swallowed it. Water used to be pure. Water used to be sacred. Now, even in the depths of the oceans, it was tainted. But still, the Ocean Mother persevered. She rolled in waves across the face of the world. She sang to my blood and reminded me of what I was.

The sky lit up with a dizzying flash of lightning and I shook my head, clearing my thoughts as I dashed for the car. A roll of thunder rumbled overhead as I sat there, clutching the steering wheel, wondering what to do.

Mitch would know, if I could bring myself to tell him. And now that we were pregnant, surely the Pod elders would come around and help us out. But somewhere deep in my heart, I knew that I'd lied. I'd lied to all of them. Would that change how they felt about me? Whatever happened, I'd never willingly give myself over to Terry. I'd die first. In fact, at one time, I'd tried and failed.

* * *

"Siobhan Morgan, you won't be defying your father." Mother shoved me back into my chair. She looked harried and tense, and I had the feeling she hadn't expected me to protest. "Terrance Fell is your betrothed and you *will* marry him. Your father and I gave our word. You're honor-bound to uphold our promise."

I closed my eyes and leaned my head against the back of the rocking chair. The walls were in need of patching, and the roof leaked, and my mother was trying desperately to sweep the floor but the dirt and sand were thick.

We'd moved into the house six years before, when Father

first brought the family out of the Orkney Islands, where we were starving, to the streets of Queenstown in Ireland. The dirt here smelled nasty, unlike the clean tang of the dirt in our old home. The house was always dusty, and too close to too many humans. I longed for the sound of rolling waves cresting on the coast of the islands, but here we had food, and my brothers and father could find work. We lived on the outskirts of the city, near the cove, keeping to ourselves as most of the roane did.

That was what our people were called here—the *roane*, rather than *selkies*, but I stubbornly held on to the name I'd grown up with. *Selkie* was comforting and familiar; *roane* was strange and confusing. As confusing as the ways of the city and the bustle of so many humans wandering through the streets. After six years, I'd adapted to living in their midst, but now I wished I'd never seen the streets of Queenstown.

"I won't marry him! I won't." Angry, I tossed the dress I was stitching to the floor and balled my hands into fists. I'd never spoken to my mother like this, and part of me felt embarrassed and ashamed, but there was too much at stake to go along quietly.

"Pick up that dress. It's your wedding gown—at least for the human ceremony." Rhiannon rested her hands on her hips and stared at me. "Siobhan, you can't betray us. Terrance is the prince of his people. He'll assure that our family will never go without. He's rich, he's well placed in both human and roane society, and he has promised that you'll never want for anything."

I pressed my lips together and snatched up the dress. The

linen crinkled in my hand and I wanted to slash it to ribbons rather than wear it for the man who had raped me. Father knew, and Mother. That was why Terrance had offered to marry me. He wouldn't have to face the Pod Tribunal then.

But *I'd* know. I'd always know that my husband had forced me and then bought me for the promise of riches. The thought of his touch made my skin crawl and I let out a sharp cry.

"We aren't roane. We're selkie. He's not one of us." The fact that my parents knew what he'd done hadn't swayed them. I'd already pleaded for them to take him before the Tribunal, but they were frightened by the power he held in Queenstown and among the roane. They tried to justify it, but I knew they didn't want to rock the boat. I was the sacrificial lamb, offered on a silver platter to keep the peace and make the prince of the roane happy.

"You're right—Terrance *isn't* one of us, and that's a good thing for the Pod," my mother said. "You know the elders are calling for new blood. We're dying, Siobhan. You can't mate with our men. Inbreeding is killing our people. That's why . . ."

She paused, then after a moment added, "That's why I joined your father's Pod. To bring new blood into the mix. No, it's set. You'll marry Terrance and become a princess, and bear his children for the good of our family and the Pod."

I didn't say anything. What could I say except to lash out at her again?

My mother paused, gazing at me out of the corner of her eye. Her voice was soft, almost gentle, as she added, "I know how you feel, my dear. I was brought into your father's Pod in much the same way. He carried me off from my family and I couldn't resist him, and so it was that I became Rhiannon of the Northern Orkney Pod. Your father married me and brought me to his people—my people, now—and we've grown to love each other over the years. The fact that Terrance agreed to align his Pod with the Cobh Selkie Pod is enough to wash away all his other sins, my daughter. We desperately need the new blood."

I stared at her for a moment. Were all the women of our Pod simply prizes for men? "Are we like the *Finfolk*, then? Do women count for nothing? Should I just roll over and let any man have his way with me if you say it's good for our people?"

"Hush. Don't say such things. It's not like that." The pained look on my mother's face made me feel good. I'd hit a tender spot. I wanted to twist the knife, but finally just shook my head.

"Then you *don't* care that he raped me. And the Tribunal closes its eyes. My own parents are content to ignore what he did in order to put food on the table and to bring new blood to the Pod?"

Rhiannon let out a long sigh. "We all make sacrifices, Siobhan. We all give up our freedom for the betterment of our families. Your family is the Pod. Your duty is to do whatever it takes to ensure the continuation of our people. Now dust off your dress and get back to your sewing."

"That's it, then?"

She shrugged to indicate the argument was over. "We're going out tonight to the waters, and you need to finish the dress before day after tomorrow. You're getting married, Siobhan.

To a prince. He's rich, and will give you children and standing. And he's joining our people. Take joy in the thought of what you can do for others, and *be glad he finds you attractive.*"

As I settled down in the rocking chair, dress in hand, my thoughts raced ahead. I had two days. Just two days in which to ensure that Terrance would never touch me again. Two days in which to change a thousand years of tradition. Or . . . perhaps . . . maybe I didn't need to change tradition. Maybe what I needed was to change myself—to put myself out of his reach.

Mulling over this new idea, I went back to my sewing, but with every stitch, I felt like I was tightening the noose on my future.

* * *

That night, standing on the edge of the harbor, I stared out over the darkened waters. Most of my family had already slipped back into their skins and returned to the sea. Selkies hid their skins when taking human form, and each of us had a safety cache in which to store them. Now I carried mine with me as the others had, in a satchel slung low on my hip.

I watched the water, mesmerized by the lapping of the waves. Then, slowly, I edged my way toward the breakers. I glanced around. Nobody near, no one to watch. I could safely change and slip out to sea, sleekly skimming through the currents. Maybe I should just keep going. Head into open ocean and see where it took me.

Chances were I'd end up shark food or caught by fishermen, but would that be worse than a life wedded to Terrance? Than bearing his hands on me night after night?

I tried to imagine what it would be like to find myself in the grips of a shark. *Fast.* It would be over soon, though I'd be alone. Could I do it? Face dying by myself? I could live without my Pod, become a rogue—that I knew I was capable of. But a painful and bloody death alone in the night sea? The thought was more than I could bear.

No, I couldn't do it. I'd always be wondering when and where the end would come, because selkies on their own didn't last long. And if the Finfolk got hold of me, it would be worse.

As I stood there, ankle-deep in the water, another thought crept into my mind. There was one option I'd overlooked. I could end it *now*. Walk into the sea in human form. Drowning was easy—just let the breath go and close my eyes as I drifted in the arms of the Ocean Mother. Everything would be over . . . all the worry, all the fear of disappointing everyone.

Marrying Terrance was out of the question, and my parents had effectively handed me over to him. Life alone at sea was too dangerous. I couldn't stay in the city—Terrance would find me. I couldn't go home to the Orkneys—he'd follow me there, too.

Dazed and feeling betrayed, I slowly began to wade into the water, the skirts of my dress floating on the surface as the chill hit me to the core. Even in June, the water was cold. As I breathlessly made my way in up to my knees, my toes curled around the silt and I reveled in the feel of the soft, wet sand.

A loud, resounding noise startled me out of my thoughts and I jerked my gaze across the cove. An ocean liner was pulling into port, returning from America, no doubt, where thousands of emigrants were flocking in hopes of better days and a life that might promise something other than poverty and starvation. *Fresh starts and new beginnings. That's what they hope for.*

For a moment, I dismissed the gigantic hull of a boat from my mind, but then . . . I looked at it again. Queenstown—or Cobh, as it had been known for centuries before some idiot human had renamed it after the queen—was an integral port to the world. And now, as I gazed at the ship, an idea began to form. What if *I* was on that boat when it sailed? The liner would leave soon—they were sailing quickly, to meet the demand. What if I booked passage on the *Umbria* and simply vanished into a new life?

My stomach quivered. I'd be leaving my family, leaving my home for a distant shore to . . . What future did I have in America? *Any future you want to make.* The thought echoed as I turned the idea over in my mind. I couldn't really do this. *Could I?*

But if I didn't . . . Terrance's face loomed large in my thoughts again and I began to shake. I couldn't let him touch me again.

* * *

"I want you," he'd said, reaching out to stroke my cheek.

I darted away from him. Something about him made my skin crawl. I'd shaken off his hand when he tried to hold mine, but his fingers on my face felt so much more invasive. I'd gone on the walk with him only because my father insisted that I get out of the house. *Get some fresh air,* he'd said.

"Terry, I don't feel that way about you." I tried to lighten my words in order to take away the sting, but no matter how I said it, it was a rejection. "I'm stubborn, my family says. I honestly don't know what I want but I'm not really looking for marriage right now."

Not exactly the truth, but close enough. I *was* looking for love, but only with the right person. I was looking for a man who made my heart beat faster, who made my pulse race and my breath catch in my throat because I wanted him more than I wanted anybody or anything else.

Terry snorted. "You don't have to feel the same way." As he moved closer, I danced to the other side, wading through the knee-deep grass that ran along the side of the cliff overlooking the harbor.

"Look—the ships are coming into port." I tried to change the subject, calculating the distance between us as I darted out of his reach. There was something in his eyes that made me want to run home and lock the door behind me. He was ruthless, a man who would do whatever it took to get what he wanted.

"You don't have to love me. I don't care. I want you, Siobhan Morgan, and you're a fool if you refuse me. I can give you everything. I can give you riches and security. I can make you a princess. And I can protect your family. All you have to do is obey me. That's all I ask in return."

I kept my mouth shut. My family was coming off a rough spot. Six years ago, we'd been forced to leave our home in the

Orkneys because there wasn't enough to eat—even the sea had turned fickle on us. We'd come to Queenstown and found a house. My brothers had found work on the docks and my mother took in washing. My father mostly drank. We kept to ourselves and managed to survive. But life was still hard, and my mother's back was always sore.

I tried to imagine accepting his offer. What he could do for our family . . . But another look in his eyes squelched any thought I had of saying yes. My heart was pounding out a warning. Terry wasn't safe. He reminded me of the Finfolk, a deadly and treacherous man.

"No, thank you." I let out a long sigh. "But I appreciate the offer." Not good to make one of the Pod royalty angry.

He let out a sharp laugh and jumped forward, grabbing my wrist.

"Then we're into the chase," he said, his face red. I could feel the waves of excitement rolling off him and I stumbled, trying to get away. But Terry was heavier and taller than I, and before I could break his grasp, he knocked me to the ground and landed on top of me. As he pushed up my skirts, his hands fumbling along my thighs, his eyes gleamed.

"I'm glad you said no," he whispered. "I like a challenge."

I began to scream, but he clapped his hand over my mouth and gave me a wicked grin. "Now, now, you wouldn't want that sweet little brother of yours to go missing . . . to become shark food, would you?"

As his meaning echoed in my thoughts, I closed my eyes and thought of the sea. She was always there, and she would cleanse me and heal me when he was done. But Terry didn't want me to miss out on the fun, and as he drove himself into me, I let out a little cry and realized that no matter how many times I bathed, I'd never get the feel of him off me.

* * *

I parked in front of our house and raced up the stairs. The two-story cottage was modest, but it belonged to Mitch and me, and it was home. As I closed the door behind me, all I could think about was barring the past. I flipped the lock and started to call out for Mitch, but then stopped. He was off on a job. Mitch was a contractor and renovated old houses for a company of property flippers. And one other thing had occurred to me on the way home.

I'd never told Mitch the truth about my past. At first, I was afraid that if the Puget Sound Harbor Seal Pod discovered that I'd been engaged to Terry, they might make me return home and face the consequences. Then, after Mitch and I found out about our daughter, it seemed a moot point.

I forced myself into the kitchen where I put the kettle on and grabbed the chamomile tea, fumbling to get the bags out of the box. I had to calm down, to think clearly. As I slid into a chair at the table, waiting for the kettle to whistle, I pulled out my cell phone. Terrance's number came up as blocked.

So, point number one: I had no idea where he was, but he knew where I was. At least, he knew my phone number.

Point number two: He wanted me back, which meant I wasn't safe. And another little matter to consider: What would he do when he found out I was pregnant with another man's child? But even as I asked myself the question, I knew the answer. Terrance would take out his anger by forcing me to miscarry. I knew him. He was the prince of his people. And when dealing with royalty, especially in the Supe Community, bloodlines were everything. He wouldn't want another man's child crowding out his own.

I glanced at the clock as I moved to pour my tea. I *couldn't* tell Mitch, not until I knew how I was going to handle this. He'd freak out. He'd have to know at some point, but the more I thought about it, the more I realized he'd go off half-cocked and get himself hurt.

And I didn't dare go to the Pod for help—not yet. Most likely they'd protect me, but I'd been a problem for them over the years because I couldn't conceive and Mitch was in love with me. They'd tried to break us up so he could move on to another woman who could bear his children. We were together only by the grace of my unborn daughter.

No, there was only one place I could turn. Camille, Delilah, and Menolly D'Artigo were the only women I knew who wouldn't hesitate to set Terrance straight. Taking a deep breath, I punched in their number and counted the rings until they picked up.

2

As the steel gray Lexus pulled to a stop in front of the house, with a Jeep Wrangler right behind it, I sucked in a deep breath. Camille and Delilah were here. I glanced back at the phone. Mitch was supposed to call. He was due home late and he always called to let me know how long he would be. His crew had gotten wrapped up in the restoration of an original fireplace and they wanted to finish it before the week was over. Which meant that he wouldn't walk in on our conversation.

I smoothed my dress and looked around the house. We hadn't even had our official housewarming, and I'd hoped to put off entertaining guests until after the Pod priestess came to bless our new home, but this was too important. Besides, the girls would never bring anything evil with them—at least not wittingly. They were fighting a group of demons trying to break through the portals to take over both Earth and Otherworld, and I was content to sit back and let them handle it.

The doorbell rang and I let them in, motioning to the living room.

"I don't know how much time I have before Mitch gets home," I said. "He's going to be late, but I want to take care of this before he gets here, if you don't mind." I rubbed my arms, feeling chilly even though I'd turned up the heat.

"What's shaking, babe?" Camille, the oldest, looked like a raven-haired cross between a member of the Society for Creative Anachronism and an S and M bar's madame. A real vixen. Delilah, a six-one lean, athletic, golden blond werecat, followed her in. Their sister Menolly couldn't make it, though. She was a vampire and wasn't up before sunset.

"How do I begin?" I turned to them, biting my lip. How was I going to stand here and tell my good friends that I'd lied to them from the beginning, even though the lie was for self-protection. Deciding that it would be like pulling teeth—better to just yank it than try to wriggle it out—I sucked in a deep breath, and then everything spilled out in a rush.

* * *

Delilah stared at me, a dumbfounded look on her face. She slowly leaned forward, her motorcycle boots heavy on the floor as she rested her elbows on the denim covering her knees. "You mean you weren't sent over to the United States because of inbreeding?"

"Not really." I shook my head. "I ran away. I spent the

entire trip terrified that someone had slipped on board behind me and would drag me over the side and back home. But nothing happened. By the time I got to Ellis Island, I realized that I'd actually done it. I escaped."

"And your parents were going to marry you off to a rapist? How sick can you get? Although . . ." Camille glanced at Delilah and snorted, "It sure sounds like some of the families back in Otherworld. *We've* got no use for people like that. You were brave to run away."

"Brave? Maybe. But not wise enough to cover my tracks once I set out for the West Coast. Hell, some of the states were still barely coming to grips with being states. The cities here were rough-and-tumble, unlike the cities back east. I didn't think anybody would ever be able to find me and as the years wore on, I grew careless." I jumped up and paced, too nervous to sit. "But now Terrance has found me and I'm terrified."

"Try to remember everything he said on the phone. I take it you don't have his number?"

I shook my head. "He has call block."

"Great. Okay, so we go from there." Camille motioned to Delilah, who pulled out her laptop and fired it up so she could take notes. "We need to know everything about Terrance. About you running away, and the Pod you ran from. You wouldn't happen to have any pictures of him, would you?"

"No, but if he looks the same as he did back then, I can describe him. I look close to what I looked like back then, so there's no reason he shouldn't as well. Though I do dye my hair because I like this color, and I wear makeup now. That was a big no-no back then."

"Okay, ready. Give me a description of what he looked like the last time you saw him," Delilah said, her fingers poised over the keys.

I closed my eyes and thought back to the last time I'd seen Terry. It had been the day before our wedding, and he'd been angry. *Very angry.*

* * *

"What do you mean, you want to move back the wedding date?" Terry's eyes flickered, his black hair gleaming under the early-morning sun. The mist was burning off the cove and it looked like we were in for a nice day.

"I thought we could hold off. At least until the solstice. I'd like to be married on a holiday," I said, striving for some reasonable explanation. My goal: Put him off long enough to gather the money I needed for the boat ticket.

"Not going to happen," he said. "Tomorrow we marry, and then you're mine. All mine. Your family will move out of that shack, and you'll move into my house. Into my bed," he added, leering.

A goose walked over my grave and I shivered, wrapping my arms around my shoulders. "Terry, it's just another couple of weeks. Why are you so angry? You're going to get what you want, so why deny me this? Consider it a wedding present." I forced myself to look compliant and lowered my eyes so he couldn't read what I was really thinking.

But he reached out and placed his finger under my chin, tipping my head up to look me square in the face.

"I don't believe you," he said softly, leaning close. "I don't believe you for a second. I know how you feel about me and what you think of marrying me. What you don't seem to understand is that *your feelings don't matter.* I want you and I'm going to have you. You'll adjust, and in the meantime, I'll make sure you enjoy yourself. Trust me," he whispered, his lips bare inches from mine. "You'll love every moment of every night."

I pulled away, trying to keep my balance, but he was a tall man and broad-shouldered, with a narrow waist. As was the nature of the roane, his hair was jet-black, wavy and curling around his ears. A scar was the one blemish he had—a jagged cut on his throat that had come from when a shark had caught him by the neck. His kinsmen had swum in to save him, one of them losing his life in the process. But Terry had survived and healed up, with just the scar to remind him. Seal or human, it remained in both his forms.

I drank in the sight of him, wanting to remember his face when I was long gone and this was all like a bad dream. Terrance would be my reminder that evil sometimes wore a very pleasant body.

"Fine. We wed tomorrow," I said and pulled away. "Now leave me be. I have to start my preparations for the handfasting."

As I walked away, I forced myself to focus on the fact that I'd never have to look at him again. Never have to talk to him, listen to him, endure his touch. But to escape, I'd have to steal the money. I'd hoped to put off the wedding until I could sell a few things to earn my passage fare, but there wasn't time.

By the time I reached our house, everyone was gone. Like a common thief, I raided the secret stashes where my parents and brothers kept their money, ending up with a handful of change above and beyond the cost of my ticket.

I packed two satchels. The journey would be lean and cold until I found a home and a job, so most of what I took were clothes, food, and a few toiletries. I stopped, though, when I came to my mother's photo box. The pictures were expensive, but my mother had managed to afford a photograph of the entire family, and she had three copies of it. I pressed the photograph to my lips, kissing it gently, then slid the picture inside my satchel, in between two small books to keep it flat and unharmed.

After that, I tucked a small vial of sand from the Orkney's shores into my handbag, along with my seal skin. I'd brought the sand with me to Queenstown, and I'd take it with me to America.

As soon as I was finished packing, I scribbled a hasty farewell.

Dear Ma and Da,

I cannot go through with the marriage. I simply can't marry Terrance. I know you don't understand. I know you feel I let down the Pod and I expect you'll hate me for it. Please, don't bother looking for me, and don't let Terrance look for me either. You won't find me. Consider me dead if you like. I resign my ties to the Pod. I shall miss you all. As for Terrance, he can rot in the blackest depths of the sea and I would rejoice. Give my brothers lots of love.

—Siobhan

I hurried toward the port and an hour later, ticket in hand, I was bustling up the gangplank. The *Umbria* was about to set sail and I'd secured one of the last seats. It would be an uncomfortable crossing, but in less than three weeks I'd walk off the boat, into a new life.

As the ship's horn sounded and we slowly pulled away from shore, I resolutely walked to the front of the boat. With images of my family flickering through my mind, I kept my eyes on the open water as we headed out to sea.

* * *

I looked at Camille. Her eyes were filled with sorrow and I realized that they understood. They knew why I'd lied to them. Why I'd hid behind a layer of half-truths and veiled deceptions. But still . . . I had to ask.

"Can you forgive me for lying to you?"

Delilah slowly hit the Save button on her file of notes. Then she called up Google and did a search on his name to see if we could find any pictures on the Web, but there were none. Pressing her lips together, she held out her hand and drew me down to sit in the chair between her and her sister.

"We understand. And Menolly . . . she'll probably understand best of all," she said softly. "The question is, what do we do now? Does he have the right to demand you head home with him? Is there any way he could make it stick? By human rights he can't do a damned thing to you—but the Supe Community might see it otherwise. They couldn't force you to go, but they could stand by and do nothing while he took you. Or make life miserable if you refused."

"I don't know," I said softly. "The Pod is old-fashioned. We may be the Weres who cling to tradition most. Many of the selkie and roane still don't interact with humans as much as other shifters do, and to be honest, we aren't even like most other Weres. We aren't ruled by the moon—not our shifting, at least."

Camille let out a long sigh. "The Pod could also make life a bitch for your baby, and for Mitch. Speaking of, you said you haven't told Mitch about this yet? Big mistake. You can't leave him out of this or he'll resent you for it."

I shook my head. "I'm not sure what the hell to do. We're supposed to get married as soon as the baby's born. Now I wonder, will he leave me? Will he side with the Pod?"

"You're borrowing trouble. Siobhan, I know you think solving this means just getting Terrance out of the way before anybody finds out about him, but what if he moves before we can nail him? What if he calls Mitch at work or shows up at the door?"

I knew she was right, but I couldn't even begin to think about how I was going to tell Mitch I'd fabricated a large part of my past. *Sweetie, I lied to you about almost everything from my past, but it's no big deal . . .* "No. If we find Terry first—"

Delilah dove in. "That's a big *if.* You have to realize that if Terrance knows your cell phone number, he's got to have done his homework. He's been stalking you for over a hundred years, and stalkers don't usually care about the feelings of their victim's loved ones."

She motioned for me to stand and—not knowing what else to do—I stood. Delilah put her arm around my shoulder and

I stared up at the towering Amazon of a woman. When I first met her, she was gentle, a kitten at heart, but I could tell she'd hardened over the past year or so. Camille, too. They looked tired, weary even when they were laughing.

"Here," she said, easing me in front of the mirror in the hallway. "Look at yourself. Look at your tummy. You have a child inside there—one you came by only after a long, hard time. Are you going to put her in danger? Are you going to chance your daughter's survival because you're afraid your fiancé will be angry at you?"

As I stared at my reflection, I let out a long sigh. She was right. They both were, and I had to face facts. "I'll tell Mitch tonight when he gets home."

"Good. Meanwhile, we'll nose around and see what we can find. We need to know everything you can remember about Terrance's tastes, hobbies—anything that might help us get a lead on him."

As we returned to the kitchen, I realized that this problem wasn't going to disappear just because I was in denial. I sank into my seat and began to tell them everything I could remember.

"Terry liked to fish, of course—all our men were fishermen, and most of the roane, too. After all, who knows the sea better than a selkie or roane or one of the Finfolk?"

I poured tea—caffeinated for Camille, herbal for Delilah and me—and set out a plate of shortbread. I made the best shortbread in the city; of that I was sure. Coworkers were always begging me to bring a batch to parties.

"What's the difference between the Finfolk and the selkies

or roane?" Camille asked. "Back in Otherworld, selkies are considered part of the Weres rather than the Fae. But Finfolk?"

"Selkies and roane are odd among the Weres, in that we have our seal suits. We don't fully shift over like you, for example." I pointed at Delilah. "You, now, even your clothes make the shift in the form of a collar. The selkies don't have that one hundred percent transformation rate. And we don't shift on cue from the moon."

"I always wondered why."

"I have no idea," I said. "I've never known a water creature to shift fully over—at least, not a *water animal*, not one ruled by anything other than the Ocean Mother herself. But the Finfolk . . . they fully transform, but they also never take full animal form. They're part fish, part humanoid in their natural state."

"Wait—are they also called the Meré?" Camille perked up. "If so, then I understand what you're saying."

"Could be. Mermen, mermaids? They can take human form for only a short time compared to selkies—a few days in between returning to the sea. But they're . . ."

"Mean." Camille grimaced. "Mean, nasty, and up to no good. In Otherworld, the Meré are considered Fae, but they aren't welcome near most towns. In fact, most of our port cities have guards to watch out for them because the men are . . . well . . . a lot like Terrance. You're right—there is a resemblance there. I wonder if he has mixed blood. Roane-Meré?" She gave me a look that told me she really didn't want to hear a *yes.*

"That would explain a lot," I said, holding my stomach. "And if that's the case, if he even has a tiny sprinkling of Meré in his blood, then he'll rip out my child and sacrifice it without hesitation. The Meré are possessive, and once they decide something—or someone—is theirs, they do everything possible to keep it that way. A child from another man would make a Meré wild with jealousy. My baby would be a sitting duck."

"Do you think there's a chance? Even a faint one?" Delilah looked up, alert. "If so, we'd better get you some protection."

I stared at the table. Could he have Finfolk blood in his veins? It couldn't be much or he'd have to be in the water more than I remembered. But then, I hadn't known him very long. We'd gone for a walk, he'd raped me, then offered to marry me to even the score. It had taken less than a month for my parents to settle with him on the wedding payment. In all that time, I'd seen him for only a few hours here and there. Just long enough to know I wanted to kill him, but not long enough to know whether he spent a lot of time cruising the waves.

"I don't know, but it's possible." I looked up. "At this point, I'm willing to believe anything."

"Why don't you show me your computer?" Delilah said.

I led her into the living room where we kept the desk with the computer on it. "Here it is—but why?"

"Because I want to check for spyware, for Trojans, for worms, for anything he might have sent you. There are so many ways to hack into someone's computer that it's scary. And if he's after all the information on you he can find . . ." She left the thought unfinished but I saw what she was getting at.

I curled up on the sofa, not wanting to know how far Terry had insinuated himself into my life without me realizing it. As I sat there, watching Delilah tap away at the keys, the reality of what was happening began to hit home. Terrance was really back in my life.

I glanced at the clock. Mitch should be home soon and I'd have to tell him what happened. "Can you guys stick around and help me explain?" I looked at Camille, as I picked at the hangnail on my thumb. "I know you're busy but I just . . ."

"You're afraid," she said. "Not of Mitch, but of what he might say?"

I nodded. "I lied to him. Not fully, but I sure didn't tell him everything. And I know he'll understand but what if . . . what if . . ."

"What if he doesn't?"

Again, I nodded. "What if he decides to leave me? To leave his child?"

"That's not going to happen," Delilah said. "Mitch is—Hello, what do we have here? Siobhan, has your computer been running a little slow lately?"

I frowned, thinking back. Mitch mainly used it to play World of Warcraft with his buddies, but I checked my e-mail, did a little online shopping, kept my diary on it.

"Yeah, it has. For about a month. Mitch said maybe we need to defrag it but I'm not sure what that means. I can use Outlook and I can write in my journal and surf the Web but I don't know much else about how a computer runs."

"E-mail? Do you get a lot of spam mail?" She frowned, tapping away at the keys.

"Gods, yes. I delete probably fifty a day."

"You should get Gmail. It has to work better than what you're using right now. You say you do a lot of online shopping?

What about online banking?" Delilah looked worried now, the black crescent scythe tattoo on her forehead flashing silver.

"Yeah, why?" I sat up. "What's wrong?"

"I think . . ." she started to say, then paused and moved the mouse a few more times. "I think you've been hacked. There are a few processes going on in your task manager that I don't recognize and they look suspicious to me."

"Oh great gods, do you think Terrance is responsible?"

She shrugged. "Could be. I'm not positive that I'm right, though. I'd like to call Tim Winthrop over to take a look. He'd be able to tell better than me. Do you mind?"

Tim was a good friend of the D'Artigos. He was a female impersonator, though I heard he was giving it up, and he'd recently married his long-term partner, Jason Binds. Mitch and I'd been invited to the wedding.

"Sure, go ahead."

As Delilah flipped open her cell phone, I glanced at the clock again. *Mitch should have called by now.* I turned around, kneeling on the sofa to stare out the window at the rain thundering against the pavement.

Something was wrong. I could feel it in my bones. I had a sudden, intense urge to head out to the Sound, to slip on my skin and dive deep in the water, seeking shelter in the depths of the inlet. Every time I felt threatened, that was the first thing that came to mind—hide, run to the Ocean Mother's bosom, and let her hold me tight.

"Tim will be over in about half an hour," Delilah said, breaking my thoughts. "He's bringing all his diagnostic gear with him. If anybody can figure out what's going on with your computer, he can."

Camille picked up the tea tray and carried it into the kitchen. "I'll make us some more tea," she said.

"Thank you. Everything feels so surreal. I can't believe this is happening—" I was cut off by the phone ringing. Mitch! It had to be him. I grabbed the handset and punched the Talk button. "Hello? Mitch?"

The voice on the other end was one I didn't recognize. A woman, she sounded professional, and yet there was something about her voice that scared me. "Am I speaking to Siobhan Morgan?"

"Yes . . . Who's calling?" Suspicion suddenly hit me in the gut. What if she was working with Terry; what if—

"My name is Amanda Bernard and I'm a nurse with Inter-Lake Hospital. I'm calling about a Mr. Mitchell Childs. Do you know him?"

Hospital? Mitch? Oh hell.

"He's my fiancé. We live together. What's wrong? Is he okay?" Panic replaced suspicion and I stiffened, trying not to cry. The hormones from being pregnant sure weren't helping me to remain calm.

"Mr. Childs has been injured. We need you to come in and give us information on his medical background. He seems to be part of the Supernatural Community. We have an Otherworld healer on hand—an elfin doctor—but we can use any background information you can give us. He needs treatment now."

"He's a selkie. Tell the doctor that. I'll be there as fast as I can." Choking back tears, I added, "Is he . . . Is the injury serious? What can you tell me?"

Her voice was soft as she said, "You should be prepared. He's been extensively injured. I won't mince words, Ms. Morgan. He's in serious condition, though we aren't sure as to just what extent. He's unconscious at the moment. We found your name in his wallet as his emergency contact."

I hung up, a searing heat racing through me. The man I was in love with was lying in the hospital and I had the horrible feeling that it hadn't been an accident. I turned mutely to Camille and Delilah.

Camille turned off the stove. "I'll take you to the hospital. Delilah, you stay here and wait for Tim." She held up my jacket and I silently let her tuck me into it; then she gathered up my purse and pushed me gently out the door.

"Where is he?"

"InterLake Hospital," I said, trying to find my voice.

She slid me into the passenger seat of her Lexus and I fumbled for the seat belt as she jumped in the driver's seat. "Breathe, Siobhan. He's alive, and he's under medical care. I want you to get my cell phone out of my purse and look for Chase Johnson's number under my contact list. Tell him you're with me, and who you are, and ask him to bring Sharah and meet us at the hospital."

I followed directions, mouthing the words, hearing Chase's concerned voice on the other end, and then hung up. Camille didn't say anything else; she just focused on navigating through the heavy rain while I stared out the window, remembering the first time I realized I had fallen in love with Mitch Childs.

3

It was 1998, and I'd integrated myself into the Puget Sound Harbor Seal Pod. They'd accepted me as a member, with my slightly altered résumé, and I once again sank into the comfort of belonging to a tribe. It had been eighty-one years since I'd had a group to call my own, and over those intervening years, I'd worked my way down one coastline and up the other, alone and lonely.

I'd adapted as my new land grew and evolved. I'd been everything from a maid during my first few years, to a candy-and-cigarette girl at a nightclub during the war, to an admin assistant at a law firm during the sixties, to a yoga teacher during the eighties.

But I'd never applied for any job that would place me too much in the public view, and while I returned to my real name after a while, I'd managed to navigate the underground labyrinth of changing licenses and social security numbers. I flew under the radar because, like all Fae and Weres, I aged more slowly than humans. It wasn't wise to let yourself be high profile. People would start with whispers; then came the rumors. Hair dye could take care of the hair, but until recently, Botox and plastic surgery weren't viable options to explain away the smooth skin and clear eyes.

Once I found the Pod, I'd decided to stick around the Seattle area, and I applied for a job with the state. I made the decision to finally go the route of using wigs and carefully applied makeup to age myself enough to be believable until retirement, at which point I'd have a good thirty years before having to reinvent myself again.

And then, I met Mitch. Mitchell Childs, who was a sturdy, muscled selkie with blue eyes and wavy chestnut hair. He was part of the Puget Sound Harbor Seal Pod, though not highly placed. And with one look in his eyes, I was lost. Within a week, we had tumbled into a whirlwind affair.

"Siobhan," he said, wrapping his arms around me the first time we stood alone together by the side of the inlet, staring out into the moonlit night. "I've been waiting for you. I didn't know who you would be, or where you would come from, but I've been waiting my whole life for someone like you."

He kissed me, his soft lips pressing gently against mine, his arms pulling me into the heart of his embrace, and in the flow of his kiss the world stopped and I knew life would never be the same. *I* would never be the same. This was the love I'd been looking for. This was my magic man, my love from the sea, the one who could sweep me off my feet and carry me away and I'd never, ever protest.

No man had touched me since Terrance. I'd made sure of that. And there had been no one before Terrance. Terrified but unable to turn away, I'd invited Mitch into my world, let him woo me and bed me and love me. But I'd kept my secrets. My past remained sealed, behind closed doors I'd locked so tight that I thought nothing could rip them open again.

A few years later, when the portals from Otherworld opened, Supes, Fae, and vampires flooded the world, coming out of the closet in droves, and I began to think that Mitch and I could have a life together, out in the open, and that I wouldn't have to shed my persona with my skin.

Until now.

And now everything threatened to be swept away by the same malignant force that had snuffed out my life in Ireland. The Pod could revoke my membership if they wanted; they could send me away. And Mitch—would he turn his back on me and the child we'd fought so hard to conceive?

And now—now Mitch might *die.*

With tears pouring down my cheeks, images of the past flipped through my mind like a deck of cards in the wind. I *couldn't* lose him. And I wouldn't let Terrance win.

Grimly, I turned to Camille, whose gaze was fastened on the road. "Whatever it takes, I want Terrance out of the picture. I know he's involved in this. I *know* he hurt Mitch. And if I'm right, I want him dead and buried so deep he'll never climb out of the grave to see the world again. Will you help me?"

She flickered a glance my way, then back to the road. "You know what you're asking, right?"

I bit my lip. I wasn't like Camille or her sisters. My life wasn't steeped in danger every day, and I wasn't a fighter like they were. I was just Siobhan Morgan, data entry operator for the state. But I was also selkie—a daughter of the Ocean Mother—and someone I loved was in danger. Time to step up to the plate.

"I know what I'm asking. Whatever you tell me to do, I'll do it. I love Mitch, and I'm not going to let Terry ruin my life with him, or our baby's life. I don't know much about fighting, Camille, but you tell me to jump and I'll jump."

She sighed. "Well, then, I promise you this: We'll do everything possible to find him and put him out of commission. And, Siobhan, make no mistake—if we go looking for him and find him, we'll *have* to kill him. Because men like him, be they FBH—full-blooded human—or Fae . . . or Were . . . they don't give up. He's stalked you for a hundred years over thousands of miles. He's not going to quit. Especially not now that he's found you."

"I know," I said. "I know."

* * *

The nurse led Camille and me to Mitch's bedside. I'd call the Pod leader and Mitch's parents as soon as I found out what was going on, but right now, I wanted to see if he was conscious, if he could remember anything. But he lay there, silent and unmoving, his body wrapped in bandages and his eyes closed in a deep sleep.

"What's wrong?" I rushed to his side, wanting to bundle him in my arms and kiss him on the forehead, to wake him with the taste of my lips on his. But this was no fairy tale, and Mitch wasn't Sleeping Beauty. No, he was severely injured and only the doctors could lead him out of danger.

"One leg is broken in three places; the other has a fracture. His left arm was shattered and we don't know if he'll ever be able to regain use of it. We think he has internal injuries to his spleen and his kidneys. His entire abdominal area is severely bruised. We'll have to do exploratory surgery, and we're going to have to open up his arm, too, in order to repair the shattered bone."

The doctor looked at me. "Miss, I know you're his fiancée, but we need his parents here, too, if they're around."

"I'll call them right away," I murmured, staring at my love. "Why is he unconscious?"

"As to the coma, we don't know. He should be awake, but he's not, and his EKG shows some abnormal activity, but of what nature, we're not entirely sure. That's why we've postponed his surgery. Since the head medic of the Faerie-Human Crime Scene Investigation team is coming to look him over, we decided to wait for her opinion before we do anything more. We have him stabilized for now, so he should be okay until sh gets here."

I let out a long sigh. "What happen

he was injured?"

The doctor pressed his lips together.

son is on his way, I suggest you wait and

this is just a preliminary conclusion, it

Childs was assaulted." He turned away to talk softly to the nurse.

I took a quick step toward Camille, who draped her arm around my shoulder and gave me a little squeeze. "This is bad, I know it's bad, but he's alive. You have to hold on to that. Sharah's on the way and she's a brilliant healer."

I let out a little whimper, but knew Camille was right. I also knew that one of her own lovers—Trillian—was still missing on a secret mission. She was facing some of the same fears that I was.

"Thank you for being here," I whispered.

Just then, Chase strode in, followed by Sharah, the elfin medic who had helped me conceive. I gave them a strained smile and Sharah patted my arm as she slipped past, her attention focused on Mitch.

Camille motioned for me to follow her. She glanced at Chase. "We'll be in the cafeteria waiting for you."

He nodded. "See you in about ten. I just want to talk to the doctor first."

On our way to the dining hall, Camille said, "Chase is good at what he does. If he can help us, he will."

I stared at the sandwiches lining the à la carte buffet, finally choosing a tuna on sourdough. I hadn't eaten since breakfast except for a few cookies, and even though I didn't have any desire for food, I knew it would help me cope with what was oing on. I added a Jell-O salad cup to my tray and watched as nille piled hers high with a meatball sub, a Caesar salad, and le of brownies.

"If I tried to eat that much food at once, I'd throw up." I handed the teller a ten and she gave me back my change.

"All Otherworld Fae have high metabolism," Camille said. "We'd starve if we ate like the women over Earthside. I think something happened during the Great Divide to our people. Even though my sisters and I are half human, we take after our father in this regard. The downside is, our food bills are a bitch."

She flashed me a smile and I actually laughed. The release felt good, though the minute I heard myself, I sobered again.

Camille steered me to a table by the wall, out of earshot of the main room. As we settled in to our food, eating silently, the pale green of the hospital walls began to get to me. It was depressing and drab. No wonder people who were stuck in here didn't get well very fast. It should be a warm beige, or a cheery yellow—something to perk up the spirits and infuse energy into the sterile hallways and rooms.

We were just finishing when Chase came in. He hurried up to our table after stopping to get a cup of coffee and a Danish. As Camille pulled the chair out for him, he slid into it and wearily began stirring sugar into his milk-laden coffee.

Camille leaned forward. "Did you find out anything?"

Chase frowned, looking at me. "Yeah, a little. But I need to ask you, Siobhan, what's going on? Apparently Mitch was holding on to consciousness when he was brought in, enough to tell the doctor that he had to get home to you—that you were in danger. Care to elaborate on any secrets I should know?"

I bit my lip, not wanting to bring the cops in on this, but

it appeared there was no other choice. With Camille's help, I ran down everything that had happened, and why. When we finished, Chase was shaking his head.

"So this Terrance guy, he raped you and then your parents were going to marry you off to him?"

I nodded. "It's the way, in some of the Pods. While rules are different among the varying Were tribes, the selkies are old—very old—and don't adapt well to social change. You say that Mitch told the healer I'm in danger?"

Chase nodded. "He was raving, so the doc wasn't sure at first what he was talking about but apparently he kept insisting that you and the baby were in danger. The doctor asked him who did this and all he would say was one of the web-fingered caught him. Any clue as to what that means?"

I caught my breath. "*Web-fingered?* Are you sure?"

"Yeah. The doctor said it caught him off guard. He has no idea what Mitch was talking about."

I pressed my fingers to my temple, trying to forestall the looming headache. "Oh Great Mother, I need some tea. Camille?"

She nodded and slipped out of her seat. As she headed over to the beverage counter, I said, "*Web-fingered* is another name for the Finfolk. Camille and her sisters know them as the Meré. They're evil. We were thinking Terrance might have some Finfolk blood in him. It sounds as though Mitch recognized it."

"Then it's a good bet he's the one we're looking for. He really messed up your fiancé, Siobhan; I'll say that for him. And by FBH laws, I can run him down and catch him, but I have to warn you—according to treaties, the Supe Community can demand we extradite him for trial, since he attacked a Supe rather than a human. But we can at least try to catch him."

Chase flipped open his notepad. "Will you work with a police sketch artist to create a drawing of him?"

I stared at him. Extradition? I'd been afraid of that, and now the last thing I wanted was for Chase to find Terrance. If the Puget Sound Harbor Seal Pod demanded extradition, there was a chance that Terrance would be set free on the grounds that he had prior claim to me. And a *chance*—even if it turned out to be slim—was too dangerous. No, it was best if Camille and her sisters could help me find him before the FH-CSI. That way, there would be an end to this. But I didn't want to alienate the detective, so I murmured my cooperation.

When Camille returned with my tea, we promised we'd head over to the FH-CSI headquarters after we checked in on Mitch again, and after I called his parents. Chase slipped out of his seat and left, giving me a gentle nod as he went. I stirred my raspberry tea, letting the scent waft up to comfort me, wondering how the hell it had come to this, and how come *now*, when I had so much to lose?

* * *

Sharah verified what the doctor had told us about Mitch's injuries, adding that his coma was his body's way of shutting down to begin the healing process. She didn't sense any loss of function in his brain, and his silver cord was intact so he was fine—just sleeping so deeply we couldn't reach him at this point.

I called Mitch's parents and the Pod elders, and gave them the news, leaving my cell number as Camille and I headed out to talk to the sketch artist. It seemed odd, pretending to care when I fully intended to give the man a vague description. I debated whether to tell Camille that I planned to throw the sketch, but she might feel obligated to tell Chase, and he'd get angry and cause a big scene I really didn't need right now.

Instead, I asked her to call Delilah while I went in and talked to the artist. "Can you find out what Delilah and Tim have discovered about my hacked computer?"

"You're sure you don't need me for moral support?" She gazed at me and I had the uncomfortable feeling she could see through me like Saran Wrap.

"No . . . no, I'm fine. Thanks, though, for everything."

I went through the motions, giving vague answers that sounded legitimate enough to fly under the radar, and in the end, the generic-looking face on the page could have been any number of men walking through the mall. I forced a worried smile and said, "That's him, all right." The sketch artist was happy, Chase was happy, and I was relieved.

Camille was waiting for me when I came out. We headed out to her Lexus. She motioned for me to be quiet until we were safely inside the car, then said, "You were hacked, all right. Delilah thinks somebody's combed through all your files. Tim said there's a doozy of a Trojan that snuck through. You must have clicked on an attachment in some e-mail you got, and it executed a program that created a direct path into your files. There's a good chance that someone—and I think we can bet on it being Terrance—managed to download a copy of every single document and image you have on your computer."

"Then everything there . . . Terrance has snooped through

everything we have on there? My journal, our pictures . . ." My stomach lurched and I couldn't tell if it was the baby, the food, or my own feeling of being violated yet again. Mitch and I had some compromising shots of us tucked away, taken with our digital camera so we wouldn't run the risk of someone else seeing them.

"Damn it, Terry's done it again. He's invaded my life and broken my boundaries." The thought that Terrance had seen those pictures, that he had all my ID information, that he had access to our financial information and everything else that Mitch and I stored on our computer, made me want to scream.

Camille grimaced. "Babe, I hate to say this, but he probably has your passwords, too—apparently there was keystroke logger spyware bundled into the package, and so everything you typed onto the computer was logged on to a host machine. The upside is that Tim thinks he might be able to trace it, because that kind of spyware leaves a footprint. There should be a trail leading back to the IP address that the information was sent to."

"This is just getting worse and worse." I leaned my head against the seat, wanting to cry. "Can they trace the IP address to where he lives, by any chance?"

She shrugged. "That I don't know, but it gives us a place to start. And remember—maybe the techno-mages of the elves can help. They might be able to magically track him if we can't do it via the Internet."

"They can do that?" I pressed my hand to my head, trying to stave off the looming headache. Too much had happened today and I was worried about Mitch, and felt like I was coming down with the flu.

"I don't know, but it's worth a shot. Now come on; let's go home and see what Tim and Delilah have to say." She started the car and eased out of the parking spot.

"I don't want to go home. I want to stay with Mitch."

She shook her head. "You're pregnant. You're going home and we'll talk to Tim, and then you're going to take a nap. You need your rest."

I didn't bother arguing. Camille and her sisters were stubborn and I knew better than to try to change her mind. I stared out the window, wondering what the hell was happening. Had I done something to anger the gods? Had the Ocean Mother turned against me?

"Damn it," Camille muttered, a few minutes after she'd pulled onto I-5, northbound.

"What's wrong?" As I glanced over at her, she bit her lip and glanced in the rearview mirror.

"I'm not sure, but . . . I think we're being followed." She switched lanes and then sped up, passing by a line of cars before smoothly moving back into our original lane again.

After a few minutes, she shook her head. "And there they are again—don't turn around, because whoever it is has a good view of us, but there's a silver Saab to our left, one car behind us. Whoever they are, they've been on our tail since shortly after we pulled out of the hospital. They've got tinted windows, so it's hard to see who's behind the wheel."

"Aren't tinted windows illegal?" I eased a glance through

the rearview mirror to catch only a glimpse of the Saab. The windows *were* dark, too dark to see through, at least from this angle.

"Not if they fall within a certain percentage range. I had to find out for Menolly—she wanted the windows of her Jag tinted, so we had to check on the laws. They're plenty expensive, though." She darted a glance over her shoulder, then flicked on the turn signal and moved into the right lane. "Let's see if they follow us over—Yeah, here they come. Whoever they are, they're keeping pace with us, but staying one lane over."

She nodded toward the sign ahead. "We're making an unscheduled departure from the freeway," she said as she veered onto the exit ramp.

My heart began to race as we quickly paced around the winding ramp, ending up on James Street. We came to a light and had to stop, and Camille fretted as we watched the line of cars go by from the other direction. She glanced in the rearview mirror and sucked in a deep breath.

"He's there, behind us, about four cars back. I was hoping we'd lose him but somehow he managed to change lanes fast enough to make the exit." She eyed the area. "We're near Seattle University, but I don't think that's going to help us. It's too late for most classes, and I don't want to take a chance on driving into an area that isn't in full view of the public. Any suggestions would be helpful."

I frantically stared out the window, my thoughts racing, trying to remember if there was anybody I knew who lived or worked in the area. And then, a name clicked to mind. I snapped my fingers. "Get onto Twelfth and head toward East Pike. Marion has a café over there and they stay open late. They're always packed because it's a big Supe hangout."

Camille quickly turned onto Twelfth as soon as the light turned green. "Who's Marion?"

"She's a member of the Northwest Seattle Coyote Clan. They're urban coyote shifters who mainly stay in the cities. A lot of the coyote Weres have taken to doing that, along with a number of the dog and cat Weres. Lagomorphs, too."

We had to adapt to modern life, I thought. It was either that, or die out. The wilderness was shrinking and while some of the bear, wolf, and big cat tribes still kept to the sparsely populated states and wilderness areas, most of the smaller Weres had slowly begun to familiarize themselves with urban living.

As we cruised down Twelfth, trying not to let the tailing Saab spook us, I patted my belly, attempting to soothe my overworked nerves. My thoughts drifted back to Mitch and how badly he'd been injured. Somebody had roughed him up something awful. Terrance had to have a couple of goons with him to cause that much damage because Mitch could hold his own in a fight. It was bad enough to have to worry about *Terrance*, but to be forced to worry about any buddies he might be hanging with . . . The thought scared the shit out of me.

Camille turned onto East Pike and I pointed up ahead. "See, there on the right. The Supe-Urban Café. There's parking to the side, right after you pass the restaurant, so pull in there and let's get ready to run in."

I unbuckled my seat belt and grabbed both our purses as Camille swung into the side parking lot. The minute she pulled to a stop and turned off the ignition, we hit the doors. As we raced for the restaurant, she locked the car with her electronic key. We managed to slip inside just as the silver Saab slowly paced by. I lingered long enough to see it pull into the parking lot.

"They're still on our tail. Head to the back. Marion spends a lot of time in the kitchen." I handed Camille her purse and led her through the maze of tables. Business was brisk; most of the tables were filled with people, eating, drinking coffee, talking, reading. It was really more of a hangout than a restaurant and Marion told me she was making enough to put her oldest through college.

As we came to the swinging doors that led to the restrooms and the office, I pushed through and found myself face-to-face with Marion herself. She was lean, gaunt but not anorexic, and she had that hungry look in her eyes that all coyote Weres seemed to have. They never looked like they'd had enough to eat, and very seldom seemed fully happy, though most that I knew were quite content and led fulfilling lives. It was just something in their nature that led them to look like street children staring through a candy store window.

"Siobhan, I haven't seen you in—" She stopped, staring at me, her nose twitching. "You're afraid. What's made you so afraid in my restaurant?"

Camille interjected herself between the door and my back. "We're being followed by someone who's looking to harm Siobhan. Do you have a place we can hide?" Most Supe establishments had panic rooms of one sort or another.

Marion glanced from Camille to me, then back to Camille

again. She quickly turned and motioned for us to follow her. We headed into her office, where she closed the door behind her, then swiftly pulled a bookshelf away from the wall. It was hinged, though we couldn't see the hinges from the way it was attached, and a dimly lit passage showed from behind it.

"This leads to a tunnel that comes out a few blocks away in Westmeyer Park. You can either wait here for me, or you can head down there and I'll have one of my men meet you there. You can pick up your car later—who was driving?" Marion handed me a flashlight from her desk.

Camille raised her hand. "That would be me. I've got a steel gray Lexus out there." She turned to me. "Siobhan, we can call Chase. He'll bring his men and come down here and if they possibly can, they'll nab him. Because you and I both know that has to be Terrance."

I bit my lip, thinking. We could wait here, let Chase catch him. And then Chase would turn him over to the Supe Community council and he'd have a damned good chance of getting away with this crap. Of course, if he'd been the one to attack Mitch—and I was positive it was him—then maybe we could do something, but with Mitch in a coma, there was no way to prove his attacker had been Terrance.

On the other hand, if I really wanted him gone, it meant taking care of him without anybody else finding out. I shook my head.

"No. We play it the way we were thinking about. Marion, thanks for the offer, but we'll call our friends on the way and have them meet us. It's enough that you're giving us the chance to escape. I'll explain everything later." I ducked into the tunnel and blew a kiss at the Were. "Anything I can do for you, let me know."

She laughed. "Just name your firstborn after me," she said, shutting the door behind us.

As the sounds of the bar were muffled by the thick bookshelf, I let out a long sigh and flicked the switch on the flashlight. The light beat a steady beam down the corridor and I breathed a little easier.

"We've got a bit of a walk in front of us," I said, glancing down at my pumps ruefully.

Camille held out her foot. She was wearing stilettos. "Don't even talk to me about painful footwear," she said, smiling. "Come on, let's get moving. I wonder if I can get cell reception down here. If not, we'll have to wait till we come out into the open to call for a ride."

As we started through the musty tunnel, fresh air piped in from somewhere above. How many people had used this getaway? And for what? Whom had they been fleeing from? But try as I might, I couldn't get my mind off Terrance. He'd decided to make his move before I had time to plan. His call had just been a terror tactic, and it had worked. And I knew him well enough to know that he'd stop at nothing to get me back.

4

The tunnel seemed to go on forever, but in reality we were walking for only about fifteen minutes. Camille's cell phone didn't work in the underground passage, and neither did mine, so we walked in silence, pushing forward with Camille behind me, keeping an eye over her shoulder. After five minutes, I let out a long breath. After ten, I began to relax. Maybe we'd gotten away after all. I sure hoped Terrance didn't tear up Camille's car, though, in his anger that he hadn't been able to catch us.

Fifteen minutes and we were at the end of the passage, facing a series of steps that led us up to a door with a one-way lock on it. Locked from the inside, we could get out, but once we did and the door swung shut, we wouldn't be able to duck back in.

"Don't let the door close," I whispered. "Not until we know it's safe." I cautiously pushed it open a crack and peeked out.

I was looking into what appeared to be a women's restroom. There was no one in sight. I pushed the door open and stepped out. Camille followed me.

"Wait here," she said, leaving me to hold the door as she raced over to the outer door leading . . . well, wherever it led.

I glanced around the room. Four stalls, dull green, two sinks with faucets. And these were old-fashioned faucets—no *run your hands under the sink and make the water come out* technology here. A paper towel dispenser and a spartan-looking mirror hung on the wall. Track lighting illuminated the room with fluorescent lights. Windows lined the upper wall, letting in some natural light. Yeah, this was a utilitarian bathroom, all right.

Camille dashed back. "It's okay. We're in the women's restroom for Westmeyer Park. You get back in the tunnel and keep the door open a crack. I'm going to step outside and call Delilah to come pick us up."

I nodded, waiting as she disappeared out the front. A couple minutes later, she was back. "She's on her way. She left Tim at your apartment. He's still fooling around with your computer."

I let out a long sigh. "That's fine." I was tired; my back was killing me from walking in pumps—ever since I'd become pregnant I'd longed for flats, and all I wanted was to sit down somewhere and cry.

Camille noticed and wrapped her arm around me. "Oh, Siobhan, everything will be all right. You wait and see." She cocked her head. "I think I hear a car. Come on, it must be Delilah. The parking lot is just a few feet away from here."

I reluctantly let the tunnel door swing shut. The dark

passage might be creepy but it had provided us a haven, and right now I needed shelter from the storms raging in my life.

As Camille opened the outer door, she let out a startled cry. "Run! Siobhan, run!"

Someone slammed the door open, sending Camille flying against the wall. She screamed as she hit the concrete and slumped to the ground, where she shook her head, dazed.

I whirled back to the tunnel but too late—the door was closed and there was no getting in. With no other exits in the restroom, I ran toward a stall, thinking to lock myself in and maybe buy a few seconds.

The swift scent of ozone filled the air as Camille shouted and a blast ricocheted against the walls. Freezing, I paused; then a man swore and, again, Camille shrieked.

"Siobhan, you might as well give it up. You're coming with me."

That voice, I knew.

"Terrance?" I turned, knowing that no matter what I did, it would be too little, too late.

Three men stood there: Terrance, along with two other men I recognized instantly by their scent as being full-blooded Finfolk.

Terrance motioned to them. "Keith, grab the Faerie bitch. Lon, keep watch."

The one named Keith grabbed Camille up in a bear hug, clapping a hand over her mouth as she struggled. The other took up guard on the door.

I stared at Terrance as he slowly walked toward me. It had been a long time since I'd looked into those cold, blue eyes.

"Just leave us alone. I'm not going with you. You can't force me to go with you." I backed up toward the wall, petrified. The look on his face was maleficent, his lips curled into a snarl.

"Oh, you're coming with me, and as soon as we get rid of the whelp bastard you've got locked up in that oven, I'll get you with my own child and that will seal the deal." His eyes glimmered and he chuckled softly. "I've followed you for too long, over too many miles, to even think of letting you go now."

"No, don't hurt my baby. Please don't hurt my baby." I crossed my hands over my stomach. But then, fear turned to anger. This was *my child*, *Mitch's child*, and if Terrance tried to hurt it, I'd rip him to shreds. "Get out of here or I swear, Terrance, I'll kill you."

He laughed again. "Right, you go on thinking that. No, my dear, you're coming with me and so is your friend. I know plenty of people who'd pay a pretty penny to give her a ride."

"You're part Finfolk, aren't you? You've got Meré blood in you!"

As he walked me back against the wall, one step at a time, he reached out and caught my chin in his hands. He stroked my cheek with one finger, hooking it lightly over my lower lip. "You finally see me clearly, my beautiful selkie princess. Now, it's time to come home with me." The way he said the word *princess* stopped me short. It wasn't an endearment. No, there was something else behind his words.

"Princess?"

"Well, I'll be damned. Your mother never told you, did she?" Terrance laughed roughly. "Ah well, I don't blame her.

Your father's folk were a rough lot—coarse and stinking up the sea. Your mother probably thought she was doing you a favor, but the truth will out, won't it?"

"What truth?" I'd been lying so long that I half believed my own stories, but now he was claiming that my mother had lied to me?

"Your blood gives you a direct lineage to nobility on her side of the family. You're in line for the throne within the Isle of Man Selkie Pod. Since you ran away from your father's people and turned your back on them, you have the option to return home and claim your heritage and right of kinship."

He couldn't be right. My mother, a princess? And now me, in line for the throne?

"Wait—my mother! Isn't she the one who should rise to power if there's a change in rulership? If you harm her—"

He twisted my arm just enough to hurt. "Pipe down. Your mother's fine. But she knowingly turned her back on her own Pod and pledged herself to your father's people. She can't return home now."

"I'm pledged to the Puget Sound Harbor Seal Pod—"

"Ah, but you have the choice to return to your mother's people because she never told you about them. Which you will do. Then, when I marry you, I'll have one of the most powerful groups of selkies under my control, via *your own sweet self.* You, my dear, are my ticket to ruling the waves. After that, it's a short step to the Finfolk taking over your people, just like we did the Cobh roane. My father married into the Pod. He was half Finfolk, and now we control them. We'll reign terror over the seas. At last, do you understand why I chased you for a hundred years? There's more at stake than just a pretty pussy. My people wait for me back home. And your people wait in fear that I'll find you. They've finally figured out just who my family is."

"You're crazy," I said. "I'm no princess—"

"But you are, in your own right. Even if you never married me, you've got the blood of queens flowing through your body. Your father had no idea of just *who* he captured when he went seeking a mate."

I let out a small cry, thinking about my mother and what she'd told me. So she hadn't been lying. Father had stolen her away from her own people. No wonder he had no reservations about handing me over to Terrance; rape and pillage were all too familiar to his people.

"Oh yes," Terrance said softly. "I know *all about* your mother and how your father found her, raped her, and took her to wife. And the kicker is: *She never told your father she's royalty.* Probably didn't want the old man to use her like I'm planning to use you. Accept it, little selkie. Women in our world are a commodity. We men can buy you and sell you at the turn of a whim. And you, my dear, are a valuable treasure."

And then he nodded over his shoulder at Camille. "If you don't come voluntarily, she's dead. I don't care how much my men might fancy her. She's expendable, and you're not. So it's up to you. Come with me without fighting, or I slit her throat."

He pulled out a thick-bladed knife with serrated edges. I cringed. He'd make it hurt. I knew him. He wouldn't kill her quickly; he'd make me watch and she'd die in a wash of blood and water.

"No," I whispered. "Don't. Don't hurt her. I'll come with you." I'd figure a way to escape, but for now, I couldn't let him kill one of my closest friends. One of the women who'd gone out of her way to help me.

"That's better." Terrance stuck the blade back in the sheath attached to his belt. He snorted. "Amazing how soft you are. If it had been me, I'd say *go ahead and do her.* No matter. All the better for me."

"That, Terrance, is the difference between us," I said softly. "You'd let a friend die to save yourself. *I* understand the nature of loyalty."

I shuddered as he dragged me along by the wrist. His lackeys held tight to Camille, keeping her mouth covered. The one energy blast had been enough to warn them she wielded magic, and they weren't taking any chances.

And then we were headed out the door, into the rain that had once again picked up, sweeping in off the inlet.

* * *

Terrance's men shoved Camille into the back of a short RV that was waiting in the parking lot, then crawled in to gag her and tie her up. My stomach clenched. The Finfolk would have a field day with her, and Terrance wouldn't lift a hand to stop them. They'd use her, then play water games with her, letting her nearly drown over and over again until they grew tired with the sport and finished her off. Finfolk fed off of fear, and their sadistic natures weren't satisfied for long.

As Terrance shoved me toward the RV, I heard a shout and jerked around as Delilah jumped out of her Jeep. I opened my mouth and let out a sharp scream, but Terrance sent his hand whistling against my cheek, and the blow stunned me into silence. He pulled me over to the open door and tossed me in to the men. I stumbled, wrapping my arms around my stomach to protect my baby. The one called Keith hauled me inside and I had one fleeting glimpse of Delilah shouting something as she raced our way before the door slammed shut.

Terrance climbed into the driver's seat up front.

"Should we tie this one up, boss?" Lon stared at me, looking all too excited by the prospect.

"Nah," Terrance said. "She can't use magic, and she knows what I'll do to her friend if she tries anything. Just keep an eye on her."

And then, with the squeal of brakes and tires, we were zooming past Delilah. I could see her through the front windshield. In fact, Terrance took aim at her and I let out a sharp cry, but then she dove to the left at the last minute and he ignored her, plowing out of the parking lot.

Camille struggled, trying to sit up. Lon unceremoniously smacked her a good one and she fell back. He laughed as she lay prone and reached up her skirts. I let him have it right across the nose with my nails, which were nice, tough gels—hard and sharp-edged.

"Bitch!" he said, but he didn't touch me and I realized that unless Terrance gave them the go-ahead, they weren't going to mess with me. I scooted beside Camille, keeping her behind me.

"Leave her alone." I glared at Lon. He glanced over his shoulder at Terrance, who was focused on driving.

"Stupid cu—"

"Shut up back there!" Terrance didn't even turn back to see what the commotion was. "I'm trying to shake that golden-haired bitch who's on our tail."

Delilah! It had to be Delilah! The fact that she was following us gave me courage. I glanced down at Camille, who looked up in my eyes. She softly turned so that her back was facing me. I saw that they'd tied her hands behind her and realized that if I scooted closer, I might be able to work the knots free while they weren't looking. And *that* meant lulling them into the belief that I was cooperating. But I couldn't be too obvious about it.

I gazed at Lon. "I won't be a bother if you just leave us alone during the ride. Please? I'm just so tired . . . my baby . . ." I let my voice drift off and widened my eyes. Make a bully feel powerful and sometimes he'll be generous.

I was in luck. He stared at me for a moment; then a smirk settled across his face. "Yeah, sure, whatever. We'll have time enough with her soon. I wonder what she'll bring on the market."

Trying not to grimace, I checked out our surroundings. The RV had been retrofitted. It sure wasn't a luxury hangout; that was for sure. A table and bench seats, a cupboard unit, the bathroom, and a couple of other seats filled the interior, but most of the space had been gutted to make room for . . . well . . . for what, I didn't know, but there were bloodstains on the floor and I had the feeling this home on wheels had been the scene of one too many *accidents.*

Camille was lying close to the table. I leaned over her, resting my head against the wall of the RV.

"I'm just going to rest for a moment," I said.

Lon shrugged and went back to whispering with Keith. As soon as he was focused on his conversation, I slid my right hand down to Camille's ropes. I couldn't risk using both my hands—they'd notice—but if I worked slowly, inch by inch, I could loosen the knots. Selkies were good with knot work—in fact, Celtic knot work was a specialty of ours, and during the seventies I'd been a big player in the macramé craze.

I ran my fingers over the knots. Simple. Practical. Knotted for speed, not for long-term bondage. I worried the biggest knot, using my thumb to brace it while I used the nails on my index and middle fingers to dig at it. The gels were strong and after a moment or so, the knot loosened a little. After a little more picking, it was loose enough for me to get my fingers through and pry open.

Camille did her best to match my movements and ease the rope so I could catch hold of the slack. After a moment, I had the free end in my grasp and a couple of minutes later, I'd untied the knot. Camille gently worked her wrists until the binding cord fell away. I scooted forward enough to cover her so they couldn't see what we'd done. She lay very still and I knew she was planning her next move. I closed my eyes to a slit, so it would look as though I was resting, but I could still see anybody coming up on us.

After a while, the RV made a sharp curve to the right and I tensed. Even through the walls, I could smell the water. We were near the inlet, with the cloying scents of brine and seaweed decay.

I sucked in a deep breath and whispered low, hoping the men couldn't hear me, "We're near the water."

Camille nodded. "Bide your time. Wait until we stop."

I touched her arm gently, to let her know I'd heard her, and went back to gathering my strength. I wasn't sure what to do, but I'd take my cue from Camille. She was the one with experience in situations like this.

Another minute or two and we began to slow down. I raised my head and turned toward the front. Terrance was focused on pulling into what looked like it might be a parking lot, though I wasn't close enough to the windshield to see. Lon and Keith finished their talk. Keith, hunched over to avoid hitting his head on the roof, made his way up front where he slid into the passenger seat.

"Get the waterweed ready," Terrance said, and Keith grunted and returned to the back, where he foraged in the cupboard and came out with a jar full of cloudy liquid.

I cringed. The Finfolk were skilled at making potions that would allow an air-breather to live underwater, at least for a time, so they could have their fun with them. As the potion began to wear off, they'd start their drowning games until they grew bored and let their victim drown for real.

When I still lived in the Orkneys, I'd known a couple of human women who had escaped from the Finfolk—a miracle in itself—and managed to make it back to land and escape before the Meré dragged them under one last and final time.

But they'd been tortured so badly that they never fully recovered their senses.

I tensed as Keith headed our way with the vial of waterweed potion. The RV came to a stop and I realized we had to do something soon, because any moment now, they'd realize Camille had gotten free from the ropes.

I sucked in a deep breath. Camille tensed.

As Keith knelt down, I quickly backed away to give Camille room. She rolled over, arms up with fingers locked in a claw condition. In one smooth motion, she sprang into a sitting position and raked her long nails down his face, drawing blood.

Keith screamed and dropped the vial to the floor, where it smashed as he shoved himself away from her attack.

Camille leapt to her feet and I followed suit as Lon came lunging forward. She threw herself headlong at him, taking him down as she caught his legs with her foot and yanked, throwing him off balance. I frantically glanced around and saw the broken vial. Grabbing it up by the neck where it was still intact, I slashed it across his face. Blood spurted in a fountain and I stared in horror as he writhed, screaming and trying to cover his face.

Camille gave me a terse look, nodded, then raised her arms over her head. She clasped her hands into a solid fist, and brought them down hard, right across his nose. *Crack.* Flesh impacted on flesh and my stomach churned as I stared at the terrifying passion that filled her face. I was about to drop the bottle, to turn away and vomit, but she darted a glance at me.

"*Don't you dare, Siobhan!* I need your help!"

Her voice was so forceful that it startled me out of my horror—and just in time. Keith was coming around again, this time armed with a nasty-looking dagger.

We didn't stick around. Camille slammed open the door, grabbed my hand, and yanked me out into a parking lot near the Sound. The water was being whipped into a fury by the wind that had sprung up, and dusk had fallen. I could barely see the waves but I could hear them, and they called to my blood.

As soon as we landed on the ground, Terrance came around the RV, a leering smile on his face.

Camille shoved me behind her and began muttering what sounded like an incantation. I hastily put more distance between us—her spells were powerful, but sometimes they backfired and the results were seldom pretty. Terrance backed up as her voice rose, his eyes widening.

At that moment, Keith landed beside me and grabbed me, the dagger at my throat. "Stop now or the selkie gets it."

Camille whirled around, a smirk curling the tips of her lips. "I don't think so. Terrance would kill you if you harmed her." And then, without another word, she swung on Terrance and let loose a bolt of energy that lit up the gloom. Terrance shrieked and dove for cover, and in that moment, Keith let go of me and lunged for Camille, slashing at her with his blade. He caught her arm. I heard her groan and smelled blood.

At that moment, Delilah's Jeep screeched into the lot, followed by a Jaguar. Menolly was up! I almost burst into tears. The vampire could make mincemeat of our attackers all by her lonesome. As I stumbled toward Camille, Keith let go of her and began to back away.

I looked back to see not only Menolly, but also Smoky—Camille's six-foot-four, almost-albino dragon lover and husband—emerge from the car. His hair hung to his ankles, and now it swirled around him like a hundred hissing snakes. *Oh shit.* Terrance and his buddies really *were* dead men now.

I started to run toward Delilah when Terrance suddenly lunged forward and caught me around the waist. He forced something in my mouth—a sponge of some sort—and began dragging me to the railing. I struggled but he was a lot stronger than me, and even though Menolly raced toward us at breakneck speed, he was able to haul me over the railing before she got there.

I tried to scream, but the sponge began to melt and I tasted waterweed. Oh hell—he was taking me into the water as a human. I could swim, but without my seal suit, I'd be totally at his mercy. I struggled harder, scraping my shins on the wooden railing, but within seconds we were falling over the edge.

As I stared into the glassy depths rising to meet us, I realized that I was on my own for now. If I was going to survive, it would be up to me. And then we hit the water and sank beneath the waves.

5

We hit hard, jarring every bone in my body, and the world went silent; the only thing I could hear were bubbles as we sank in the turbulent water. As Terrance dragged me under, I struggled. He was starting to shift and he let go of me as the throes of transformation racked his body. Some shifters went through a lot of pain when changing; others barely felt a thing. Finfolk suffered; selkies didn't.

I kicked away from him, propelling myself through the water. While I was a good swimmer, though much better in seal form, once he'd managed to shift over, I'd be no match for him.

Finfolk were strong, ungodly so, and their powerful tails acted akin to a propeller on a motorboat. They couldn't go as fast as a boat, but they could move and dart through the sea with barely a blink.

I tried not to look back as I forced my way toward the surface, chilled to the bone by the icy water. I could breathe, thanks to the waterweed sponge. But that didn't mean it would help me survive the depths unless I miraculously found my seal coat, or unless the Finfolk water witches gave me the protection they usually offered their victims. Toys were no fun if they died early.

Whatever the case, I expected Terrance had something planned, which meant there were probably other Finfolk in the area. Not good for the Pod, and not good for human swimmers. Too many *accidental* drownings occurred due to their interference.

The water boiled as Terrance thrashed, the currents pressing against me as I broke the surface and screamed for help. Waterweed didn't prevent an air-breather from breathing above water, the one saving grace for me right now.

But as soon as I'd shouted, a splash beside me told me I was in trouble. Terrance popped up next to me, transformed and feral, like some primal cross between fish and man. His skin was pale silver like that of a trout's, and a scaled tail joined what had been his legs. He had genitals, though, and all his other features remained intact except his hair was darker and his eyes were luminous. Gills slatted the side of his neck and I screamed as he reached for my wrist.

"Come on, baby," he said.

"Leave her alone!" Menolly's voice echoed from above and I gazed up to see Delilah, frantically flashing a light to find me. Oh hell—I knew Delilah could swim, but she was terrified of water. And Menolly would sink like a stone—vampires couldn't float.

And then, I saw Smoky, teetering on the edge of the railing with Camille by his side. As they leapt over the edge, Terrance made another grab for me and this time wrapped his arm around my waist. With a sudden rush, he yanked me below the surface and we were off, into the depths.

From somewhere behind us, I could feel the splash as Camille and Smoky landed in the water. But would they be able to keep up with Terrance? This was his world. And without my seal suit, I was as alien to it as were they. I scrambled to think of any advantage I had; then it occurred to me that I knew the inlet better than Terrance. I'd lived here for several decades and he'd just arrived. If I could get away from him long enough, I could use that knowledge to hide.

We wove through the dark water, silent and swift, Terrance holding me against him with one arm while steering with the other. His tail acted like a rudder, shifting our direction, sending us deeper and deeper with its powerful motion. The cold began to seep into my bones, and I felt myself going numb. It wouldn't be long before I passed out.

The water was like a black veil, everything that was familiar to me, everything that I associated with riding the waves gone, stripped away by my human form. I could feel my baby stirring, and wondered if she could feel the arms of the Ocean Mother embracing us. She would be a selkie, born in the ocean, and she would return to it time and again. She would revere it and worship it and love it, but only if I managed to survive.

Terrance suddenly halted and I vaguely saw another shape near us. Another of the Finfolk. The woman reached out and stroked my hair, then raked her nails down the side of my face, not enough to make me bleed but enough to hurt. As she did so, I could feel an energy surrounding me and then—within seconds—the numbing chill fell away and I was warm and comfortable. She was a sea witch, then, and dangerous. I let out a faint shudder and Terrance pulled me closer and started off again.

He let out a series of chirps and clucks. I knew enough of his language to recognize the meaning. Apparently we were heading toward open water, and he said something to his companion about a boat. So that was how they were stealing me away. Via boat. At least I wouldn't be riding the waves across the ocean. In human form, I wouldn't survive it.

We glided through the glassy depths, turning slightly as Terrance's silent, powerful fin steered us northward. I tried to remember my geography. Were there locks? Were there places where we'd be forced to get out of the water and transform?

Finfolk possessed exceptional strength and Terrance would be able to swim for a long time before needing to rest. My bet was that we wouldn't stop until we reached Whidbey Island, which would be the perfect place for him to have a boat waiting if he wanted to sail out through the Strait of Juan de Fuca.

But could he really mean to cross the Pacific? If so, he'd better have one hell of a boat.

I tried to work out how far we'd come, but my sense of timing was off. Time shifted in the water—as if the clock slowed to a crawl.

And then I glanced up. The shadow of something low-flying and big was skimming along the surface. What the hell? Before I could blink, there was a huge displacement of water as a large white form dove deep, coming up to grab Terrance and me in one gigantic claw. As we were swept up out of the water, I gasped. *A dragon.* Smoky! And astride his back, thoroughly soaked and clinging to him for dear life, sat Camille, looking dazed and cold in her dripping chiffon and leather.

Terrance began to flail and Smoky eased open his claws long enough for the Meré to slip through and fall hard into the water. I held tight to the talons gripping me by the waist, praying that my baby was all right.

With wings steadily gliding on the chill breeze, we were over land within minutes, back over the park from where Terrance had kidnapped me. As we landed, Delilah and Menolly ran over to us, pulling Camille off Smoky's back and wrapping her in a blanket, and wrapping me in another. I stared at them, horrified, trying to comprehend everything that had happened.

"She's in shock," Delilah said, and her voice seemed to be coming from a long, long way away, from down a long, dark tunnel.

"You're right. We need to get her to the FH-CSI and have her checked out." Menolly gazed at me, her eyes burning bright and brilliant, red as fire, red as blood. She leaned forward and I couldn't look away.

"Sleep," she whispered.

And I did.

* * *

I woke to the smell of tea and toast, and pushed myself up on my elbows. I was in my house, and soft whispers filtered in from the other room. The clock told me it was near eight, and a glance at the window told me the night had passed and we were into morning.

As I slipped out from beneath the quilt, I saw that I was dressed in a loose gown—a soft robe that Mitch had bought me when I started getting too big for my pajamas. My slippers were by the foot of my bed, and I slid them on, then hurried into the bathroom to pee. As I headed toward the kitchen, the voices grew louder.

Camille was at the table, looking dry and fresh, and Delilah was beside her, along with Smoky. Iris, the house sprite who lived with them, brought over a plate of bacon, eggs, and toast. She set it in front of me, then patted my shoulder as I slid into a chair.

"Has the hospital called? Is Mitch still . . . ?" My voice faltered. I couldn't say the words. I couldn't ask if he was still alive because I was afraid of the answer.

Iris nodded, her cheeks rosy from standing over the range. No doubt she'd used my step stool to reach the stovetop. "Yes, he's still alive. They performed the exploratory surgery yesterday. Good news—the medic says they won't have to remove the spleen after all. It was damaged, but should recover. His kidneys are bruised but will also recover."

"What about his arm? It was shattered."

"They went in early this morning. He should be out of surgery in an hour. He's going to need time to heal up, though. He'll be in the hospital for a while—a couple weeks at least."

I pressed my hands to my lips. Two surgeries in two days. Two too many. "Terrance is going to pay for this."

"By the way, we took you to the FH-CSI medical unit last night. You and your baby are fine, so no worries there." Camille leaned over my shoulder and gave me a hug. "We decided not to wake you out of the trance that Menolly put you in. You were in shock and desperately needed rest. Sharah says the baby is fine, and she countered the waterweed in your system. It really shouldn't be used by pregnant women, but she doesn't think any damage was done."

I blinked back tears. "Thank you," I whispered, not wanting to think about the past twenty-four hours. "What about Terrance?"

"He and his men are still out there," Smoky said from the head of the table. "I had to drop him for fear he might hurt you."

"Is it true? Camille told us that Terrance claims you're heir to a throne?" Delilah asked.

I shrugged. "I suppose so. I don't think Terrance would have bothered chasing me through all these years and over all those miles without some ulterior motive like that. He's always been a control freak, grasping for power. And I'm the key to that power."

A sudden chill washed over me. "If we don't find him, I'll never be able to stop looking over my shoulder. My daughter will be in danger; Mitch will be in danger, because Terrance will never, ever stop. He'll come back, again and again, until I kill him or he kills me. I won't let him take me back as the key to enslave my mother's people."

The eggs and toast were threatening to pay a return visit, but Camille brushed my hair back and gently ran her hand over my forehead, and my nausea began to subside. Her skin was cool against the heat flaring on my face.

"Everything will be okay." She gently rubbed my neck, easing the knots that had built up. "We're here to help. We won't let him hurt you."

I glanced up in time to see Delilah frown at her.

"I won't hold you to that. I won't hold anybody to a promise like that. But I thank you. For being here. For putting yourselves on the line. So . . ." I sucked in a deep breath and slowly exhaled. Time to pull myself out of the mire and face reality. "What do we—*I*—do next?"

"Terrance isn't stupid. What's the one way he could break your spirit, besides harming your daughter?" Smoky leaned across the table, and gently took my hand, his fingers light on my wrist. I stared at his hands. They were strong but unblemished, so far from the taloned claws they'd been the night before, and yet—and yet I could feel the nature of the dragon emanating from every pore.

"I say this not to frighten you," he continued, "but because I understand opportunistic males. I understand those who grasp and yearn for something or someone they do not possess. I grew up around them. If we can identify your vulnerabilities, then we've identified the potential targets on whom your enemy will set his sights."

I slowly raised my eyes to meet his. "You know what my one vulnerability is, besides my child. Mitch. Mitch is my life, my love. I fell in love with him the first moment I met him, and when we thought the Pod would separate us because I couldn't bear a child, I was about to go mad with grief. He means the world to me. I chose him for my mate, and I can't imagine giving him up without a fight."

"Then we haul ass to the hospital," Camille said as Smoky quietly nodded and let go of my hands. "Because you know damned well Terrance is going to be down there, looking to finish what he started. He's not going to wait for us."

As I hustled back to the bedroom to change and make a quick call to work to let them know that Mitch had been hurt and I wouldn't be in, I stopped to pick up a picture on the nightstand.

Mitch and me, standing at the edge of the Pacific over in Ocean Shores. The dunes were shifting with the wind that day as the waves rolled in to crash along the beach. That was the day when everything fell into place. That was the day when I told him we could finally plan on being together forever.

* * *

Mitch was flying a kite, laughing as he ran. The kite—a chimera—had taken him four weeks to build and now the winds tossed it around like so much wrapping paper. But he was having fun, and I was videotaping him, waiting for just the right moment to tell him my news.

He came racing up to me, and dropped in the sand, slowly beginning to reel in the kite as the stiff breeze dropped and the sun began to warm up the chilled air. I opened the basket and spread out our picnic—thick tuna sandwiches, freshly sliced cucumbers, potato chips and pickles, and a cherry pie.

"What, no wine?" Mitch anchored the kite so it wouldn't blow away. He leaned back in the sand, shading his eyes as he stared out at the ocean. "Shall we go swimming later?" He pointed to his pack. "I brought my suit; did you bring yours?"

I nodded softly and handed him a paper plate with one of the sandwiches on it. "Yes, as long as nobody sees us *change*. But eat first. And no, I didn't bring any wine. I did bring sparkling cider. I just felt . . . I don't feel like alcohol right now, you know?"

With a shrug, he accepted the plate and piled it high with chips and cucumbers. "Not a problem. But you brought cookies, right?"

The hopeful note in his voice made me laugh. Mitch was a sucker for anything with peanut butter. "Yes, I brought some fresh peanut butter cookies along with the pie. They're in the cooler."

We ate slowly, listening to the mournful call of the gulls as they swirled around our heads. Seabirds knew we weren't human; they could sense our connection to the Ocean Mother and they flocked to our side, waiting for us to recognize them as allies, as compatriots. I'd never figured out the connection, but it didn't matter. We liked the gulls and they liked us.

I pulled out a spare loaf of bread and began tearing it up, tossing the chunks to the birds, who immediately swarmed the crumbs, ignoring all sense of propriety.

Mitch laughed and sat up. "They sure like people."

"No, they like *food*," I said, closing my eyes against the warmth of the sun as it played along my face, kissing me softly with its rays. "Mitch, I have some news—and I want you to really listen to me."

He dropped the book he'd picked up and turned to me, wrapping his arms around his knees as he brought them to his chest. "What is it, love?"

I took a deep breath. This was it. Make or break time. "You know how the Pod keeps trying to break us up since I can't get pregnant?"

"Oh gods," he said, groaning. "Not again—what have they done now?"

With a soft smile, I said, "Nothing."

"Then what?"

"They can't touch us now. I'm pregnant. I found out yesterday—Sharah checked me out and—"

I couldn't get another word out because Mitch tossed his plate away and leapt up, pulling me to my feet. He danced me around, covering my face with kisses. His lips were soft against my skin and I melted into his embrace, listening to his giddy laughter.

"My Siobhan, my love, is it true? You're sure?" He pushed me away, to arm's length, holding me by the shoulders and staring into my eyes. He looked afraid, as if I might suddenly tell him it was all a joke.

"I'd never lie about something like this, not even in jest. It's true. I'm pregnant, and I'm going to have a little girl. I'm only a couple months along, but Sharah said the pregnancy has taken hold, and everything's going along just fine." I started to cry. "Now they can't take you away from me. The Pod can't tell you to leave me and take a new lover."

He stopped then, and tipped my chin up to gaze at me. "Siobhan, I don't care what the Pod says. Either way. I'd leave them before I'd give you up. I thought you knew that. You're my soul mate, my love."

Sniffling—whether it was the way he said it, or the hormones, I wasn't sure—I nodded and wiped my nose on a paper towel. "I know . . . I know you said that but when push comes to shove . . ."

"When push comes to shove, I shove back. I'm thrilled you're pregnant. I wanted this, too, but I want you most of all. And nothing would make me leave if you were truly infertile. Not the Pod, not my parents, not the Ocean Mother herself."

And then he dropped to one knee and pulled out a velvet box from his pocket. "I was waiting to show you this—to see if we'd have to run away from the Pod first. But now there's nothing they can do to stop me. Siobhan Morgan, will you do me the honor of becoming my wife and mate?"

As he opened the box, an emerald-cut aquamarine inset in platinum shimmered under the sun. Seafoam trapped in a crystal. I gasped as he slid it onto my finger. "Please, please say yes."

"You know the answer to that already, Mitchell Childs. You know the answer." And then, with no one else on the beach, he laid me down on the blanket and made love to me by the ocean's side.

* * *

"Siobhan? Siobhan? Are you ready?"

I glanced up to find Camille standing at my door, hesitantly peeking in. I was dressed, but had been lost in the memory of that day. Mitch, my life and soul, who would have left his family and home for me. Mitch, who would have given up being a parent because he loved me so much. And now he was lying in a hospital bed, in danger because of a cruel and vicious man from my past.

"I'm ready," I said, gathering my purse and keys. I checked to make sure the stove was off and slid on a warm jacket. "Let's go find Terrance. I don't want the sun to set again while he's still alive."

Camille gave me the thumbs-up. "You've got it, babe. You've got it."

6

We drove to the hospital in two cars. I went with Camille and Smoky in Camille's Lexus, while Delilah and Iris went together in Delilah's Jeep. I was wearing a pair of maternity jeans and a loose top, so at least I could move if I had to. I wasn't at the waddling stage yet, but I was starting to show and my regular clothes were all a little too snug for comfort now.

As the buildings passed by in a blur, I sucked in a deep breath. Amazing what sorrow twenty-four hours could bring. Amazing what panic a phone call could presage. The thought of trying to hide in today's world was terrifying. In 1907, I blended into the crowd and vanished. That luxury didn't exist today. I had to stay close to the coastlines, which cut out a lot of hiding places.

The day was overcast as usual, but the sun was trying to break through and I regarded it with suspicion. Right now I wanted the cloud cover and the fog, anything to make me feel less exposed.

"So what, we just watch Mitch?" I finally asked.

"No, we slip a webcam in his room and the rest of us watch from another part of the hospital while you stay with him, making for two tempting targets in one place. Either we can set it up or Chase can, your choice." Camille swerved to avoid the remnants of a tire on the road and smoothly shifted lanes to take the next exit, which would lead us to the hospital.

"Not Chase. He'd try to take Terrance into custody. And I don't want Terrance in custody." I glanced at the back of her head, and she looked at me through the rearview mirror. "We do this ourselves, if you're still willing."

Camille nodded. Another ten minutes and we pulled into the parking lot of the hospital.

She turned around in her seat. "Listen, Delilah is going to install the webcam, but she'll be coming in dressed as a nurse. Terrance would probably recognize me, and there's no way anybody could overlook Smoky, so we're going to sneak in a different way."

She didn't say just how they were planning on doing so, and I had the feeling it was on a need-to-know basis.

I nodded. "What about me?"

"You go in, in plain sight. You head to Mitch's room and you sit with him. If anybody else is in there—from the Pod or his parents—somehow, you encourage them to leave. Delilah will be in shortly but don't act like you know her."

Camille let out a long sigh. "Terrance will probably strike during the night, and probably soon, since he knows we're onto him. We need the hospital to agree to let you stay with Mitch. Being his fiancée, that shouldn't be too hard for you to arrange. Tell them that last night, you were too distraught over his injuries and your doctor made you stay home, but that you can't stand being away from him tonight."

I slipped out of the car and grabbed my purse. As I swung the door shut, I whispered a quick, "Thank you. For everything."

They waved me off and I headed toward the hospital.

* * *

I didn't have much trouble convincing the nurses and Mitch's Otherworld doctor that I needed to stay with him. In fact, his doctor thought it would be a good idea.

"The surgery on his arm went just fine, but at this point, we still don't know how much use he'll recover. The bone was shattered and his arm is full of pins. To be honest, I haven't the faintest idea of how that will affect him when he shifts into selkie form. For now, he needs your comfort and support."

The elfin doctor flipped through Mitch's chart as he walked us into the room, his footsteps making no noise on the sparkling linoleum. "He's still very groggy from the pain medication and surgery, but he'll know you're here. He seemed disturbed last night, as if he was afraid of something."

I frowned, glancing around. We were on the third floor, but that didn't preclude Terrance using some supernatural way to climb up the outside wall. Most likely, though, Mitch was just afraid that Terry would hurt me. If he'd picked up on the fact that I was the Finfolk's target, and he knew he couldn't do anything about it, he would be terrified and feeling helpless. And a helpless man made for an angry man.

I hurried over to Mitch's side. His arm and both legs were in casts—the kind where they could be removed to change the dressings and examine the injuries. Mitch blinked, looking up at me through glazed eyes. He was drugged, all right. I took his hand and leaned over to kiss his forehead.

"It's okay," I whispered. "Everything's going to be all right. The D'Artigo sisters are helping us. Don't worry, okay?" I kept my voice low, but forgot the doctor was from Otherworld.

"Is something wrong, Ms. Morgan? You having problems with someone?" Dr. Elanya set down the clipboard and turned to me.

"Why do you ask?"

"Because someone injured him. Mitch didn't beat himself up. And if you know who did it, then you'd better speak to Detective Johnson so they can catch the lowlife before he hurts someone else."

Even though he was wearing Earthside clothing and had the letters *D* and *R* planted before his name, he was still an elf. And elves always seemed bent on playing by the rules. I smiled weakly and eased my way into a chair.

"We think it may be an old boyfriend of mine, out for a little revenge. I've already talked to the authorities." I shrugged.

Dr. Elanya looked at me and I knew he didn't believe me, but there was no graceful way to call me a liar and get away with it.

"All right, then," he said after a moment. "I'll have the nurse bring you a blanket. You can use the bed next to him.

I doubt we'll have enough emergencies to need it. Besides, in your condition, you should get as much rest as you can." And with that, he snapped the chart shut and left the room.

I followed him to make sure he was gone and then returned to Mitch's side. "Honey, I have so much to tell you but I'm afraid you won't remember it if I tell you right now. Just trust me. Please . . . You trust me, don't you?" I strained, holding his uninjured hand, waiting for an answer.

Mitch's brilliant baby blues stared up at me for a moment, questions warring in his gaze, but he finally nodded and squeezed my hand. He opened his mouth and struggled until a faint "I trust you" came out, followed by, "I love you."

I wanted so badly to tell him what was going on, but in his condition, he needed to rest. So I kissed his lips and adjusted his covers and watched as he slid back into a drug-filled sleep.

As I lowered myself into the chair and picked up the remote control, wondering what to do with myself all day, the door opened and a tall, blond nurse bustled into the room, pushing a cart with a beautiful potted plant on it.

"Hey." I started to stand but Delilah motioned me back into the chair. She shook her head and pressed a finger to her lips.

"Ms. Morgan, I'm just delivering this plant that one of Mitch's friends sent. What a beautiful philodendron." She glanced around, then motioned to the dresser that was opposite Mitch's bed, beneath the TV mounted on the wall. "Why don't we put it there? I think it would be just perfect."

As I gathered my purse from off the dresser, I noticed a tiny camera nestled in the ceramic pot. It was aimed directly toward the door and from what I could tell, the view would include Mitch as well. I gazed at it for a moment, then stood back.

"You're right; that's the perfect spot." I gave Delilah a quick nod to show her I'd seen it, and stepped back. "Thank you. I know Mitch will appreciate it when he wakes up."

"If that's all, then, I'll be going. May I speak with you outside for a moment?" she asked. "It's nothing important, but you need to sign a form if you're going to stay here overnight."

I followed her into the hall and she motioned me off to one side and pressed a small pager into my hand.

"Camille and Smoky are hanging out on the roof, and I'm going to be hiding in cat form down the hall. There's a room nobody seems to use and I can sneak in there behind one of the old beds. Camille has a monitor linked to the webcam, and we both have pagers linked to yours. You press the alert button, we'll come running."

I examined the pager, then slid it into the side pocket of my top. "What about the webcam? Wireless?"

"Entirely. It's all set up. Camille and Smoky are watching right now. You hang out here today, read, relax, maybe get in a nap in case Terrance makes his move tonight. You'll want to be refreshed." She glanced over her shoulder at a group of nurses who were passing by. They gave us an odd look, but left us alone.

"What if he doesn't come tonight?" I both feared he would, and feared he wouldn't. Either way would be a mess.

Delilah shrugged. "Then we deal with it tomorrow. But I think . . . I have a hunch that he's around. I'm a cat; I can still smell that briny scent he had yesterday when we were fighting in the park. There was something about him—the smell of salt and seaweed and decay—and I can smell that now. Faint, but it's here, in the hospital."

"Can you track it?" If she could, maybe we'd be in luck.

But she shook her head. "No, it's too weak. But it's recent. Trust us on this one. Camille's intuition's pretty damned fine-tuned, and I've got a nose that won't quit."

I nodded. "I do trust you. That's why you're here with me now and not Chase. As nice as the man is, he just wouldn't understand." I paused, then laid a hand on Delilah's arm. "Thank you. Thank you for everything."

She smiled. "Thank us after it's over. Now go back in there and try not to worry." As she turned and headed down the hall, I returned to Mitch's room. All well and good to say, *Don't worry.* Following her advice was an entirely different matter.

* * *

I opened my eyes to the sound of someone entering the room. For a moment, I wondered where the hell I was—this wasn't my own bed—and then I remembered. *Mitch. The hospital. Terrance.*

I slowly took in my surroundings, keeping still to avoid warning the intruder that I was awake. And then, remembering what Delilah said, I inhaled a long, slow breath, trying to concentrate on weeding out the scents surrounding me.

I could smell the bleach they used to clean the bathroom, and the medications that Mitch had dripping through his IVs.

I could smell the attempts at sterility the hospital made, but they'd never realize just how far they fell short, for beneath the cleansers were the odors of illness and injury, of old vomit and stale urine.

Lowering myself another layer, I let the next level of scent waft over me, forcing myself to remain still as the door opened another inch.

And there it was. *Brine. Seaweed. Mussels. The decay of the sea.* Terrance was here.

It took every ounce of courage I had not to leap up, to scream for help. Instead, I forced myself to pretend to sleep while I stealthily reached for the pager that I'd stashed in my robe. But when I reached into the soft cotton pocket, the pager wasn't there.

Shit! It must have fallen out while I was sleeping! What the hell was I going to do?

I fumbled around, trying to sense whether anybody was near me, and to find out where the damned pager had gone to. I prayed that I hadn't knocked it off the bed while I was sleeping. Of course, there was the webcam, but I didn't trust Camille and Delilah to get here before Terrance had a chance to kill Mitch. And he would. I knew he would.

As the door swung open all the way, soft footsteps slipped into the room, followed by a second pair. If it had been a nurse, she would have come in matter-of-fact. The night nurse had already woken me up once when she came to check on Mitch. And the lights stayed off this time, so it was a pretty good bet that whoever this was, was up to no good.

And then I felt the pager. *Damn it!* The thing was down by my left foot. If I scrunched down to get it, Terrance would notice. If I tried to move it up to my hands using my feet—

again, he'd notice. What the hell was I going to do? The minute I gave myself away, he'd go after Mitch and then after me. There was only one thing I could think of—scare the hell out of him, then take off running and pray he'd follow me and leave Mitch alone.

I dreaded the onslaught of nurses we'd face—they'd immediately call Chase. But I had no choice. The question was, would it work? Could I startle him enough to give me time to punch the button on the pager and get out the door before he caught me? There was only one way to find out.

I sprang up as fast as I could—which wasn't as fast as I'd hoped—let out one piercing shriek, and grabbed the pager. As I punched the red button, I expected to hear a commotion outside, but instead all I heard was Terrance letting out a blast of obscenities that would have made even Camille and Menolly blush.

"You want me so bad, you come and get me," I shouted, running for the door.

Terrance—I could see him clearly now; he was with Lon—looked at Mitch, then back at me, then at Mitch again. As I thundered out the door, he growled and motioned to Lon.

"Get her. We'll deal with him later. We can't have her spreading the alarm." He headed my way and I darted into the hall, looking around frantically for something to use as a weapon.

Then I noticed: There were no nurses at the nursing station. *Where the hell—*

"I'm going to make you wish to hell you'd never laid eyes on me," Terrance said as the door swung shut behind him. "Make it easy on yourself and stop right now. Obey, and I'll kill him neat and clean. If you make me chase you, I promise you the stupid seal will feel every single cut I put into his body, and you'll be there watching. And I'll make sure that before he dies, he knows exactly what I did to you back in Cobh, and what I'm going to do to you now. You and that whelp in your belly. You'll bear a child, all right. *Mine.*"

I backed up against the wall, counting the seconds. Where were they? Where were Delilah and Camille and Smoky? They promised they'd be here!

Whimpering now as fear set in, I backed up against a cart full of meds. I glanced down and saw two syringes there—fully loaded with . . . whatever was in them. It looked like the night nurse had just left the cart sitting in the hall as she was making her rounds.

I slipped in front of the cart and slid my hands behind me, grabbing one of the syringes. It could have anything from vitamins to sleeping meds in it. The former would be only of shock value when I hit him with the needle. The latter might actually do some good.

I sidestepped my way to the wall beside the cart, and backed up against it, hiding the syringe behind me. "Terrance. Please rethink this. Don't do this—it's been a hundred years. For all you know, my mother's people might have died out. Why bother? We live in a different age. Hell, if you want to rule so badly, head over to Otherworld. The world's a lot harsher there, and a lot more welcoming to our kind."

He arched one eyebrow. "If I wanted to go to Otherworld, I would. And your mother's people are alive and thriving. Do you really think I'm that stupid? I have a network of informants scattered from here to Ireland. I'm a prince among my own people, remember? While it may not mean much to some selkies, the crown still counts for something with the Finfolk and the roane."

I moaned gently as he lithely stepped in front of me. "Okay, bitch. It's time to leave. Let's go say good-bye to your boyfriend and then be on our way."

As he reached for me, I panicked and brought the syringe around, stabbing hard and deep into his neck and pressing the plunger. He screamed and backhanded me, knocking me against the wall. Lon stared dumbly at me, then at his boss, obviously not knowing what to do.

At that moment, I heard a high-pitched warning cry and looked up to see Delilah, Camille, and Smoky hurtling down the hall. Smoky passed right by me and grabbed Terrance around the waist, squeezing with a mighty grunt. Terrance turned blue and fainted.

Lon wheeled around, intending to run, but I was feeling my oats now, and I stuck out my foot and tripped him. He went sprawling at Delilah's feet, and she promptly gave him a kick so hard I could hear bones breaking. I shuddered as Camille took me by the hand and moved me to the side.

Smoky looked around. Still no one in sight. He frowned, then turned back to me. "What do you want me to do with him?"

I stared at the dragon. He was offering me what I wanted. What I needed. But could I ask someone else to kill for me?

If I let Terrance live, there was a chance the Pod would vote to let him go. There were still plenty of members there—mainly female—who resented the fact that my infertility problem had been cured and that Mitch was off the market now. Some selkies mated with whomever they wanted, but Mitch and I . . . he was my one and only. And I was his. I sucked in a deep breath, not knowing what to say.

As I knelt beside his prone form, trying to build up my nerve to do the job myself, he suddenly went into convulsions. I jumped back, not sure what was going on, and we watched as Terrance spasmed again, then fell silent.

Camille felt for a pulse. "He's dead," she said, standing up. She picked up the needle that I'd stabbed him with. "What's this?"

"I don't know—I was using it to try to buy time so I could get away. What does it say on the cart? It was in that tray right there." I pointed to the tray.

She glanced at the label on the tray, then looked at me. "Insulin—meant for a Juanita Chalker. And a hefty dose, at that. Must have thrown him into a hypoglycemic shock and killed him."

I stared at Terrance's body. He was dead. I'd killed him. I glanced at Lon, who was staring at me, pale and wan.

"Call Chase," I said. "I guess there's no harm in telling him what happened now. Turn Lon over to him. Meanwhile, where are the nurses that work this floor?"

Lon groaned from the floor. "They're locked up in the cleaning closet. Terrance and I forced them in there. He didn't want any interference and figured we'd be long gone by the time they broke out."

Smoky reached down and lifted Lon by his collar, letting the man dangle with his feet a good ten inches above the ground.

"You not only endangered the two selkies, but also the lives of every patient on this floor. I should just crisp you and eat you right here, but I think I'll let the humans have their way with you. But mind you this—if you're *ever* set free, and you ever come near this selkie and her mate again, I'll find you and use your bones as toothpicks. Understand, *little man*?"

Lon nodded, his eyes wide, and I felt a rush of warmth in my heart for Camille's big lug of a husband.

* * *

The sun was setting over the water as Mitch, in his wheelchair, and I stood at the edge of a grassy area just beyond the Daybreak Star Indian Culture Center in Discovery Park, staring out over the Shilshole Bay. Camille and Delilah were a little ways away, sitting on the grass. We were all bundled up. It wasn't cold, but a chill definitely hung low in the air.

Mitch reached up with his uninjured arm to take my hand. I leaned down and pressed a kiss to his forehead. We still didn't know what would happen when he tried to shift—the pins in his other arm were there for good and the elders of the Pod couldn't give us an answer, either.

Luckily, marine Weres—unlike most other Weres—weren't affected by the full moon. Why, we didn't know, but we shifted when we wanted. Perhaps it was because the ocean was already aligned to the moon, with its effect on the ebb and flow of the tides. Or maybe we weren't truly Weres, but some other type of shifter . . . But the upshot was, Mitch wouldn't have to transform until he felt ready. I could feel his longing, though, to bathe himself in the Ocean Mother's waters.

Camille brushed her hair out of her eyes and looked over at us. "So is everything okay?"

Mitch and I glanced at each other; then Mitch nodded. "Yeah . . . I understand why Siobhan kept her past a secret."

"I wanted to forget the past," I said. "I almost had myself convinced that all my lies were real, that what happened with Terrance had been a nightmare. But I guess you can never run away from your problems. Sometimes you have to face them head-on and defeat the demons that reach out of the dark to grab hold of you."

"What happened to Terrance's cronies?" Delilah stood up and sucked in a deep lungful of air, keeping a wary eye on the water. Even though the waves were a good distance from us, I could see her pull back. I wondered what it would be like to be so afraid of the water. For me, the ocean was an embracing mother, a refuge and sanctuary.

"Chase wrote it up as self-defense, and the Pod's indicted Lon for attempted murder and kidnapping. They also caught the other one—Keith—and both of them are going before the Tribunal. I doubt they'll make it out alive."

"Good riddance," Camille said. After a moment, she turned a dazzling smile our way. "So, did I hear talk of a trip to Scotland?"

"In a bit." I tried to repress a smile, but it broke through anyway. "But first, we're going to Ramsey, on the Isle of Man, where my mother will meet us. Her people still live there, and so I'll be able to meet my relatives on her side. This is the first time I've spoken to her in over a hundred years. She thought I was dead all this time."

Mitch laughed. "I still can't believe I actually married a princess."

"I'm not a princess, you doofus." I grinned.

"Yes you are, or you will be, once they verify your birth with your mother." He shrugged, then winced. "Ouch, remind me not to do that again."

"I take it you're reclaiming your rightful heritage?" Delilah clapped her hands. "It's just like a Cinderella story!"

"Cinderella story, my ass," I said, snorting. "Prince Charming can go suck rocks. I've met my true love and he's a contractor."

After a moment, my smile faded. "Seriously, I have no idea what will come of this. My mother can visit her homeland, but she can't rejoin her people—it's been too long and they're pissed at her for keeping it a secret from me."

"What about her parents? How do they feel?"

"My grandmother insists that I be entered into the rolls of the Pod, even though I was born into my father's people. She says since my mother was abducted, I didn't have a choice as to birthplace, and that I'll be given dual status with both the Puget Sound Harbor Seal Pod—my Pod of choice—and the Isle of Man Selkies—my mother's people. We'll fly there about six weeks before our daughter is born. And she'll be born into my grandmother's people, and given dual status, too."

"What if they want you to return home to rule someday?" Camille dusted off her dress as the clouds began to roll in.

I stared at the water as it broke along the shore. What *would* I do? Would I ever return to my mother's people to accept the crown? I loved it here; I loved the freedom that being just *Siobhan Morgan* gave me.

Queen and princess—those titles required a certain loss of freedom. Did I want that? Would Mitch ever accept that?

"I have no idea. Our daughter can make up her mind when she comes of age—we won't influence her either way. But for me . . . I think I'd like to stay here, if I can. But who knows what will happen?"

"What about Terrance's people? Will they come after you for revenge?" Delilah asked.

I shook my head. "No, not if everything goes right. They think he died in an accident. That way the Cobh Selkie Pod and the Finfolk won't take revenge on my mother's people. But someday, if my grandmother calls me to help her, I may not have a choice." I looked down at Mitch and he squeezed my hand. "Would you go with me if that happened? If I'm called to lead a war?"

"I told you before," he said quietly. "I'll follow you anywhere. You're my mate, my love. If you rise to be a queen or a warrior princess, I'll be at your side. You and our daughter come before anything or anybody . . . or any *place*."

A sharp breeze picked up and I felt the tides of change whip in on it. The world wasn't what it used to be. Times were changing. If I ever became queen of my people and one of our women was stolen away, we'd do everything in our power to rescue her—and with technology, we'd stand a good chance. No more marriages-by-capture for me or my kind.

The Supes and Fae of the world were adapting along with the humans, and our cultures had to adapt. It was imperative, if we expected to thrive.

A sharp kick against my stomach startled me and I laughed.

"She's going to be a fighter, our Marion is," I said, patting my belly.

"So you're naming her after the café owner?"

I nodded. "She helped us in our time of need. I'm going to honor her request. Our Marion will grow up knowing that she's a new breed of selkie—that the old ways are changing. She'll be on the cutting edge of that change, and I hope, one day, she'll leave her mark on the world."

Mitch kissed my hand and I leaned down and locked his lips with my own, savoring the kiss, savoring his love, savoring my freedom. Yes, it was a good day, and while I knew that *happily ever after* never came easily, I thought we stood a pretty good chance of making it happen.

The Tangleroot Palace

MARJORIE M. LIU

1

Weeks later, when she had a chance to put up her feet and savor a good hot cup of tea, Sally remembered something the gardener said, right before the old king told her that she had been sold in marriage.

"Only the right kind of fool is ever going to want you."

Sally, who was elbow-deep in horse manure, blew a strand of red hair out of her eyes. "And?"

"Well," began the elderly woman, frowning. And then she seemed to think better of what she was going to say, and crouched down beside her in the grass. "Here. Better let me."

They were both wearing leather gloves that were stiff as rawhide, sewn in tight patches to reach up past their elbows. Simple to clean if you let them sit in the sun until manure turned to dry flakes, easy to beat off with a stick. Sally, who did not particularly enjoy rooting through muck, was nonetheless pleased that the tannery had provided her with yet another new tool for her work in the garden.

"You know," Sally said, "when I told the stableboy to take care of my new roses, this is not what I meant."

The gardener made a noncommittal sound. "There were ravens in my dreams last night."

Sally finally felt something hard and stubbly beneath her fingers, and began clawing manure carefully away. "I thought we were talking about how only a fool would ever want me."

"All men are fools," replied the old woman absently, and then her frown deepened. "They were guarding a queen who wore a crown of horns."

It took Sally a moment to realize that she was speaking of the ravens in her dream again. "How odd."

"Not so odd if you know the right stories." The gardener shivered, and glanced over her shoulder—but not before her gaze lingered on Sally's hair. "Sabius is coming. Your father must want you."

Sally craned around, but the sun was in her eyes. All she could see was the blurry outline of a bowlegged man, stomping across the grass with his meaty fists swinging. She glanced down at herself, and then with a rueful little smile continued clearing debris away from her roses.

"Princess," said Sabius, well before his shadow fell over her. "Your father requests your . . . Oh, dear God."

The gardener bit her bottom lip and kept her head down, long silver braids swinging from beneath her straw hat. Sally, gazing with regret at the one little leaf she'd managed to expose, leaned backward and tugged until her arms slid free of the rawhide gloves—left sticking from the manure like two hollow branches. Her skin was pink and sweaty, her work apron brown with stains.

"Oh, dear God," said her father's manservant again; and turned his head, covering his mouth with a hairy, bare-knuckled hand better suited to brawling than to the delicately scripted letters he often sat composing for the king. He made a gagging sound, and squeezed shut his eyes.

"Er," said Sally, quite certain she didn't smell *that* bad. "What does my father want?"

Sabius, still indisposed, pointed toward the south tower. Sally considered arguing, but it was hardly worth the effort.

She shrugged off her apron and dropped it on the ground. Smoothing out her skirts—also rather stained, and patched with a quilt work of silk scrap from the seamstress's bin—she raised her brow at the gardener, who shook her head and returned to digging free the roses.

The king's study was on the southern side of the castle, directly below his bedchamber, which was accessible only through a hidden wall behind his desk that concealed a narrow stone staircase. Not that it was a secret. Everyone knew of its existence, what with the maids scurrying up and down in the mornings and evenings: cleaning, folding, dressing, doing all manner of maid, and maidenly, things that Sally did not want to know about.

Her father was just coming down the stairs when she entered his study even more slowly than she had intended, having been stopped outside the kitchen by two of the cook's young apprentices from the village, who, in different ways, could not help but try to clean her up. First with scalding-hot water and crushed lavender scrubbed into her face, then her loose hair tugged into a respectable braid. The other girl fetched a fresh apron from the kitchen, which was not fine, and certainly not royal, but was clean and starched, and certainly in line with Sally's usual apparel. No use wasting fine gowns on long walks, or earth work, or even just reading in the library.

Her one concession to vanity was the amethyst pendant she wore against her skin; a teardrop as long as her thumb, and held in a golden claw upon which half of a small wooden heart hung, broken jaggedly down the middle. Her mother's jewelry, and precious only for that reason.

"Salinda," said her father, and stopped, sniffing the air. "You smell as though you've been sleeping beneath a horse's ass."

"Do I?" she replied airily. "I hadn't noticed."

The old king frowned, looking over her clothing with a great deal more scrutiny than was usual. He was a barrel-chested man, tall and lean in most places, except for his gut and the wattle beneath his chin, which he tried vainly to hide with a coarse beard that was fading quickly from black to silver. He moved with a limp, due to an arrow shot recently into his hip.

Sally had been frightened for him—for as long as it had taken the old king to wake from the draught the doctor had poured down his throat in order to remove the bolt. His temper had been foul ever since. Everyone was avoiding him.

"Don't you have anything nicer to wear?" he asked, a peculiar tenseness in the way he studied her that made Sally instantly uneasy. "I pay for seamstresses."

"And I have fine clothing," she replied cautiously, as her father had never commented on her appearance, not once in seventeen years. "These are for everyday."

The old king made a small, dissatisfied sound, and limped past her to his desk. "I suppose you heard about the skirmish at old Bog Hill? Men died. More good men every day. Little weasel bastard Fartin throwing gold at mercenaries to test our borders. But"—and he smiled grimly—"I have a solution."

"Really," Sally said, suffering the most curious urge to run.

"Your darling mother, before we married, had a very dear friend who was given to one of those southern tribal types as part of a lucrative alliance. She bore a son, who just so happens to be a very powerful man in need of a wife."

"Oh," Sally said.

Her father gave her a stern look. "And I suppose he's found one."

"Oh," Sally said again. "Oh, no."

"Fine man," replied the old king, but with a glittering unease in his eyes. "That Warlord fellow. You know. *Him*."

Sally stared, quite certain that bumblebees had just committed suicide in her ears. "Him. The Warlord. Who commands all the land south of the mountains to the sea; who leads a barbarian horde of nomadic horsemen so fierce, so vicious, so *perverse* in their torments, that grown men *piddle* themselves at the thought of even breathing the same air? *That* Warlord?"

"He does sound rather intimidating," said her father.

"Indeed," Sally replied sharply. "Have you lost your mind?"

"Amazingly, no." The old king rubbed his hip, and winced. "I haven't felt this proud of myself in years."

Sally closed her eyes, grabbing fistfuls of her skirt and squeezing. "I think *I'm* losing my mind." She had heard about the man for as long as she could remember. Warlord of this and that: colorfully descriptive names that were usually associated with pain, death, and destruction. Sally had vague memories of her mother speaking of him, as well, but only in association with *his* mother. He would have been a small child at the time, she thought. Nice and innocent; probably skinning dogs and plucking the wings off butterflies while suckling milk from his mother's teat.

"What in the world," she said slowly, fighting to control her temper, and rising horror, "could a man like that possibly want from a woman like me? He could have anyone. He probably *has* had everyone, given his reputation." Sally leaned forward, poking her father in the chest. "I will not do it. Absolutely not. You are sending me to a short, hard, miserable life. I'm ashamed of you."

Her father folded his arms over his chest. "Your mother's best friend was sent to that short, hard, miserable life—and she thrived. *Your* dear, late, lovely mother would not have lied about that." He turned and fumbled through the papers on his desk. "Now, here. The Warlord sent a likeness of himself."

Sally frowned, but leaned in for a good long stare. "He looks like a dirty fingerprint."

"Of course he doesn't," replied her father, squinting at the portrait. "You can see his eyes, right there."

"I thought those were his nostrils."

"Well, you're not going to be picky, are you? At least he has a face."

"Yes," Sally replied dryly. "What a miracle."

The king scowled. "Spoiled. I let you run wild, allow you teachers, books, a lifestyle unsuitable for any princess, and this is how you repay me. With sarcasm."

"You taught me how to think for myself. Which never seemed to bother you until now."

He slammed his fists onto the desk. "We are being overrun!"

His roar made her eardrums thrum. Sally shut her mouth, and fell backward into the soft cushions of a velvet armchair. Her knees were too weak to keep her upright. Terrible loneliness filled her heart, and sorrow—which she bottled up tight, refusing to let her father see.

The old king, as she stared at him, slumped with his arms braced against his desk. Staring at maps, and embroidered family crests that had been torn off the clothing of the fallen soldiers; and that now were scattered before him, some crusty with dried blood.

"We are being overrun," he said again, more softly. "I know how it starts. First with border incursions, and petty theft of livestock. Then villages ransacked, roads blocked. Blamed on vandals and simple thieves. Until one day you hear the thunder of footfall beyond the walls of your keep, and all that you were born to matters not at all."

He fixed her with a steely look. "I will not have that happen. Not for me, not for you. Not for any of the people who depend on us."

Sally swallowed hard. Perhaps she *had* been spoiled. Duty could not be denied. But when she looked at the small portrait of the man her father wanted her to marry, terrible, unbending disgust filled her—disgust and terror, and a gut-wrenching grief that made her want to howl with misery.

Married to *that.* Sent away from all she knew. Forced to give up her freedom. No matter how fondly her mother had spoken of her friend, that woman's son had a reputation that no sweet talk could alter. He was a monster.

The old king saw her looking at the Warlord's likeness, and held it out to her with grim determination. She did not take it, but continued to stare, feeling as though she were going to jump out of her skin.

"I can't tell anything from that," she said faintly. "His artist did a terrible job."

"Probably because he never sits still," replied her father sarcastically. "Or so I was told. I assume it's because he prefers to be out killing things."

Sally grimaced. "You're not seriously considering this?"

"Darling, sweet child; you golden lamb of my heart; my little chocolate knucklehead: I did consider, I have considered, and the deed is done. His envoy should be arriving within the week to inspect you for marriage and sign the contracts."

"Oh, dear." Sally stared at her father, feeling as though she hardly knew him—quite certain that she did not.

And, since he was suddenly a stranger to her, she had no qualms in grabbing a nearby candle, and jamming it flame first into the tiny portrait he held in his hand. Hot wax sprayed. She nearly set his sleeve on fire. He howled in shock, dancing backward, and slammed his injured hip into the desk. He yelled even louder.

"And that," Sally said, shaken, "is how *I* feel about the matter."

* * *

She was sent to her room without supper, which was hardly a punishment, as the idea of food made her want to lean outside her window and add bile to the already bilious moat; which, briefly, she considered jumping into. Unfortunately, she had a healthy respect for her own life, and if the fall did not kill her, swallowing even a mouthful of that stinking cesspool probably would.

So she paced. Ran circles around her chamber, faster and faster, until she had to sit down in the middle of the floor and hold her head. No tears, though her eyes burned. Just a lump in her throat that grew larger and harder, and more sour—until she did bend over and gag, covering her mouth, trying to be quiet so that no one would hear her.

Her father, she thought, was not a bad man. But he was desperate, and had no son, and while that had not bothered him when she was young, now that he was getting on in years—hounded by insipid little squirts invading his borders—he had clearly lost his mind, and his heart, and if she did not control her temper, perhaps some other vital body parts.

Clearly, something had to be done.

Selfish, she thought. *You know he needs this alliance. He would not have gone to such extremes otherwise.*

Of course not. But that did not mean that she had to put

up with it. Being married to a warlord? And not just any warlord, but the Warlord of the South, with his endless army of barbarians, witches, and wolves? Even the horses were said to eat meat (an exaggeration, she knew that for a fact), and the Warlord himself lived in a tent so that he could up and move at the change of the wind, or if a good pillage was scented; and to evade all the assassins sent to take his head. *That* much was not an embellishment.

She wouldn't last a week. It was a death sentence.

So go, she thought. *Leave your father to his own devices.*

Leave the father whom she loved. Betray him to his enemies. Allow him to stand before the envoy of the most hated, villainous man to haunt the South, and say that his daughter had up and run—with apologies for having made the envoy make the trip for nothing. Yes, that would work perfectly.

Sally sighed, pounding her fists against her legs in frustration. She could not do that to her father. But she could not marry the Warlord, either. There had to be another way.

Except there was nothing.

Nothing, unless you turn to magic.

Simple, stupid, magic. Probably her imagination. Magic was something folks whispered about only when they were frightened; and then, if it was dark, only as ghouls and flesh suckers, or men who transformed into wolves. Which wasn't even magic, in Sally's opinion. Just other kinds of people. Who probably didn't exist.

Magic was something else. Magic was power, and thought, and miracle. Magic could spin the threads of the world and make something new. Magic could circumvent the future.

Sally's mother had dabbled in magic; or that was how Sally remembered it, anyway: small things that her father called *eccentricities*. Like singing prayers to roses, or speaking to the frogs in the pond as though they were human. Sketching signs over her chest when passing certain trees, or laying her hands upon others, with a murmur and a smile. Cats had enjoyed her company, as did fawns from the wood (although, as the deer on her father's land were practically tame anyway, that was hardly evidence of the arcane); and sometimes, in a storm, with the lightning flickering around her, she would stand on the balcony in the rain and wind, staring into the darkness as though searching, waiting for something she thought would come.

Which was why she had died, some said. Being in the wind, chilled until a cough had found her; and then fever.

Many little things. Many memories. Her mother had been a witch, according to a very few; born in the heart of the Tangleroot Forest. But Sally knew that was a lie. Her mother had merely lived and died with farseeing eyes, able to perceive what others could not. Sally wished she had those eyes. Her mother had said that she did, but that was cold comfort now.

If there was such a thing as magic, it was not going to save her. She'd have better luck asking bluebirds or goldfish for salvation.

So Sally went for a walk.

Night had spun around, with stars glittering and the moon tipping the edge of the horizon, glimpsed behind the trees. Sally strode down to the garden, led by habit and soothing scents: lavender and jasmine, roses full in bloom. She passed the kitchen plot, and plucked basil to rub against her fingers and nose; and a carrot to chew on; and listened to pots banging, cooks arguing; and to the wind that hissed, caressing her hair, while frogs sang from the lilies in the pond. Sally followed their croaks, lonely for them; and envious. She felt very small in the world—but not small enough.

Several ancient oaks grew near the water. Some said they had been transplanted as seedlings from what was now the Tangleroot Forest, though after three hundred years, Sally could hardly imagine how anyone could be so certain that was the truth. She had a favorite, though, a sleeping giant with fat coiled roots that were too large for the earth to contain. She imagined, one day, that her gentleman tree would wake, believing he was an old man, and try hobbling away.

Her mother had often laid her hands upon this tree. Sally perched on the thick tangle of his once-and-future legs, bark worn smooth from years of her keeping company with his shadow, and leaned back against the trunk with a sigh.

"Well," she said. "This is a mess."

The oak's leaves hissed in the wind, and then, quite surprisingly, she heard a soft female voice say, "Poor lass."

Sally flinched, turning—but it was only the gardener who peered around the other side of the massive oak. The old woman held a tankard in her wrinkled hands, her silver eyes glittering in the faint firelight cast by the sconces that had been pounded into the earth around the castle, lit each night and burning on pitch.

"I heard," said the gardener. "Thought you would come here."

Sally remembered the first time she had seen the old woman,

who looked the same now as she had fifteen years ago when Sally had first tottered into her domain, sticky with pear juice and holding the tail of a spotted hunting dog, her mother's finest companion besides her daughter and husband. The garden had been a place of wonderment; and the gardener had become one of Sally's most trusted confidants.

"You've always been a friend to me," she said. "What do you think I should do?"

The old woman pushed back her braids, and took a brief sip from the tankard before passing it on to Sally, who drank deeply and found cider, spicy and sweet on her tongue. "I think you should be useful to yourself."

"Useful to my father, you mean?"

"Don't be dense," she replied. "You know what you want."

Sally did. What she wanted was simple, and yet very complicated: freedom, simply to be herself. Not a princess. Just Sally.

Except that there was a cost to being free, and in the world beyond this castle and its land, she was useful for very little. She could garden, yes, and cook; or ride a bucking horse as well as a man. But that was hardly enough to survive on. She was Sally, but also a princess—and that had never been clearer to her than now, when she thought of what she might be good for, out in the world.

"Useful," Sally said, after a moment's thought. "Useful to myself and others. That's a powerful thing."

"More than people realize," said the gardener. "Everyone has got something different to offer. Just a matter of finding out what that is."

She sipped her drink. "I was the youngest of seven children.

A good, hardy farming family, but there wasn't enough for all of us to eat. So I left. Took to the road one day and had my adventures. Until I came to this place. They needed a person with a talent for growing things, and that I had aplenty. I was useful. So I stayed.

"I'm a princess. I have duties."

"That you do," said the old woman. "But following the duty to yourself, and the duty to others, doesn't have to be separate."

Sally narrowed her eyes. "You know something."

The gardener smiled to herself, but it was sad, and vaguely uneasy. "I dreamed of the queen and her crown of horns, sleeping in the forest by the silver lake. Guarded by ravens, who keep her dreams at bay."

She spoke the words almost as though she were singing them, and Sally found herself light-headed, leaning hard against the oak, which seemed to vibrate beneath her back. "But that's just a dream."

"No," whispered the gardener, fixing her with a look. "Those of us who ever lived in the shadow of the Tangleroot know of odd truths, and odder dreams that are truth, echoes of a past that slumbers; and of things that walk amongst us, fully awake. Stories that others have forgotten, because they are too strange."

Sally rubbed her arms, chilled. "The Tangleroot is only a forest."

"Is that why no one enters it?" The old woman's smile deepened, but with a particular glint in her eyes. "Or why no one cuts its trees, or stands long in its shadow? You know that much is true."

Sally did know. The Tangleroot was an ancient forest,

rumored to have once been the site of a powerful kingdom. But a curse had fallen, and great battles had raged, and what was mighty had decayed; until the forest took root, with trees rising from the bodies of the dead. To cut a tree from the Tangleroot, some said, was to cut a soul—and bring down a curse upon your head.

Whether mere fancy or not, Sally had never met a man or woman who did not take heed of the old warnings. And it was true, too, that strange things seemed to happen around that forest. Lights, dancing in the shadows, and unearthly voices singing. Wolves who were said to walk as men, and men small as thimbles. Those who entered did not often come out; and the lucky few who walked free were always changed: insane or wild, or aged in unnatural ways.

Sally began to suddenly suffer the same uneasiness that had filled her just before the old king had announced his plan to marry her off. "Why are you telling me this?"

"Because there are answers in the Tangleroot, for those who have the courage to find them. Answers and questions, and possibilities."

"And dreams?" Sally asked.

"Dreams that walk," whispered the old woman, staring down into her tankard. "Your mother would have understood. She had been inside the forest. I could see it in her eyes."

Sally went still at the mention of her mother, and then placed her hand over her chest, feeling through her dress the pendant, warm against her skin; the wooden heart, especially. "If I go there, will I find something that can help me? And my father?"

"You'll find something," she replied ominously, and pointed at Sally. "The Tangleroot calls to some, and to others it merely answers the desire that it senses. You want that forest, and it'll bring you in, one way or another. It is a dangerous place, created by a dangerous woman who lived long ago. But there's danger in staying here, too. You can't stop a plant that wants to grow. You'll only crush it if you try."

Sally had felt crushed from the moment her father had mentioned marriage, but now a terrible restlessness rose within her, crazy anticipation feeding a burst of wildness. Her entire body twitched, as though it wanted to start walking, and for a moment she felt a strange energy between herself and the oak. Like something was waking.

Fool's errand, she told herself. *Magic, if it exists, won't save you.*

But she found herself saying, "And all I would do is enter the Tangleroot? There must be more than that. I wouldn't know what to look for, or how to start."

"Start by not making excuses. Go or stay." The gardener stood on unsteady legs, and handed Sally her tankard. "Princess or not, duty or no, you were born with a heart and head. Which, in my experience, is enough to make your own choices about how to live your life."

The old woman touched Sally's brow, and her fingertips were light and cool. "You have a week before the envoy arrives."

"That's not much," Sally said.

"It's a lifetime," she replied. "Depending on how you use it."

2

Sally used it that night, when she slipped out of the castle and ran away.

She did not take much with her. Bread, cheese, dried salted beef; a sharp knife; and warm clothing that consisted of a down vest, a woolen cloak, and cashmere knitted leggings worn beneath her work dress, which still smelled faintly of manure. She took gold coins, and left behind her horse. If she was going to venture inside the Tangleroot—and that remained to be seen—she did not want to worry about leaving the animal behind. That, and it was harder to hide with a horse when one traveled the road.

The borders of the Tangleroot were everywhere, scattered and connected, twisting through the countryside across numerous kingdoms. The closest edge of the ancient forest was more than a day's walk to the south, a little farther if Sally stayed off the main road and traveled one of the lesser-used trails. Which she did, guided by the light of the moon, and the stars glimpsed through the leaves of the trees.

She moved quickly, almost running at times, afraid that she would hear the silver bells attached to her father's saddle; or the familiar call of his deep voice. Part of her wished that she would hear those things; not entirely certain that she would keep on running.

She was terrified. This was a fool's journey. No direction, save faith in the unknowable, and the possibility of something miraculous.

But she did not stop. Not once. Afraid that if she did, even for a moment, she would turn around and return home. Like a coward, without even trying to fight for her freedom. The gardener was right: Sally had a week. One week to find an alternative, be it magic or simply inspiration—neither of which she was going to discover back home.

Near dawn, she found a small clearing behind a thicket of blackberry bushes that had lost their flowers. It was a cool night, and she curled deep inside her cloak to eat bread and cheese. Forest sounds filled the air: the hiss of the wind, and the crunch of a hoof in the leaves. Owls hooted. Sally was not frightened of the night, but sitting still made her think again of what she was doing, and that was far more terrifying. She shut her eyes and tried to sleep.

And dreamed of a queen.

Dawn, and though it is spring, there is ice on the lake, a sheen of frozen pearls smashed to dust, compacted into a shield against the undercurrent, dark water. A sleeping time: the fog has not yet burned away, and everywhere a glow, an otherworldly gleam.

It is not safe to walk on the ice. Ice belongs to the sleeping queen, the horned woman of the southern shore, who wears a crown to keep her dreams inside her head. Such dangerous things, her dreams. Like her voice, which makes thunder, raining words that drown.

She is silent now. Shackled, sleeping. Wearing the crown that binds her. A crown that has a lock. A lock that has a key.

A key that can be found.

Sally was still trying to find that key when something tugged her from the dream. She opened her eyes, and found herself staring into the face of a little girl.

It was an unexpected sight, and it took Sally several long moments to pull away from the dream and convince herself that she was not yet still asleep. It should have been dawn, sun high, but the sky was dark with night. And yet the air was cool on her face, and there was a rock digging into her hip; and when she dug her nails into her arm, she felt the pinch.

The little girl was naked, her dark hair long and matted with leaves, brambles, and feathers. Hard to see much of her, as the shadows loved her face, but she was a healthy, round little thing, not much older than five or seven, with sylphlike features and eyes that were huge and gray.

When Sally began to sit up, the little girl scuttled backward, half crouching, each movement graceful and wild, but fraught with a startled energy that reminded her of a deer. She did not walk, but jolted; she did not crawl, but leapt; and the moon that dappled her skin with light seemed instead like the spots on a fawn, drifting sweetly across her smooth, soft flesh.

"Hello," Sally whispered.

The little girl flinched at the sound of her voice, swaying backward as though she wanted to run. Sally held her breath, afraid of moving; but, after a moment, let her hand creep slowly toward the satchel lying on the ground at her elbow.

"Are you hungry?" she asked the child. "Food?"

The little girl did not react, not even a blink. Sally fumbled inside the bag, and removed the half-eaten loaf of bread. The child showed no interest. Instead, she reached deep inside her matted hair, and pulled out a small speckled egg. Sally stared, astonished, as the little girl placed it on her palm, and held it up at eye level, peering at Sally over the round, pale surface; like a small spirit, gazing over the curve of the moon.

And then, with hardly a wasted motion, the little girl popped the egg inside her mouth, crunched down hard—and ran.

Sally sat, stunned. Watching as that fleet-footed little girl slipped into the night shadows like a ghost, so quick, so graceful, that for one brief second Sally wondered if she was not hallucinating, and that she had instead seen a deer, a wolf, some creature beyond human, beyond even life.

She struggled to her feet, sluggish, as though her limbs had been dipped in cobwebs and molasses, and when she finally stood, the world spun around her in waves of moonlight. She gathered up her belongings and stumbled down the path that the little girl had taken.

It was down the same trail she had been traveling, but the moonlight made it feel as though she walked upon silver, and the shadows glistened as though edged in pearl dust, or stars. Ahead, a glimmer of movement, a flash like the tail of a rabbit; and then a breathless stillness. The little girl stood in the path, staring at her, tiny hands clutched into fists.

"Wait," Sally croaked, holding out her hand, but the child danced away. This time, though, she stopped after several long, leaping steps, and glanced back over her shoulder. Poised, lost in shadow, so that all Sally could see was the high bone of her cheek and the glint of a single eye.

I am sorry, whispered a sweet voice. *But she wants you.*

Sally tried to speak, but her throat closed and the only sound she could make was a low, strained croak. She managed to take a step, and then another, and it suddenly seemed like the most important thing in the world that Sally reach that little girl, as if night would crush them both if she did not.

But just before she could touch the child's shoulder, she sensed movement on her right, deep within the moonlit shadows of the forest. Sally froze, terrified to look, heart pounding. Finally unable to help herself.

She saw children in the forest. Boys and girls who wavered in her vision, wild and tangled as the roots they stood upon. Small hands faded and then reappeared, clutching at the trunks of trees, while mice poked their heads from nests of hair, and small birds fluttered free.

The little girl leapt out of reach, and stared at Sally with eyes so ancient, so haunted, her human body seemed little more than a fine shell, or a glove to slip on. Her small fingers traced patterns through the air, above her chest—as Sally remembered her mother doing.

Hurry and wake, whispered the little girl, just as Sally heard a thumping roar behind her, like the beating of a thousand wings. She could not turn—her feet were frozen in place—but the sound filled her with a cold, hard terror that wrapped around her throat in a choking, brutal grip.

The children covered their faces and vanished into the trees. The moon disappeared, and then the stars, and the trail she stood upon transformed into a ribbon of dark water. A raven cawed.

Sally found her voice, and screamed.

* * *

Later, far away, she heard men speaking. There was nothing she could do about it. Her arms were too heavy to move, and she could hardly feel her legs. Swallowing was difficult because her throat was sore, mouth dry, lips cracked and bleeding. Thirst burned through her, and she made a small sound; a croak, or whimper.

A strong, warm hand slid under her neck, and the cool rim of a tin cup touched her lips. Water flooded her mouth, and she choked on it; but she tried again, greedily, and managed to swallow every last drop. The effort exhausted her, though. Sally fell back against the rocky ground, eyes closed, too weak to care where she was, or whom she was with. All she could see inside her mind were the children, and one in particular: the little girl, wild-eyed and inhuman, whispering, *Hurry.*

"Hurry," Sally heard a man say.

Strong arms slid beneath her body, lifting her off the ground. Her head lolled, and another set of hands, smelling of horse and ash, pushed under her neck, supporting her. She was carried a short distance, and her eyelids cracked open just enough to see sunlight filtering through the leaves, green and lush, whispering in the wind.

Sally was placed on another flat surface that was considerably softer than the ground, and felt as though it had been padded with blankets, bags of meal, hay, and several sharp objects that jutted uncomfortably into her side.

A man's face suddenly blocked the sun. Sally could see nothing of his features, but he held up her head again to drink from the same tin cup, and then wiped her mouth with the edge of his sleeve.

"Damn," said a gruff voice. "This *is* a strange place."

"Just drive," replied the man beside her, with a distinct weariness in his voice. Reins cracked, and the surface upon which Sally rested lurched with a groan. The leaves began moving overhead.

The man who had helped her drink water lay down beside her with a tired sigh. He did not touch her. Sally tried to look at him, but her eyes drifted shut, and her head felt too heavy to move. She heard the man humming softly to himself. His voice carried her into sleep, though she dreaded the darkness. She was afraid of her dreams.

But when she opened her eyes again, she remembered nothing of her sleep. The sun was still up. She stared at the branches of trees, and the wind was blowing. But the wagon had stopped, and the man who had lain beside her was gone.

Sally smelled woodsmoke. She rolled over on her side, and found that she still had her belongings; even the gold coins in her pouch. She checked her throat for her necklace, and pulled it out from beneath her neckline. Amethyst glittered, though her eyes were drawn to the tiny remains of the wooden heart, the grains of which suddenly seemed threaded with gold.

Sally tucked the necklace back inside her dress, and peered over the wagon wall. She saw a clearing surrounded by oaks and dotted with clumps of bluebells; and a man who was juggling stones.

Quite a lot of stones, all of them irregularly shaped, as if he had just gathered them up from the ground and started juggling on the spot. His hands were a blur, and he was sitting in front of a small crackling fire. Except for the juggling, he was utterly unassuming in appearance, neither tall nor short, big nor small, but of a medium build that was nonetheless lean, and healthy. His hair was brown, cut unfashionably short, and he wore simple clothing of a similar color, though edged in a remarkable shade of crimson. A silver chain disappeared beneath his collar.

Several horses grazed nearby. Sally saw no one else.

The man suddenly seemed to notice that she was watching him, and with extraordinary ease and grace allowed each of the rocks flying through the air to fall into his hands. He hardly seemed to notice. His gaze never left hers, and Sally found herself thinking that his face was rather remarkable, after all—or maybe that was his eyes. He looked as though he had never stared at anything dull in his entire life.

His mouth quirked. "I wondered whether you would ever wake."

Sally was not entirely convinced that she had stopped dreaming. "How long was I asleep?"

He hesitated, still watching her as though she were a puzzle. "Since we found you yesterday. Just on the border of the Tangleroot. Another few steps and you would have been inside the forest."

Sally stared. "Impossible."

He tossed a rock in the air, and in an amazing show of agility, caught it on the bridge of his nose—swaying to hold it steady. "Which one?"

"Both," she said sharply, and tried to sit up. Dizziness made her waver, and she clung to the wagon wall, gritting her teeth. "When I stopped . . . when I stopped yesterday to rest, I was nowhere near that place."

"Well," said the man, letting the rock slide off his face as he stared at her again, thoughtfully. "Things happen."

And then he looked past her, beyond the wagon, and smiled. "What a surprise."

Sally frowned, and struggled to look over her shoulder. What she saw was indeed a surprise—but not, she thought, any cause for smiles.

Men stood on the edge of the clearing, which she realized now was beside a narrow track, hardly used by the length of the grass growing between the shallow wagon tracks. The men were dressed in rags and leather, with swords belted at their waists and battered packs slung over lean shoulders. Some wore bent metal helms on their heads, and their boots seemed ill-fitting, several with the toes cut out.

Mercenaries, thought Sally, reaching for the knife belted at her hip. A small scouting party, from the looks of them. Only four in total, no horses, little to carry except for what they could scavenge. Sally had no idea how far she had come from home, but she knew without a doubt that she was still well within the borders of the kingdom. Her father had been right: one day soon there would be the sound of hard footfall outside the castle; and then it would be over.

The mercenaries walked closer, touching weapons as their hard, suspicious eyes surveyed the clearing. The man by the fire started juggling again, but with only two rocks—a slow, easy motion that was utterly relaxed, even cheerful. But something about his smile, no matter how genuine, felt too much like the grin of a wolf.

And wolves, Sally thought, usually traveled in packs.

"You've come for entertainment," he said to the mercenaries, and suddenly there was a red ball in the air, amongst the rocks. Sally could not guess how it had gotten there. The mercenaries paused, staring, and then began smiling. Not pleasantly.

"You could say that," said one of them, a straw-haired, sinewy man who stood slightly bent, as though his stomach hurt. He gave Sally an appraising look. She refused to look away, and he laughed, taking a step toward her.

By the fire, the juggler stood and kicked at the burning wood, scattering sparks and ashes at the mercenaries. They shouted, jumping back, but the juggler kept his rocks and red ball in the air, and added something small and glittering that moved too quickly to be clearly seen. He began to sing and stood on one leg, and then the other, hopping in one place; and finally, just as the mercenaries were beginning to chuckle coarsely and stare at him as if he were insane, the juggler threw everything high into the air, twirled, and flicked his wrist.

Sally almost didn't see him do it. She was crawling from the wagon, taking advantage of the obvious distraction. But she happened to look at the juggler just at that moment as the rocks and red ball went up—taking with them the mercenaries' attention—and caught the glint of silver that remained in his hand.

The straw-haired man staggered backward into his companions and fell down, twitching, eyes open and staring. A disk smaller than the mouth of a teacup jutted from his forehead, deeply embedded with edges that were jagged and sharp, as irregularly shaped as the points on a snowflake. His companions stared at him for one stunned moment, and then turned to face the juggler. He was tossing rocks in the air again, but was no longer smiling.

"Accidents," he said. "Such a pity."

The mercenaries pulled their swords free. Sally scrambled from the wagon, but did not run. Her dagger was in her hand, and there was a man in front of her with his back exposed. She could do this. She had to do this. It was she or they, them or the juggler—even though everything inside her felt small and ugly, and terrified of taking a life.

But just before she forced her leaden feet into a wild headlong lunge, a strong hand grabbed her shoulder. She yelped, turning, and found herself staring into brown hooded eyes, almost entirely obscured by coarse, bushy hair and a long braided beard shot through with silver.

A human bear, she thought, with a grip like one. He held a crossbow. Beside him stood another man, the tallest that Sally had ever seen, whose long blond hair and strong chiseled features belonged more to the ice lands than the green spring hills of the mid-South. His hands also held a bow, one that was almost as tall as him.

Startled, sickening fear hammered Sally's heart, but the bearded man gave her a brief beaming smile, and fixed his gaze on the mercenaries—who had stopped advancing on the juggler, and were staring back with sudden uncertainty.

"Eh," said the bearded man. "Only three little ones."

"I'm going back for the deer," replied the giant, sounding bored. He glanced down at Sally. "Congratulations on not being dead. We took bets."

He turned and walked away toward the woods. Sally stared after him, and then turned back in time to see a rock slam into a mercenary's brow with bone-crushing force. She flinched, covering her mouth as the man reeled to the ground with a bloodless dent in his head that was the size of her fist.

Pure silence filled the air. Sally was afraid to breathe. The juggler was now tossing the red ball into the air with his left hand, holding his last rock in the other. He stood very still, staring with cold hard eyes at the two remaining mercenaries—both men obviously rattled, trying to split their attention between him and the bearded man, who patted Sally's shoulder and pointed his crossbow at their chests.

"I think," said the juggler, "that you should consider your options very carefully. My hands are prone to wild fits, as you've seen—which I have most humbly come to suspect are possessed occasionally by various deities in lieu of hurling thunderbolts."

"In other words," said the bearded man, "you should drop your weapons and strip. Before he kills you."

"But not in front of the lady," added the juggler.

"Don't mind me," replied Sally weakly.

The mercenaries looked at each other, and then at their dead companions on the ground, both of whom had finally stopped twitching.

Slowly, carefully, they put down their swords, unbuckled their knives, dropped their helmets and then their trousers (at which point Sally had to look away, because a nude man was not nearly as startling as one that appeared to have never washed), and pulled off the rest of their raggedy clothing, which gave off a remarkable odor that would have been funny if Sally had not still been so shaken by everything she had just witnessed.

"Run along," said the juggler, when they were finally disarmed, and disrobed. "I hope you meet some lovesick bears. 'Tis the season, and you would make excellent fathers."

The mercenaries ran. Sally watched them go, but only until she was convinced that they would not be returning. Humans, she thought, were far more attractive with clothes than without.

She sagged against the wagon's edge, unpeeling her fingers from the knife hilt. Her knees felt shaky, and she was breathless. She glanced at the dead, who were being searched by the bearded man, and had to look away.

A water skin was shoved in front of her face. It was the juggler, peering down at her with a peculiar compassion that was utterly at odds with the coldness she had seen in his face; or the wolf's smile; or the cheerful, even madcap glint that had filled his eyes while distracting those mercenaries with his tricks.

"You've been ill," he said. "I'm sorry you had to see that."

"I would be sorrier if I hadn't," she replied. "Who are you?"

"Oh," he said, with a grin. "We're just actors."

3

They were the Traveling Troupe of Twister Riddle, which was a name that Sally told them made no sense, but that (when they prodded her for additional commentary) was rather catchy, in a crazed sort of way. The juggler was supposed to be Lord Twister Riddle himself, though his real name (or as real as Sally could only assume it to be) was Mickel Thorn.

The small bear of a bearded man was called Rumble, and the giant—when he returned from the forest with a deer slung over his shoulders—introduced himself as Patric. Neither seemed capable of performing anything more complicated than a good beating, but Sally knew better than to judge.

"There used to be more of us—" began Mickel.

"But there's no such thing as loyalty anymore," interrupted Rumble. "One little whiff of gold—"

"And the years mean nothing," said Patric, who folded

himself down upon on a fallen tree to begin skinning the dead animal. "They left us for another troupe. Without a word, in the night. I nearly drowned in tears."

He said it with a straight face. Sally frowned, unsure what to make of them. They were most certainly dangerous, but not rough or coarse, which was an odd contradiction—and an odd atmosphere between them all. She had always considered herself to be a good judge of character, but that had been at home—and she had never, not once in seventeen years, been on her own beyond the protection of her father's lands. Sally was not entirely certain she could trust her judgment. And yet she thought—she was quite sure—that she was safe with these men.

For now. She thought of her dream, her dream that had felt so real: that little girl with her ancient eyes, and the children in the trees. A shiver ripped through her, and she gritted her teeth as she glanced behind at the woods—feeling as though someone was watching her. The hairs on her neck prickled. It was not quite the afternoon, and the weather was chilly, though clear. If she could backtrack to the Tangleroot . . .

"I should go," Sally said reluctantly. "But thank you for your help."

Patric's hands paused. Rumble gave her a quick look of surprise. Mickel, however, reached inside his coat for a small metal spoon, which he waved his hand over. It appeared to bend. "Are you running from something?"

"Of course not." Sally peered at the spoon, trying to get a closer look. Mickel hid it in his fist, and when he opened his hand it had vanished.

"You're a trickster," she said. "Sleight of hand, games of illusion."

"Not magic?" Mickel placed a hand over his heart. "I'm shocked. Most people think I have unnatural powers."

Sally tried not to smile. "You have an unnatural gift for words. Anything else is suspect."

Rumble grunted, picking at his teeth. "Won't be safe with mercenaries still out there. Not for you, lass."

"Too many of them," Patric said absently. "More than I imagined."

Chilly words. Her father was losing control over his land. For a moment Sally considered returning home, but stopped that thought. She would have to make a choice soon—but not yet. Not until she stepped into the Tangleroot and discovered whether a power was there that could make a difference.

Sally forced herself to stand. Her legs were still unsteady. Mickel stood as well, and kicked dirt over the fire. "We were also leaving." Rumble and Patric stared, and he gave them a hard look. "What direction are you headed?"

Sally folded her arms over her chest. "South."

"Remarkable. Fate has conspired. We're also headed that way."

Rumble coughed, shaking his head. Patric sawed at the deer a bit harder. Glancing at them, Sally said, "Really."

"And tomorrow we'll begin ambling north." Mickel tilted his head, his gaze turning thoughtful. "Where are you from?"

"I don't think it matters," she replied curtly. "If I asked you the same question, I suspect you would feel the same."

"Home is just a place?" he replied, smiling. "You're jaded."

"And you smell," Rumble said, peering up at her.

"Like manure," Patric added. "Very alluring."

Sally frowned. "You three . . . saved my life. I think. And I appreciate that. But—"

"But nothing. No harm will come to you. If you travel with us, you are one of us." Mickel held her gaze, as if he wanted her to understand. When she finally nodded, he turned away to nudge Rumble with his boot. "Come on, then. We'll go to Gatis. It's not far."

No, not far at all. Only two days' ride from home. She could be recognized, or her father might find her there—assuming he had begun looking.

But it was also close to the Tangleroot.

Sally held out her hand to Mickel, who stared for one long moment before taking it with solemn dignity. His grip was warm and strong, and a tingle rode up her arm. From the way he flinched, she thought he felt it, too.

"My name is Sally," she told him.

"Sally," he said quietly. "Welcome to the family."

* * *

She began seeing ravens in the trees as they drew close to Gatis. Hardly noticeable at first, until one of them launched off a branch in a burst of black feathers, cawing in a voice so piercing, the sound seemed to run straight down into her heart. Images flashed through her mind—ravens and horns, and silver frozen water—making Sally sway with dizziness. She leaned hard against the edge of the rickety wagon, holding her head.

Mickel rode close on a swift black mare that was surprisingly fine-boned and sleek; a lovely creature, and a surprise. She had seen such horses only once before, those from a trader who had come from south of the mountains. The Warlord's territory.

She would not have guessed a mere performer would have such a horse; nor Patric or Rumble. Rumble's mount was tied to the back of the wagon. He sat up front, holding the reins of the mules.

Sally caught Mickel's eye. "You said you found me near the Tangleroot."

"Yes," he said, drawing out the word as though it made him uncomfortable. "You were unwell."

"Unconscious, you mean."

Mickel rubbed the back of his neck. "Not quite."

"You were screaming," Rumble said, turning to look at her. "It's how we found you. Just standing as you please in front of the border of that cursed forest, making the most bloodcurdling sound I've ever heard. And I've heard plenty," he added, a moment later.

Sally stared at him. "I was . . . screaming."

"Quite a fighter, too," Patric said, guiding his horse past the wagon.

She blinked, startled. "And I fought?"

"You were delirious," Mickel told her. "Simple as that."

"You were trying to enter the Tangleroot," Rumble said. "Almost did. Took all three of us to hold you down."

"Stop," Patric called back, over his shoulder. "You'll scare her."

"No," Mickel said slowly, watching her carefully. "No, I don't think you will."

Sally, who had no idea what her expression looked like, had nonetheless been thinking that it would have been a great deal easier if they had just let her go. Perhaps more terrifying, too, given what she remembered of her dream. If it had been a dream.

But she did not like having her thoughts written so clearly upon her face. She studied her hands, noting the dirt under her nails, and then looked back up at Mickel. He was still watching her. She studied him in turn, and suffered a slow rush of heat from the boldness of his gaze—and her own.

Gatis was a rambling village built into the high hills of a river valley, a place that had belonged to shepherds for hundreds of years, and still belonged to them; only now they lived in comfortable cottages with fine large gardens bordered by stone, and fruit orchards growing on the terraced hills that dipped down to the Ris, its winding waters blue and sparkling in the late-afternoon sun.

Sally had been to Gatis years before with her family—while her mother was still alive. The villagers were known for the quality of their yarn and dyes, and the fine craftsmanship of their weaving. Her cloak and vest were Gatis-made, and likely the cloth of her dress, as well. She pulled up her hood as they neared the village, hoping that none would remember her face. She had been only ten at the time. Surely she looked different.

The road sloped upward around a grassy hill covered in boulders, and at the crest of it, Sally saw the border of the Tangleroot. It was far away, but there was no mistaking those woods, however distant. The border was black as pitch, a curving wall of trees that looked so thick and impenetrable, Sally wondered how it would even be possible to squeeze one arm through, let alone travel through it.

Seeing the forest was like a slap in the face. She had known that one of the borders to the Tangleroot was near this village, but looking at it in broad daylight twisted in her gut like a knife. Sally felt afraid when she saw the faraway trees; fear *and* hunger. She closed her eyes, hoping the sensation would fade, but all she saw was the little girl, running fleet-footed down the moonlit path.

It made Sally wonder, briefly, about her mother—if it was true that she had been inside those ancient woods; and if so, what she had seen. The young woman wondered, too, if coming to Gatis had bothered her mother, what with the Tangleroot so close. She had died soon after that trip, though until now, Sally had never thought to associate the two. Perhaps there was still no reason to.

A hand touched her shoulder, and she flinched. It was Mickel, riding close beside the wagon. He looked away from her at the distant forest, sunlight glinting along the sharp angles of his face, and highlighting his brown hair with dark auburn strains.

"Not all trees are the same," he murmured. "Something I heard, growing up. Some trees are bark and root, and some trees have soul and teeth. If you are ever foolish enough to encounter the latter, then you'll know you've gone too far. And you'll be gone for good."

Sally had heard similar words, growing up. "It seems silly to give a forest so much power."

He shook his head. "No, it seems just right. We are infants

in the shadows of trees. And those trees . . . are something else."

"Some say they used to be human."

"Souls stolen by the forest of a powerful queen. Roots that grew from bones and blood, and imprisoned the spirits of an entire people." Mickel smiled. "I've heard it said that red hair was a common trait amongst them, and that descendents of those few who escaped the curse, who battled the queen herself, still bear that mark."

Sally brushed a strand of red hair self-consciously from her eyes. "You and your stories. How could something like that be true?"

"Maybe it's not. But either way, something about you is affected by that place, even by looking at it."

She began to deny it. He touched a finger to her lips. The contact startled her, and perhaps him. His hand flew away as though burned, and something unsettled, even pained, passed through his gaze. Sally suddenly found it hard to breathe.

"You think too much in your eyes," he said quietly. "I can practically read your thoughts."

"How terrifying," she replied, trying to be flippant; though hearing herself was quite different: she sounded serious as the grave.

A rueful smile touched his mouth, and he stroked the neck of his horse. He hardly used a saddle, just a soft pad and a molded piece of pebbled leather. He held the reins so lightly that Sally thought he must be guiding the horse with his legs. "Yes, it is frightening."

Sally fought the urge to touch her warm cheeks. "Why do you do this?"

"Perform? Create masks for a living? Haven't you ever wanted to be someone else?" Mickel's smile deepened. "No, don't answer that. I can see it in your eyes."

Sally thought she should start wearing a blindfold. But before she could ask him more, he said, "So what are you useful for? Are you good for anything?"

"I can read," she said, stung. "Garden, cook, ride a horse—"

"All of which are admirable," he replied, far more gently. "But I was referring to skills that would be useful in a . . . performance setting."

"Performance," she echoed, eyes narrowing; recalling overheard discussions between her father's men about "performances" involving women. "What kinds of skills do you think I might have?"

Rumble, who had been silent, began to laugh. Mickel shook his head. "Reading, I suppose, would be enough. Precious few can do that. If you know your letters, you might earn your keep writing messages that we can carry along the way."

"Earn my keep? You expect that I'll be traveling with you for much longer?"

Rumble glanced over his shoulder and gave the man a long, steady look. As did Patric, who was suddenly much closer to the wagon than Sally had realized. Both men had messages in their eyes, but Sally was no good at reading them. Mickel, however, looked uncomfortable. And, for a brief moment, defiant.

It's all right, she wanted to say. *I'll be gone by tonight.*

Ahead, a small boy stood in the road with several sheep and a dog. He stared at them as they passed, and Mickel's hands were suddenly full of small colorful balls that flew through the air with dazzling speed. He did not juggle long, though, before catching the balls in one large hand—and with the other, tossing the boy something that glittered in the sun. A silver mark, though the cut of it was unfamiliar. The child stared at it with huge eyes. Sally was also impressed, and puzzled. The coin, though foreign, would buy the boy's family at least a dozen fine sheep, or whatever else they needed.

"You run ahead," Mickel said, in a voice far deeper, and more arrogant, than the one he had just been speaking with. "Let your village know that the Traveling Troupe of Twister Riddle has arrived for their pleasure, and that tonight they will be *dazzled*, *astonished*, and *mystified*."

The boy gulped. "Magic?"

"Loads of it," Mickel replied. "Cats chasing kittens will be coming out of your ears by the end of the night."

"Or more silver!" he called, when the boy began running down the road, halting only long enough to come back for his sheep, which had scattered up the hill behind him, herded by the much more diligent dog.

Patric chuckled quietly to himself, while Mickel gave Sally an arch look. "Warming up the crowd is never a bad thing."

"That was an expensive message you just purchased."

"Ah," he said, rubbing the back of his neck. "We've performed for many important people."

"I'm surprised, then, that the rest of your troupe left you behind, even for the promise of yet more riches." Sally frowned. "I also thought actors were supposed to be poor."

"We're immensely talented."

"Is that how you afford such lovely horses?"

Rumble coughed. "These were a gift."

"A gift," she echoed. "You've been south of the mountains, then."

Mickel gave her a sidelong look, followed by a grim smile. "You have a keen eye, lady."

"I have a good memory," she corrected him. "And I've seen the breed."

"Have you?" he replied, with a sudden sharpness in his gaze that made her uncomfortable. "So go ahead. Ask what's really on your mind."

She frowned at him. "The Warlord. Did you see him?"

Rumble started to chuckle. Mickel gave him a hard look. "We performed for him."

Heat filled her, fear and anger and curiosity. Sally leaned forward. "I hear he sleeps with wolves in his bed and eats his meals off the stomachs of virgins."

Patric laughed out loud. Rumble choked. Even Mickel chuckled, though he sounded incredulous, and his nose wrinkled. "Where did you hear such nonsense?"

"I made it up," she said tartly. "But given how other men speak of him, he might as well do all those things. Such colorful descriptions I've heard. 'Master of Murder.' 'Fiend of Fire'—"

"Sex addict?" Rumble said, his eyes twinkling. "Ravisher of women? Entire villages of them, lined up for his . . . whatever?"

Mickel shot him a venomous look. Patric could hardly speak, he was laughing so hard. Her face warm, Sally said, "You disagree?"

"Not at all," he said, glancing at Mickel with amusement.

Sally drummed her fingers along her thigh. "So? Was he truly as awful as they say?"

"He was ordinary," Mickel said, with a great deal less humor than his companions seemed to be displaying. "Terribly, disgustingly ordinary."

"Or as ordinary as one can be while eating off the stomachs of virgins," Rumble added.

"This is true," Mickel replied, his eyes finally glinting with mischief. "I can't imagine where he gets all of them. He must have them grown from special virgin soil, and watered with virgin rain, and fed only with lovely virgin berries."

"Now you're making fun of me," Sally said, but she was laughing.

Mickel grinned. Ahead, there was a shout. Children appeared from around a bend in the road and raced toward them. The boy who had been given the silver mark was in the lead. Sally thought they resembled little sheep, stampeding.

"Damn," Rumble said, slowing the mules as Patric whirled his horse around and galloped back to the wagon. "You and your bright ideas."

"Brace yourself," Mickel said.

But Sally hardly heard him. She had looked up into the sky,

and found ravens flying overhead; a handful, soaring close. She swayed, overcome with unease, and touched her throat and the golden chain that disappeared beneath the neck of her dress.

Two of the birds dove, but Sally only saw where one of them went—which was straight toward her head. She raised her hands to protect herself, but it was too little, too late. Sharp claws knocked aside her hood and pierced her scalp, ripping away a tiny chunk of hair. Sally cried out in pain and fear.

Her vision flickered. Inside her head, she glimpsed images from her dream, which swallowed the wagon, and Mickel, and the sun with all the steadiness of something real: a silver frozen lake, and a woman sleeping within a cocoon of stone, her head dressed in a crown of horns. An unearthly beauty, pale as snow.

But the woman did not stay asleep. Sally saw her again, standing awake within a dark, tangled, heaving wood, gazing from between the writhing trees to a castle shining in the sun; an impossibly delicate structure that seemed made of spires and shell, built upon the green lush ground. But in the grass, warm and still, were the fresh bodies of fallen soldiers, so recently dead that not even the flies had begun buzzing. Amongst them stood women, strong and red-haired and bloody. Staring back with defiance and fury at the pale queen of the wood.

Sally felt a pain in her arm, a sharp tug, and the vision dissolved. She fell back into herself with a stomach-wrenching lurch, though she could not at first say where she was. The sun seemed too bright, the sky too blue. Her heart was pounding too fast.

Mickel's fingers were wrapped around her arm. She peered

at him, rubbing her watery eyes, and was dimly aware of the other men watching her, very still and stunned; and the children below, also staring.

"I wasn't screaming, was I?" Her voice sounded thick and clumsy; and it was hard to pronounce the words.

Mickel shook his head, but he was looking at her as no one ever had; with surprise and compassion, and an odd wonder that was faintly baffled. Blood trickled down the side of his face. He looked as though he had been pecked above the eye.

"You're hurt," she said.

"I got in the way," he replied, and reached out to graze her brow with his fingers—which came away bloody. Sally touched the spot on her head and felt warm liquid heat where part of her scalp had been torn off. Pain throbbed, and she swallowed hard, nauseous.

"You are a curious woman," Mickel said quietly. "Such a story in your eyes."

"Magic," Rumble muttered. "When a raven sets its sights . . ."

But Patric shook his head, and the older man did not finish what he was going to say. Mickel murmured, "The raven who attacked you spit out your hair. I could almost swear he simply wanted to taste it . . . or your blood."

The children scattered, melting away from the wagon. Perhaps afraid. Sally did not want to look too closely to know for certain. She shut her eyes, feeling by touch for the hem of her skirt. She tore off a strip of cloth, and bundled it against the wound in her head.

"I should go," she mumbled.

"Rest," Mickel replied. "Dream."

No, she thought. *You don't understand my dreams.*

But she lay down in the wagon bed, thinking of ravens and her father, and her mother, and little girls with wild hair and wilder eyes; and slept.

4

Sally danced that night. It was not the first time she had ever danced, but it was the first beyond the watchful eye of home, in a place where she was not known as the eccentric tatterdemalion princess—but as Sally, who was still a mystery, and unknown, without the aura of expectation and distance that so many placed on her. If anyone recognized her face—and there were several older women who gave her and her clothing sharp looks—no one said a word.

And no one seemed to be aware of the encounter with the ravens; nor commented on the wound in her head. She thought the children must have talked, but the people of Gatis were either too polite, or too used to strange occurrences, to make much of it.

Instead, she was treated as another Twisting Riddle, a woman of letters, who held children in her lap while she transcribed messages on the backs of flat rocks, smooth bark, and pale tanned hide; listening with solemn patience to heartbreak, tearful confessions, stories that would be amusing only to family and friends; news about births, livestock, weather; and the growing mercenary presence with pleas attached to be safe, be at ease, stay out of the hills. *I love you,* people said. *Write that down*, they would tell her. *I love you.*

And all the while, Mickel juggled and sang, and juggled and danced, and juggled some more: no object was too large or small, not even fire. The other two men were also gifted, in surprising ways. Rumble dragged a stool into the heart of the gathered crowd, where he slouched with his elbows on his knees and began reciting, halfheartedly, a well-known fable that also happened to be utterly boring. But at the end of the first verse his hand suddenly twitched, and the ground before him exploded with sparks and fire and smoke.

The crowd gasped, jumping back, but Rumble never faltered in his story, his voice only growing stronger, richer, more vibrant. More explosions, and he began striding forcefully across the ground, punctuating words and moments with clever sleights of hand; cloth roses pulled from thin air, along with scarves, and coins; small hard candies, and once a rabbit that looked wild and startled, as though it couldn't quite believe how it had gotten there.

Patric was a marksman. Daggers, arrows, any kind of target. Sally was convinced to stand very still against a tree with a small soft ball on her head—holding her breath as the blond giant took one look at her, and threw his blade. She felt the thunk, listened to the gasps and cheers, but it was only when she walked away that she was finally convinced that she'd survived.

The men had other acts that impressed—shows of horsemanship, riddles, recitations of famous ballads (during which Sally beat a drum)—indeed, several hours of solid entertainment that no one in Gatis would likely forget for a long time to come. Nor would Sally. And, when the show was over, it seemed only natural that the village treat the little troupe to dinner (at which Patric's catch of venison was sold), and to a performance of their own—as all the local musicians took up a corner of the square, and began playing to their heart's content.

It was night, and the air was lit with fire. Sally danced with strange smiling men, and then Rumble and Patric; but she danced with Mickel the longest, and he was light on his feet, his hands large and warm on her arms and waist. She felt an odd weight in her heart when she was close to him, a growing obsession with his thoughts and the shape of his face; and it frightened her, even though she could not stop what she felt. She thought he might feel the same, which was an even graver complication. His eyes were too warm when he looked at her—cut with moments of flickering hesitation.

But neither of them stopped, and when the music slowed, Mickel twirled her gently to a halt, as Sally spun with all the careful grace she possessed and had been taught.

"Well," he said hoarsely, standing close.

"Yes," Sally agreed, hardly able to speak past the lump in her throat.

The people of Gatis offered them beds in their homes that night. The men politely refused. Sally helped them pack the wagon, including fine gifts of cloth and wine, and then the troupe followed the night road out of the village, toward the north. Sally kept meaning to jump out and head in the opposite direction, but her heart seemed to be heavier than her body, and refused to move from the wagon bed.

"Why did you leave?" she asked Mickel.

"It's never good to overstay," he replied, sounding quiet and tired. "What feels like magic one night becomes something cheap the next, if you don't take care to preserve the memory. Familiarity always steals the mystery."

"Always?"

"Well," he said, smiling. "I believe you could be the exception."

Sally smiled, too, glad the night hid her warm face. "Who taught you all these things?"

"We learned on our own, in different places," Rumble said, the bench creaking under him as he turned to look at her. "All of us a little strange, filled with a little too much wild in our blood. Got the wanderlust? Nothing to do but wander. Now, Mickel there, he comes from a long line of those types. Knows how to recognize them. He put us all together."

"And how long have you been at this?"

Patric flashed white teeth in the dark. "How long have you? You were quite good tonight."

"I read. I held children and beat a drum, and stood while you threw a knife at my face."

"But you did it easily," Mickel said. "You made people *feel* at ease. Which is not as simple as it sounds. I know what Patric means. You have it in you."

"No," she replied. "I was just being . . . me."

"As were we."

"Mostly," Rumble added. "I don't usually keep chickadees in my pants, I'll have you know."

"That," Sally said, "was a remarkably disgusting trick."

"It only gets better," Patric replied dryly.

They set up camp near the road, beside a thick grove of trees that was not the Tangleroot, but nonetheless made her think of the ancient forest. It was somewhere close, but if she kept going north with these men, she would lose her chance, lose what precious time she had left.

Perhaps it was for nothing, anyway. Despite her strange dreams and the behavior of the raven (her head still ached, and she could not imagine her appearance), the longer she was away from the gardener and her words, the less faith she had in her chance of finding something, anything, that could help her in the Tangleroot. It might be a magical forest, filled with strange and uncanny things, but none of that was an answer. Perhaps just another death sentence.

You think too much, she told herself. *Sometimes you just have to feel.*

But her feelings were not making anything easier, either.

Rumble and Patric rolled themselves into their blankets as soon as they stopped, and were snoring within minutes. Mickel stayed up to keep watch, and Sally sat beside him. No fire, just moonlight. He wrapped himself in one of the new cloaks the villagers had given them, and fingered the fine heavy cloth with a great deal of thoughtfulness.

"This is a good land," he said. "Despite the mercenaries."

Sally raised her brow. "You say that as though you've never been here."

He shrugged. "It's been a long time. I hardly remember."

"So why did you come back?"

"Unfinished business." He met her gaze. "Why are you running? More specifically, why are you running to the Tangleroot?"

"My own unfinished business," she replied. "I have questions."

"Most people, when they have questions, ask other people. They do not go running headfirst into a place of night terrors and magic."

Sally closed her fists around her skirts. "I suppose you're lucky enough to have people who can help you when you're in trouble. I'm not. Not this time."

"Apparently." Mickel did not sound happy about that. "Perhaps I could help?"

I wish, she thought. "I doubt that."

"I have two ears, two hands, and I have seen enough for two lifetimes. Maybe three, but I was very drunk at the time. Certainly, I could at least lend some advice."

Sally hesitated, studying him. Finding a great deal of sincerity in his eyes. It almost broke her heart.

"You don't understand," she began to say, and then stopped as he held up his hand, looking sharply away, toward the road. Sally held her breath, listening hard. At first she heard only the quiet hiss of the wind—and then, a moment later, the faint ringing of bells.

Sally knew those bells.

She stood quickly, weighing her options—but there were none. She turned and began running toward the woods. Mickel leapt to his feet, and chased her. "Where are you going?"

"Horses," she muttered. "Deaf man, there are horses coming."

"And?"

She could hardly look at him. "My father. My father is coming to find me, and when he does, he will drag me home, stuff me in a white dress like a sack of potatoes, and thrust me into the arms of the barbarian warlord he has arranged to marry me."

Mickel, who had been reaching for her, stopped. "Barbarian warlord?"

"Oh!" Sally stood on her toes, and kissed him hard on the mouth. Or tried to. It was the first time she had ever done such a thing, and she was rushed. Her lips ended up somewhere around his cheek, left of his nose. Mickel made an odd choking sound.

"I do like you," she said breathlessly. "But I have to go now. If my father finds me with you and your men, he'll assume you all have dispossessed me of my virtue, in various unseemly ways. And then he'll kill you."

Mickel still stared at her as though he had been hit over the head with one of the rocks he was so fond of juggling. "I have a strange question."

"I probably have a strange answer," she replied. "But unless you want to see your man parts dangling around your neck while my father saws off your legs to feed to his pet wolves, I'd best be going. Now."

He followed her, running his fingers through his hair and pulling so hard she thought his scalp would peel away. "Why would your father need to make an alliance with a warlord? He sounds perfectly ghastly enough to handle his enemies on his own."

"Oh, no," she assured him, walking backward toward the woods. "That's me. I have a much better imagination than he does."

A pebble was thrown at them, and hit Mickel in the thigh. Rumble poked his head out from beneath the covers. "Eh! Shut up, *shut up!* I'm trying to sleep! Can't a man have a decent night's—"

Mickel found something considerably larger than a pebble, and threw it back at him. Sally heard a thump, and Rumble shut his mouth, grumbling.

"You can't go," he said.

"Oh, really." Sally marched backward, pointing toward the forest. "Well, here I am, *going*. And you should be thanking me."

Mickel stalked after her. "You are the craziest woman I have ever met. You make *me* crazy. Now come back here. Before I . . ."

"Do something crazy," Rumble supplied helpfully.

"If you're so crazy, dear man," she said quickly, "I don't think that would be prudent."

And she turned and ran.

Mickel shouted, but Sally did not look back. She wanted to, quite badly, with all the broken pieces of her grieving heart.

But her father *would* find her if she stayed with him, and she liked Mickel too much to subject him to the harm that the old king most certainly would inflict. He might not be an imaginative man, but he was thorough. And a princess did *not* travel with common performers, not unless she wanted to become a . . . tawdry woman.

Which, she thought, sounded rather charming.

The forest was very dark, and swallowed her up the moment she stepped past its rambling boundary, suffocating her in a darkness so complete that all she could do was throw up her hands, and take small, careful steps that did not keep her safe from thorns, or the sharp branches that seemed intent on plucking out her eyes. She had to stop, frequently—not for weariness, but because she was afraid, and each step forward was a struggle not to take another step back.

Or to simply hide, and wait for dawn, until her father passed.

But that would not do, either. Returning to Mickel and his men would endanger them, and she could not tell them who she was. No man—no common, good men—would want to deal with a princess on the run. All kinds of trouble in that, especially for one who was betrothed to the Warlord of the Southern Blood Wastes, Keeper of the Armored Hellhounds, Black Knight of the Poisoned Cookies—or whatever other nefarious title was attached to his name.

Sally could depend only on herself. She had been foolish to imagine otherwise, even for a short time.

And, like the gardener enjoyed saying, life never fell backward, just forward—growing, turning, spinning, burning through the world day after day, like the sun. One step. One step forward.

Until, quite unexpectedly, the forest became something different. And Sally found herself in the Tangleroot.

She did not realize at first. The change was subtle. But as she walked, she found herself remembering, *Some trees are bark and root, and some trees have soul and teeth*, and she suddenly felt the difference as though it was she herself who was changing, transforming from a human woman into something that floated on rivers of shadows. It became easier to move, as though vines were silk against her skin, and she listened as words riddled through the twisting hisses of the leaves, a sibilant music that slid into her bones and up her throat: in every breath a song. Sweet starlight from the night sky disappeared. The world outside might as well have been gone.

Sally had journeyed too far. The Tangleroot, she had thought, lay farther away—but the ancient had reached into the new, becoming one.

She was here. She had been drawn inside. Nor could she stop walking, not to rest, not even to simply prove to herself that she could, that her body still listened to her. Because it did not. Her limbs seemed bound by strings as ephemeral as cobwebs, tugging her forward, and though she glimpsed odd trickling lights flickering at the corners of her eyes, and felt the tease of tiny invisible fingers stroking her cheeks and ankles, she could not turn her head to look. All she could see was the darkness in front of her.

And finally, the children. Tumbling from the trunks of trees like ghosts, staring at her with sad eyes. Tiny birds fluttered around their shoulders, while lizards and mice raced down their limbs; and though there was no moon or stars to be seen through the canopy, their bodies nonetheless seemed slippery with light: glimpses and shadows of silver etched upon their skin.

The little girl from her dream appeared, dropping from the branches above to land softly in front of Sally. She was different from the others, less a spirit, more full in the flesh. More *present* in her actions. Her matted hair nearly obscured the silver of her eyes. She crouched very still, staring. Sally could not breathe in her presence, as if it was too dangerous to take in the same air as this child.

The girl held out her hand to Sally. Behind her, deep in the woods, branches snapped, leaves crunching as though something large and heavy was sloughing its way toward her. She did not look, but the children did, their eyes moving in eerie silent unison to stare at something behind her shoulder.

The girl closed her hand into a fist, and then opened it urgently. Swallowing hard, Sally grabbed her tiny wrist—suffering a rapid pulse of heat between their skin—and allowed herself to be drawn close, down on her knees.

The girl reached out with her other hand, and hovered her palm over Sally's chest. Warmth seeped against her skin, into her bones and lungs. She became aware of the necklace she wore, and began to pull it out. The girl shook her head.

Better if you never had the desire to find this place, came the soft voice, drifting on the wind. *She would not have heard your heart.*

"Who are you?" Sally whispered. "*What* are you?"

The child glanced to the left and right, at the watching, waiting children. *I am something different from them. I was born as I am, but they were made. Forced into the forms you see. They were human and dead, but the trees rose through them, around them, and trapped their souls in this tangled palace, from which they can never leave.*

"The queen," Sally said.

She sleeps, and yet she dreams, and though the crown that shackles her mind weakens her dreams, her power is still great through the green vein of the Tangleroot. You have entered her palace, you redheaded daughter, and you will escape only through her will.

Sally leaned back on her heels, feeling very small and afraid. "Why are you telling me this?"

The child made an odd motion over her chest; as though sketching a sign. *Because you have lain in my roots from babe to woman, and it is my fault the queen heard your desire. I could not hide your heart from her mind, though I tried. As I try even now, though I cannot disobey her for long.*

Sally's breath caught. "You are no tree."

But I am the soul of one, replied the little girl, and tugged Sally to her feet. *Beware. She will try to take you, and what you love. And we will have no choice but to aid her.*

"No," Sally said, stricken. "How can this be? I came here for help."

There is no help in the Tangleroot. Do not trust her bargains. All she wants is to be free.

And the child forced Sally to run.

She lost track of how long they traveled, but it was swift as a bird's flight, and silent as death. The girl led her down narrow corridors where the walls were trees and vines, and the air was so dark, so cold, she felt as though she was running on air, that beneath her was the mouth of a void from this world to another, and that if she fell, if the child let go, she might fall forever.

Beyond them, in the tangle of the forest, she glimpsed clearings shaped like rooms, replete with mushrooms large as chairs, and steaming pools of water within which immense scaled bodies swam. She glimpsed other runners, down other corridors, ghosting silver and slender, limbs bent at impossible angles that startled her with fear. Voices would cry out, some in pain or pleasure, and then fade to an owl's hoot. And once, when a wolf howled, its voice transformed into slow, sly laughter, accompanied by the whine of a violin; clever music that women danced to, glimpsed beyond a wall of vines: breasts bare with nipples red as berries, faces sharp and furred like foxes, and eyes golden as a hawk.

Sally saw all these things, and more; but none seemed to see her. It was as though all the strange creatures within the Tangleroot abided in separate worlds, lost in the maze that was the queen's dreaming palace. It was haunting, and terrifying. Sally was afraid of becoming one of those lost living dreams, sequestered and imprisoned in a room made of vines and roots, and ancient trees.

But the little girl never faltered, though she looked back once at Sally with sadness.

Finally, they slowed. Ever so delicately, Sally was pulled through a wall of trees so twisted they seemed to writhe in pain. Even touching them made her skin crawl, and she imagined their leaves weeping with soft, delicate sobs. And then

Sally and the girl broke free, and stood upon the edge of a lake.

It felt like dawn. A dim silver light filled the air, though none had trickled into the forest. She had thought it was night until now—and perhaps it was still, on the other side of the Tangleroot.

No birds sang, no sounds of life. The water was frozen and the air was so cold that Sally could see each breath, and her face turned numb. When she looked up, examining the rocky shore, she thought that the trees still carried leaves, black and glossy, but then those leaves moved—watching her with glittering eyes—and she realized that the branches were full of ravens. Hundreds of them, perhaps thousands, sitting still.

It made her feel small and naked. Fear had been her constant companion for the last several days—but now a deeper, colder terror settled in her stomach. Not of death or pain, but something worse that she could not name, worse even than those rooms in the forest filled with strange beings. It had not seemed such a bad thing before, to enter a place and come back changed—but she had been a fool. Sally felt as though she sat on the edge of a blade, teetering toward sanity or madness. One wrong slip inside her heart would be the end of her.

The little girl pointed at the ice. Sally looked into her silver eyes, uncertain.

Only through her, whispered words on the wind, though the child's mouth did not move. *She has you now.*

Sally gazed out at the frozen lake, which shone with a spectral glow. Far away, though, the mists parted—and Sally glimpsed a long dark shape on the ice.

She found herself stepping onto the ice. The little girl did not follow, nor did the ravens move. She walked, sliding and awkward, terror fluttering in her throat until her heart pounded so hard she thought it might burst. And yet she could not stop. Not until she reached the coffin. Which, when she arrived, was not a coffin at all, but a cusp of stone jutting from the water, dark with age and carved to resemble the bud of a frozen flower. It seemed to Sally that the stone might have been part of a tower—the last part—reaching through the ice like a broken gasp.

Sally peered inside. Found a woman nestled within. She knew her face from dreams: pale, glowing, with a beauty so unearthly it was both breathtaking and terrifying. There was nothing soft about that face, not even in sleep; as though time had refined it to express nothing but truth: inhumanly cruel, arrogant, and cold.

She wore a crown of horns upon her head, though they seemed closer to branches than antlers, thick with lush moss covered in a frost that enveloped much of her body; painting her dark brow and hair silver, and her red dress white, except for glimpses of crimson. The crown seemed very tight upon her head, and there was a small heart-shaped groove at the front of it, set in wood.

The lock for a key.

Sally could hardly breathe. She started to look behind at the shore to see if the little girl was still there, but a whispering hiss drew her attention back to the sleeping queen. Her eyes were closed, her mouth shut, but Sally heard another hiss, and realized it was inside her head.

I know your face, whispered the sleeping queen. *I know your eyes.*

Sally stared at that still, pale face, startled and terrified. "No. I have never been here."

I know your blood. I know your scent. You bear the red hair of the witches who imprisoned me. So, we are very close, you and I. I know what you are.

A chill beyond ice swept over Sally. "Is that why you brought me here?"

You wanted to come, murmured the queen. *So you have. And now you stand upon the drowned ruins of the old kingdom, amongst the souls of the long dead. You, who share the blood of the dead. You, whose ancestors escaped the dead. And left me, cursed me, bound me.*

Sally trembled. "I know nothing of that. I came for answers."

Release me, and I will give you answers.

Her hand tightened, and she realized that she was holding her mother's necklace, squeezing it so forcefully the chain was digging into her hand. She was almost too afraid to move, and glanced back at the shore—glimpsing movement amongst the trees. Children. The little girl. Ravens fluttering their wings. She did not know how it all pieced together. It was too strange, like a dream.

Someone else stumbled from the woods, down to the edge of the lake.

Mickel. He had followed her into the wood.

5

Mickel saw her, and tensed. He did not appear hurt, but even from a distance she could see the wildness of his eyes, and the determined slant of his mouth.

I am the Tangleroot, whispered the queen, frozen as the ice within her tomb. *This forest is my dream. All who touch it belong to me. My trees who were human, who became my children. My trees, whose roots reach for me, though ice confines them.*

Release me, she breathed. *Or I will make him mine.*

"Why do you think I can release you?" Sally forced herself to look at the queen, feeling as though her feet were growing roots in the ice—afraid to see if that was her imagination, or truth. "I am no one."

My ravens tasted your blood. You are born of a witch, and I feel the key. Sweet little girl. Release me.

Mickel stepped on the ice and fell to his knees, sliding with a quiet grunt. Sally tried to move toward him, but her feet refused to budge.

He, too, whispered the queen. *His blood is also sweet.*

"And if you were free?" Sally asked hollowly, still staring at Mickel.

A great hiss rose from the ice, a terrible, vicious sound that might have belonged to a snake or the last breath of the dead. Onshore, children swayed within the shadow of the wood, covering their hearts.

Little hearts. Sally looked down at her necklace, and the broken remnants of the wooden heart dangling from the precious amethyst. A heart the size of the indent in the queen's crown.

Mickel rose to his feet, half crouched. His eyes were dark and hard, cold as the ice. Silver glimmered in his hands.

"Sally," he said.

"Stay there," she said hoarsely. "Run, if you can."

But he did not. Simply walked toward her, his unsteadiness disappearing until it seemed that he glided upon the ice, graceful as a dancer. He never took his gaze from her, not once, until he was close to the tomb. And then he looked down at the queen, and flinched.

"Whatever she wants," Mickel said, gazing down at the sleeping woman with both horror and resolve, "don't give it to her."

"She wants her freedom," Sally whispered, almost too frightened to speak. "She thinks I can give it to her."

I came searching for freedom, she thought, and realized with grim, bitter irony that whatever happened here would be a far worse, and more irreversible, loss than any she might have faced outside the wood.

The ice rumbled beneath their feet. Sally fell forward against the stone tomb. She gripped its dark, cold edge with both hands, and the necklace swung free. Mickel made a small sound, but she could not look at him. The queen commanded every ounce of her attention, as though the roots she had felt in her feet were growing through her neck, up into her eyes—forcing her to stare, unblinking, at that frozen, chiseled face.

The key, whispered the queen. *It has been broken.*

Sally gritted her teeth, sensing on the periphery of her vision the split, jagged remains of the heart swinging from the chain. "Then it is no use to you. Let us go. Let *him* go and keep me, if you must. But stop this."

"Sally," Mickel said brokenly, but he, too, seemed frozen in spot.

Another terrible hiss rose from the ice, vibrating beneath her feet. *Half is better than none at all. Perhaps I will find enough power to break free. Place it in my crown, witch. Do this, and I will let him go free.*

Sally hesitated. Mickel whispered, "No."

A terrible cracking sound filled the air, as though the world was breaking all around them. But it was not the world. Mickel cried out, and Sally watched from the corner of her eye—suffocating with horror—as the ice broke beneath his feet, and he plunged into the dark water.

Swallowed. His head did not reappear.

A scream clawed up Sally's throat, and she gripped the edge of the stone tomb so tightly her nails broke.

Give me the key and I will save him, whispered the queen in a deadly voice. *I will save him.*

"No," Sally snapped, anger burning through her blood with such purity and heat that she felt blinded with it. Her hands released the stone. Her feet moved. Her head turned, and then her body. She could move again.

Sally jumped into the icy water.

It was dark beneath the ice. Pressure gathered instantly against her lungs, immense and terrible, but she did not swim back to the hole of light above her head. She kicked her legs, fighting the painful cold, and searched the drowning void for Mickel. Desperation filled her, and despair; there was nothing of him. He was gone.

Until, quite suddenly, a ghost of light glimmered beneath her. Just a gasp, perhaps a trick. But Sally dove, feet kicking off the ice above her, and swam with all her strength toward that spot where she had seen the light. Her lungs burned. Her eyes felt as though they were popping from her skull. She was going to do this and die, but that would be another kind of freedom, and no doubt better than what the queen had in store for her.

She saw the light again, just in front of her, and then her hands closed around cloth, and she pulled Mickel tight against her body. He moved against her, his hands weakly gripping her waist—which surprised her—though not nearly as much as the light that glowed from a pendant that floated free from a chain around his neck.

A teardrop jewel, like her own—which she realized was also glowing. She stared, stunned, discovering the jagged half of a heart that was linked to his pendant.

She tore her gaze away to stare at Mickel's face, and found him ghastly. Alive, though, barely. More lights danced in her vision, but that was death, suffocation. Sally kicked upward, and after a moment, Mickel joined her. His movements were awkward, almost as if his strength and grace had been sapped away even before plunging into the water and losing air. The queen had her hold on him.

The light in the ice was very far away, but the light around their necks, much closer. Sally heard voices whispering deep in the darkness, almost as if the water was speaking, or the palace that had drowned and whose last spire entombed the queen. Visions flickered, and Sally saw her mother's face, soft with youth, and another at her side—two girls, little enough for dolls, holding hands and standing on the ice. Red hair blazing. Jaws set with stubbornness, though their eyes were frightened.

She is strong in her tangled palace, even in dreams, murmured a soft voice, *but this is also where she fell, and where her greatest weakness lies. She was bound by a crown made from her own flesh, bound in the blood of those who captured her.*

She cannot touch you, said another voice, sweeter than the other. *She cannot touch either of you, if you do not bend. Your blood makes you safe to all but the fear and lies that she puts into your heart. What flows through your blood made her crown.*

Choose, whispered yet another. *Choose what you want, and not even she can deny you.*

I want to live, Sally thought with all her strength, as darkness fluttered through her mind, and her body burned for lack of air. *I want* him *to live.*

Light surrounded her then. Cold air, which felt so foreign that Sally almost forgot to breathe. But her jaw unlocked, and she gasped with a burning need that filled her lungs with fire. She dragged Mickel up through the hole in the ice, and he sucked down a deep breath, coughing so violently she thought he might die just from choking on air, rather than water. His skin was blue. So was hers.

Somehow, though, they dragged themselves from the water onto the ice, and when they were free, collapsed against each other, chests heaving, limp with exhaustion. Cold seeped into her bones, so profound and deadly she was almost beyond shivering.

"Sally," Mickel breathed.

"Come on," she whispered. "We have to move."

But neither did, and all around them the ice shook, vibrating as though a giant hand was pounding the surface in rage.

Free me, snapped the queen, *and I will give you anything. Deny me and I will kill you.*

"No," Sally murmured, her eyes fluttering shut. "We'll be going now."

A howl split the air, a heartrending cry jagged as a broken razor. Sally closed her eyes, pouring all of her remaining strength into holding Mickel's hand. His fingers closed around her wrist as well, tight and close as her own skin. A rumble filled the air.

And suddenly they were moving. Rolled and rippled, and shrugged along the ice, until rocks bit through their clothing, and their bodies were lifted into the air. Sally tried to hold fast to Mickel's hand as they were carried through the wood, flung hard and thrown to sharp hands that pinched her body and dragged claws against her skin. She heard voices in her head, screams, and then something quieter, softer, feminine: her mother, or a voice close enough to be the same, whispering.

Her bonds are renewed as though she is winter lost to spring. You have bound her again. You have raised the borders that had begun to fall.

She was already bound, Sally told that voice. *Nothing had fallen.*

Nothing yet, came the ominous reply. *Her strength is limited only by belief.*

But Sally had no chance to question those strange words. She heard nothing more after that. Nor could she see Mickel, though she caught glimpses of those who touched her—golden, raging eyes and silver faces—and felt the heat and deep hiss of many mouths breathing. Mickel's hand was hard and hot around her own, but Sally was dying—she thought she must be dying—and her strength bled away like the air had in her lungs, beneath the crushing weight of water. Her heart beat more slowly, as though her blood was heavy as honey, and warm inside her veins, full of distant fading light.

Mickel's hand slipped away. She lost him. Imagined his broken gasp and shout, felt her own rise up her throat, but it was too late. He disappeared from her into the heaving shadows, and no matter how hard she tried, she could not see him.

And then, nothing. Sally landed hard on her back within tall grass, and remained in that spot. Small voices wept nearby, and another said: *You found your answer, I think.*

But the souls, the children, thought Sally. *Mickel.*

Rest, whispered the little girl. *Someone is coming for you.*

"Mickel," breathed Sally, needing to hear his name.

But she heard bells in the night, and hooves thundering; and she could not move or raise her voice to call out. Nothing in her worked. Her heart hurt worse than her body, and made everything dull.

Sally tried to open her eyes and glimpsed stars. A shout filled the air. Warmth touched her skin. Strong hands.

"Salinda," whispered a familiar voice, broken and hushed. "My dear girl."

Her father gathered her up. Sally, unable to protest, fell into darkness.

* * *

She came back to life in fits and gasps, but when her eyes were closed she did not dream of tangled forests and queens, but of men with dark eyes and fierce grins, who juggled fire and stone, and riddles. She grieved when she dreamed, and her eyes burned when she awakened, briefly, but there was nothing to do but rest under heavy covers, and recover. She was suffering from cold poisoning, said her father's physician—something the old man could not reconcile, as it was spring, and the waters had melted months ago.

But it was cold, he said, that had damaged her, and the prescription was heat. Hot water, hot bricks, hot soup poured down her throat, along with hot spirits. Sally grew so hot she broke into a sweat, but that did not stop the shivers that racked her, or the ache in her chest when she breathed.

A cough took her, which made the old king flinch every

time he heard it, and would cause him to roar for the physician and the maids, and anyone else who cared to listen, including the birds and stars, and the moon. He did not leave her side, not much, but once after a brief absence she heard him whisper to Sabius, "Not one person can explain it. Mercenaries were crawling past the border only days ago, but now not a sign of them. Some of the locals say they found swords and horses near the Tangleroot."

"Pardon me saying so, sire, but it used to be that way when your queen still lived. It seemed that nothing wicked could touch this kingdom."

But her father only grunted, and Sally glimpsed from beneath her lashes his thoughtful glance in her direction.

She received preoccupied looks from the gardener, as well, who would slip into the king's chair while he was away, and hold Sally's hand in her dry, leathery grip.

"You knew," Sally whispered, when she could finally speak without coughing. "You knew what would happen."

"I knew a little," confessed the old woman. "Your mother told me some. She said . . . she said if anything ever happened to her, that I was to point you in the right direction, when it was time. That I would know it. That it would be necessary for you; necessary for the kingdom."

She leaned close, silver braids brushing against the bed-covers. "I had red hair once, too, you know. Many who live along the Tangleroot do. It is our legacy. And for some, there is more."

More. Warmth crept into Sally's heart, a different heat than soup or hot bricks, or the fire burning near her bed. There was honey in her slow-moving blood, or sap, or lava rich from a burning plain; felt in brief moments since her rejection from the Tangleroot, as though something fundamental had changed within her.

"Tell me what you mean," Sally said, though she already knew the truth.

The gardener held her gaze. "Magic. Something your mother possessed in greater strength than anyone believed."

Sally looked away, remembering her vision of two little girls facing the queen of the Tangleroot. Seeing herself, for a moment, in that same place—but holding hands with a strong young man.

Some days later, Sally was declared fit enough to walk, though the king refused to hear of it. He had a chair fashioned, and made his men carry the princess to her favorite oak by the pond, where she was placed gently upon some blankets that had been arranged neatly for her. Wine and pastries were in a basket, along with pillows that the gardener stuffed behind her back. It was a warm afternoon, and the frogs were singing. Sally asked to be left alone.

And when finally, after an interminable time, everyone did leave her—she tapped the oak on its root. "I know you're in there."

There was no wind, but the leaves seemed to shiver. Sally felt a pulse between her hand and the root. Soft fingers grazed her brow. She closed her eyes.

"What happened in that place?" Sally whispered. "What happened, really?"

I think you know.

She could still feel those hands on her body, carrying her from the forest. "Her strength is limited only by belief."

You wear a key, whispered the little girl. *Or so the queen believes. But there is no such thing. No key. Just lies. What binds the queen is only in her mind, and the greatest trick of all. The witches who bound her used magic . . . but only enough to convince her that she had been caught. The queen gave up.*

Sally opened her eyes, but saw only green leaves and the dark water of the pond. When the frogs sang, however, she imagined words in their voices, words she almost understood. "You mean that she could be free if she wanted to be?"

If she believed that she was. When she is denied her freedom, as you denied her, she gives up again. And so binds herself tighter to the lie. There is a duty to confront the queen, once a generation. To strengthen the bonds that hold her. You fulfilled that duty as the women of your line must.

"What of them?" Sally whispered. "Those souls imprisoned in the Tangleroot?"

Time answers all things, said the little girl. *They are tragic creatures, as are all who become imprisoned in the palace of the queen. But nothing lasts. Not even the queen. One day, perhaps a day I will see—though surely you will not—she will fall. But the Tangleroot will outlast her. She has dreamed too well. Magic has bled into the bones of that forest, into the earth it grows from. Magic that is almost beyond her.*

But not beyond you, she added. *You are your mother's daughter. You are a daughter of the Tangleroot.*

Sally stared down at her hands. "Did my mother know you?"

But the little girl who was the soul of the oak did not answer. Nearby, though, Sally heard a shout. Her father. Sounding frantic and angry. She tried to sit up, concerned for him, and saw the old man limping quickly down the path to the pond. She heard low cries of outrage behind him—gasps from the maids, and more low shouts.

Her father's face was pale and grim. "Salinda, I am sorry. I have been a fool, and I pray you will forgive me. When you left, when I almost lost you, I realized . . . oh, God." He stopped, his expression utterly tragic, even heartbreaking. "I will do everything . . . everything in my power to keep you safe from that man. I should not have agreed to such a foolish thing, but I was desperate; I was—"

Sally held up her hand, swallowing hard. "The Warlord's envoy is here?"

"The Warlord himself," hissed the old king, rubbing his face. "I looked into his eyes and could not imagine what I was thinking. But your mother . . . your mother before she died spoke so fondly of her friend and her son, and I thought . . . I was *certain* all would be right. It was her idea that the two of you should meet one day. *Her idea.* She could not have known what he would become."

Sally held herself very still. "I would like to meet him."

"Salinda—"

"Please," she said. "Alone, if you would."

Her father stared at her as though she had lost her mind—and perhaps she had—but she heard footsteps along the stone path, and her vision blurred around a man wrapped in darkness, flanked by a giant and a bear. Sally covered her mouth.

The old king stepped in front of the Warlord and held out his hand. "Now, you listen—"

"Father," Sally interrupted firmly. "Let him pass. I'm sure you don't want to test those homicidal tendencies that the man is known for. What is he called again? Warlord of Death's Door? Or maybe that was Death's Donkey."

"Close enough," rumbled the Warlord, a glint in his eye as the old king turned to give his daughter a sharp, startled look. "Your majesty, I believe I have an appointment with young Salinda. I will *not* be denied."

"You," began the king, and then glanced at Sally's face and closed his mouth. Suspicion flickered in his gaze, and he gave the Warlord a sharp look. "If you hurt her, I will kill you. No matter your reputation."

"I assure you," replied the Warlord calmly, "my reputation is not nearly as fierce as a father's rage."

The old king blinked. "Well, then."

"Yes," said the Warlord.

"Father," replied Sally, twitching. "Please."

She felt sorry for him. He looked so baffled. He had tried to marry her off to the man, and now he wanted to save her. Except, Sally no longer wanted to be saved. Or rather, she was certain she could save herself, quite well on her own.

The old king limped away, escorted by the bear and giant, both of whom waved cheerily and blew kisses once his back was turned. Sally waved back, but halfheartedly. Her attention was on the man in front of her, who dropped to his knees the moment they were gone, and laid his large strong hand upon her ankle.

"Sally," he said.

"Mickel," she replied, unable to hide the smile that was burning through her throat and eyes. "I thought you might be dead."

He laughed, but his own eyes were suddenly too bright, and he folded himself down to press his lips, and then the side of his face, upon her hand. A shudder raced through him, and she leaned over as well, kissing his cheek, his hair, his ear; spilling a tear or two before she wiped at her eyes.

"You're not surprised," he said.

"The pendant." Sally fingered the chain around his neck with a great deal of tenderness and wonderment. "I had time to think about it, though I wasn't sure until I saw you just now. I couldn't believe. *Why*? Why the illusions?"

He rolled over with a sigh, resting his head in her lap. "When people hear there is a warlord passing through, they tend to get rather defensive. Pitchforks, cannons, poison in the ale—"

"They hide their daughters."

He smiled, reaching up to brush his thumb over her mouth. "That, too. But you find the most interesting people when you're a nobody."

Sally kissed his thumb. "And the names? The reputation?"

Mickel closed his eyes. "My people are decent fighters. Really very good. You couldn't find better archers or horsemen anywhere. But that doesn't mean we want to fight, or should have to. So we lie when we can. Dress men and women in rabbit's blood and torn clothes, rub soot in their faces, and then send them off into the night blubbering senselessly about this *magnificent* warlord who rode in on a fire-breathing black steed and set about ravaging, pillaging, murdering, and so forth, until everyone is so worked up and piddling themselves that all it takes to win the battle is the distant beating of some drums, and the bloodcurdling cries of my barbarian horde."

He opened his eyes. "You should hear Rumble scream. It gives *me* nightmares."

"That can't work all the time."

"But it works enough. Enough for peace." Mickel hesitated, giving her an uncertain look. "You ran from the man you thought I was. You were so desperate not to marry me, you were willing to enter the Tangleroot."

"And you agreed to marry a woman sight unseen." Sally frowned. "You seem like too much a free spirit for that."

"Our mothers were best friends. Growing up, all I ever heard about was Melisande and how brave she was, how good, how kind. How, when there was trouble, she was always the fighter, protecting my mother. And vice versa." He reached beneath his leather armor and pulled out a pendant that was an exact mirror of her own. "I never knew. I never imagined. She was devastated when she learned of Melisande's death. I think it hastened her own."

"I'm sorry," Sally said.

He tilted his shoulder in a faint shrug. "She told me that Melisande had borne a daughter, and that one day . . . one day she would like for us to meet. And so when your father advertised the fact that he was looking for a husband for his daughter—"

"Advertised," she interrupted.

"Oh, yes. Far and wide. Princess. Beautiful. Nubile. Available to big strong man, with even bigger sword." Mickel thumped his chest. "I was intrigued. I was mortified. I thought I would save the daughter of my mother's best friend from a fate worse than death."

"And if I had been a loud-mouthed harridan with a taste for garlic and a fear of bathing?"

"I would have been the Warlord everyone thinks I am, tossed her aside like a sack of potatoes in a white wedding dress, and asked for the hand of a peculiar redheaded woman I met on the road."

Sally smiled. "And if she said no?"

"Well," Mickel said, kissing her hand. "I may not be the Warlord of the Savage Belly Ache, but I am exceptionally brave. I would fight for her. I would battle magic forests and sleeping queens for her. I would plunge into icy waters—"

"—and be rescued by her?"

"Oh, yes," he whispered, no longer smiling. "I would love to be rescued by such a fair and lovely lady. Every day, every morning, every moment of my life."

Sally's breath caught, and Mickel touched the back of her neck and pulled her close. "You, Princess, are far more dangerous than any Warlord of Raven's Teeth, or Ravisher of Dandelions." Again, uncertainty filled his eyes. "But do you still want me, knowing all this?"

"I never wanted a warlord," Sally said. "But you . . . I think you'll do just fine. If you don't mind having a witch as your bride."

"Queen Magic and Warlord Illusion," he whispered, and leaned in to kiss her.

Sally placed her hand over his mouth. "But I want another name."

Mickel blinked. "Another?"

She removed her hand and grinned against his mouth. "Well, the Warlord must have a wife who is equal to his charms, yes?"

Mickel laughed quietly. "And what will I call you? War Lady? My Princess of Pain?"

"Just call me yours," she whispered. "The rest will take care of itself."

And it did.

The Wrong Bridegroom

SHARON SHINN

1

THE BEAUTIFUL PRINCESS

This was the proclamation sent out to all corners of the land: *I, King Reginald, have decreed that I will wed my daughter, Olivia, to the man who passes three tests that prove he is brave, strong, and clever. All men are invited to Kallenore Castle to compete for the very fairest prize.*

Sounds romantic, doesn't it? I thought so at first, until I started appraising some of my suitors. They didn't arrive armed only with weapons, courage, and intelligence. A good number of them also brought lust, greed, ambition, and a few other unsavory traits. For Kallenore was a lush and prosperous land, and I was my father's only child—and people have been telling me since the day I was born that I'm beautiful. I have to admit I secretly believe it's true. My hair is black, my eyes are blue, and my skin has been free of those appalling blemishes for four years.

After the first round of competition—a standard if very energetic joust—eliminated more than half of the contestants, I began to think seriously about what it would mean to be married off to someone I didn't know and might not like. I was particularly worried about two of the combatants who had survived the rounds of fighting. One was a large, brutish man who looked like he could tear apart the palace's foundation stones with his thumb and forefinger. He had bulging eyes, greasy hair, and a beard that might not have been trimmed since the day it first started to show. I comforted myself with the thought that he didn't look bright enough to pass the test that relied on brains.

But the second contestant who caught my eye most assuredly *was* that intelligent, and I didn't want to marry *him*, either. In fact, my refusal to be betrothed to Sir Harwin Brenley of Brenley Estates was what had precipitated this whole not-so-romantic-after-all competition in the first place.

I had known Harwin my whole life. His father, Sir Milton, was the most significant property owner in the kingdom, a lord who by turns was my father's greatest ally and chief adversary. The day I was born, our parents decided that Harwin and I should marry. Harwin had never seemed as horrified at the idea as I had.

Well, he wouldn't. He was too dull to whip up an emotion like horror. He was placid and stolid and measured and practically *bovine* in his level of insensate calm. He could be quite stubborn in failing to yield a point or change his mind, but he never argued; he never shouted or threw things or stalked from the room spitting curses. He wasn't, I suppose, hideously unattractive, for he was tall, and athletic enough to acquit himself on a jousting field, and his face didn't have any scars or squints or disproportionate features. He just *was*—this big, solid, boring clump of a human being.

I mean, I couldn't possibly marry him.

What if he passed all three of my father's tests?

I would run away. I would. My father couldn't make me marry someone against my will.

My father had never been able to make me do anything I didn't want to do. Which was probably the reason he detested me as much as I detested him.

There was a knock on the door, which I ignored, but the person in the hallway came inside anyway. I glared at her. I usually went to some trouble to avoid spending any time with my stepmother, Gisele, more out of principle than because of any active dislike. Well, she was only five years older than I was, small and dainty and well behaved. Her dark brown hair always lay sleek against her cheeks; her black eyes were always watchful. She made me look like a big galumphy girl when I stood beside her, and even when she wasn't criticizing me out loud, her expression was generally reproving. And she had married my father, which I couldn't imagine any woman of sense wanting to do. Ever since she had moved into the palace three years ago, I had refused to respond to any of her attempts to win me over. She had mostly given up trying.

Today it seemed like she might be trying one more time. Her face wore a more urgent expression than usual. "Olivia," she said. "It's not too late."

I had been standing at the window, watching the bustle in

the palace courtyard, where most of the contestants had set up tents and pavilions. There were still probably two dozen remaining, and at least half of them were milling around in the warm golden light of an autumn afternoon. The whole scene of color and endless motion was amazingly inviting, and I longed to be down there with my suitors instead of up here with my stepmother.

I turned my back to the pageantry outside and said in the surly voice I usually employed while speaking to Gisele, "It's not too late for what?"

"To accept Harwin," she said.

I let out a gusty breath of surprise. "I am *not* going to marry Harwin!"

She went on as if I hadn't spoken. "Have you taken a good look at some of the individuals who have come to the palace with the intention of winning your hand? Even if you ignore the obvious fact that they would be unqualified to rule at your side once you inherit your father's throne, they would be *nightmares* to share your bed with for the next fifty years. I know you think Harwin is a charmless bore, but he is not cruel, he is not stupid, and he is nowhere near as oafish as you believe. Whereas some of these men—"

I stiffened my back. I would not let her see that her alarm was echoing my own uneasiness. "The competition has already started," I said. "It would not be honorable to cancel it now."

"You'll be thinking a lot less about honor once you find yourself married to a man you cannot tolerate," Gisele said grimly. "You'll be wishing yourself safely wed to Harwin Brenley, for all his bland conversation."

I actually stamped my foot. "I do not *choose* to marry Harwin," I said. "A woman should have some *choice* in the matter of her marriage!"

"She should, which is why she should say yes when the choice she is offered is a tolerable one," Gisele replied.

"Is that how you ended up married to a king?" I said in a rude voice. "Because you turned down the other matches your father would have made for you?"

She watched me steadily with those dark, unreadable eyes. "Do you think your father is the person I would have married had I been given the choice?"

I hunched a shoulder. "You married him fast enough. My mother had only been dead six months."

"My father and your father strode from the crypt to the chapel, already making plans," she shot back. "I would have been here six *days* after her death if they had had their way."

I shrugged again. What did it matter? She had been eager enough to jump into the marriage bed with a man old enough to be her father. "At any rate, you can see why I am not so interested in *your* advice on how to make a happy marriage."

She continued to keep her gaze on me. "Your father wants a son," she said. "The minute he has one, you will be shoved aside—forgotten. I recommend that you make sure you are safely married off to a man you like and admire before your father gets his son, or your life will become wretched in the extreme. There. I have just given you another piece of good advice that you will no doubt ignore."

"I suppose it's very lucky for me that you have so far failed to provide him that son," I said.

"I suppose it is."

I spread my hands in an impatient gesture. "Why do I find it so hard to believe that you have my best interests at heart?"

"I don't know," she replied. "Why do you?"

Shrugging again, I turned my back on her and once more gave all my attention to the tumble and gaiety in the courtyard. "Thank you for your concern," I said, my polite voice obviously insincere. "But I think I can manage my life without your interference."

* * *

I waited till after dark. And then I put on a plain, brown cloak, pulled the hood over my head, and stole down the servants' stairways, out the kitchen exit, and into the vast courtyard. Soon I was winding my way through the variegated tents, jostling bodies, and loud merriment that had taken over what was normally a very formal space.

It was hard to take it all in. Servants and pages were racing past the irregular campfires, carrying messages and fetching food. Some of the men were outside their tents, arguing and practicing swordplay. Some were inside; I could see their shadows leap and gesture on the cloth walls, lit from within. The smells were diverse and suffocating—smoke, meat, ale, mud, horse, leather, and excrement, from man or beast or both. Now and then I heard a woman's laugh or high-pitched squeal over the lower rumble of men's voices.

The sounds surprised me and I found myself frowning. I had a low opinion of any man who brought a doxy to a competition to win the hand of a princess. Shouldn't all my suitors be pure of heart as well as strong and brave and brilliant? I would have any man disqualified if he consorted with low women while he was wooing me. If, of course, I could figure out which ones they were.

I had wound my way halfway through the courtyard when I spotted the big bruiser who had caught my eye during the joust. He was sitting on an overturned barrel, but he was so heavy it looked as though his body weight was slowly forcing it into the ground. In one hand he held a hunk of charred meat hacked off the bone; in the other, he held a slovenly woman whose breasts were so big her dirty white camisole could hardly contain them. Three comrades lounged nearby, calling out advice. I hurried on before I could quite decipher what that advice pertained to.

No. *He* would not be an acceptable bridegroom by any measure.

He could not win my father's competition, could he?

I wandered on, drawing my cloak more tightly around my body to fend off the chill of the autumn evening. I was a little reassured to come upon a corner of the camp where no one was wolfing down overcooked meals or enjoying the attention of questionable women. There were plenty of sober-looking young men sitting contemplatively before their fires, or oiling their blades or mending their tack. I even saw one reading a book. He was a tall, lean fellow who looked to be mostly ribs and elbows. I couldn't imagine how he'd made it through the joust without being unhorsed, but I guessed he would fare well during the test of intelligence. Standing in the darkness, I studied his face by flickering firelight. He looked humorless, severe, fanatical. I would not want to be married to him, either.

Though I would choose him over the big brute with the greasy skin.

If I was allowed to choose.

I pushed away my anxiety and moved on.

At the very last tent pitched just inside the palace gate, I saw a man practicing magic.

It was difficult at first to get a glimpse of him, because he had drawn a small crowd of onlookers who ringed him about, murmuring astonishment. I found a discarded trunk with a broken lock and stood on it to get a better view. And then I, too, was gasping with delight at the show unfolding before me.

A slim, handsome young man stood in a circle of spectators, his face and body lit by the curiously brilliant flames of a low fire. But no—it was not an ordinary fire; it was a blaze made of jagged blocks of golden quartz, each tendril of flame tapered to a point, the whole thing glowing like a harvest moon. While we watched, he twisted his outstretched hands, and the colors within surged to red and hunkered down to purple. He snapped his fingers and the light disappeared completely—and then suddenly sprang back to life, crackling and leaping like an ordinary little fire.

"How'd you do that?" someone asked in a stupefied voice, speaking for all of us.

"Magic," said the young man, and then he laughed.

He was plainly visible in the light from the natural fire, and he was adorable. His shoulder-length blond hair had a rogue curl; his face wore a rascal's smile. The mischievous look was counteracted somewhat by deep-set eyes, a generous mouth, and a patrician nose. His hands were elegant and expressive; he reached for the sky and I swear every person in the audience looked up to see what he might pluck from the air. A bird, as it happened, squawking and indignant, who shook itself and leapt from his palm to wing back into the night. He laughed to see it go, his expression purely joyous.

"Are your tricks real or just illusions?" someone demanded.

"What makes you think illusions are not real?" he replied. He picked up a block of rough firewood and squeezed it in his hands; it lengthened and changed colors and leafed out between his fingers, becoming a switch of live greenery covered with white flowers. Just as I had convinced myself that this was a mere visual trick, he snapped off one of the blossoms and presented it to a woman in the audience, a little older and a little less debased than the one I had seen on the big fellow's lap. She cooed and tucked the bloom into the front of her bodice, then shared a kiss with a man who had his arm around her waist.

"What else can you do?" someone called out.

"What would you like to see me do?"

"Can you change coppers to gold coins?" another man spoke up.

The blond man laughed. "I've found that it never pays to tinker with the king's coin," he said. "So the answer is no."

"Can you turn water into ale?"

"Make a woman love you?"

"Heal a broken limb?"

"Change a person's face?"

It was this last request that interested him. "Whose face? Your own? Come closer and let me look at you."

A young man broke free of the shadows and stepped into the circle of firelight. He was of medium height, a little heavy-set, with an unfortunate collection of features. Droopy eyes under thick brows, a nose both large and broad, huge ears, bad teeth, the whole covered with a pocked and scarred layer of skin. "I wouldn't ask to be made a handsome man," the youth said in a quiet voice, "just better-looking."

The magician studied him. "I believe I can improve you without making you unrecognizable to your friends."

Again the crowd murmured, a little bit awed, a little bit unnerved. I had to admit my own emotions were much the same. "How long would such a magic last?" the boy asked.

The blond man shrugged. "Forever. It will be as if your face was resculpted, down to the blood and bone."

The homely boy took a deep breath. "Then change me, if you will."

Someone behind him called out, "Calroy, you fool, you didn't ask him for his fee first!"

The magician laughed again. "There's no fee. I'll do it for the challenge alone. Hold still now." And Calroy closed his eyes and turned motionless as a tree stump. The blond man frowned in concentration and laid his hands over Calroy's jaws, his eyes, his unruly hair. Everyone in the audience, myself included, was leaning forward to watch, but Calroy's back was to most of us and there was very little to see. Another flutter of his fingers and then the magician stepped back.

"Don't turn around yet," he ordered. "My sister will hand you a mirror. If you don't like what you see, I'll change you back."

Calroy stood obediently passive, while a woman sitting at the back edge of the circle came to her feet. *Sister*? I thought with some derision, remembering my walk through camp. But this one looked enough like the magician to make the blood tie plausible. By firelight, her hair was redder, thicker, and without that springy curl. But the curve of her mouth and the line of her profile matched his own, and her smile looked just as playful. In her hand was a small mirror, which she angled for Calroy's view.

He bent forward, and then he gasped, his hands flying up to touch his face. "Show us!" someone from the audience demanded, and Calroy pivoted on one foot.

There was first silence and then a murmur that was half admiration and half fear. For Calroy stood before us definitely altered and yet still clearly himself. The heavy brow had been shoved back, the outsize eyes reshaped. The nose was much refined, and the mouth—stretched wide in a smile—showed even teeth without a hint of decay. He certainly wasn't a man who would turn the girls' heads, but neither would he draw the mockery of young boys. He was a little better than ordinary, with a look of happiness that gave him extra appeal.

"Well?" asked the magician. "Are you satisfied?"

"More than satisfied. Thank you—thank you—I do have

a few coins with me, not nearly enough to pay for something like this—"

The magician waved a dismissive hand. "The work of a few moments. I was glad to do it. All I would ask is that if you have the chance to do an easy kindness for someone else, you take that chance."

"And this will be my face from now on? For the rest of my life?"

"Forever," the magician confirmed.

"I must go show my brother," Calroy exclaimed, and dove through the crowd and disappeared.

The others drew back to let him pass, and then turned to one another to express their amazement at what they had just witnessed. I had jumped off my trunk, ready to sneak away, but I got caught in the general disorganized movement of the crowd. A few murmured apologies, a few bodies gently pushed aside, and I suddenly found myself a few feet from the magician and his sister. I could not see them through the press of bodies, but I recognized his voice and guessed at hers.

"That was the most fun magic has brought me for a while," he said in a jaunty tone.

Her voice was a lilting alto. "I suppose you're hoping Princess Olivia will hear of your kind deed and favor your suit?"

He laughed. "Yes, or her father. Why should they not learn that I am gifted and generous? Who would not want such a man for a husband?"

"I love you, Darius, but you would make a very bad husband. And an even worse king. I don't know why you're even in this competition."

"Have you seen her, Dannette? She's beautiful. That hair! That skin!"

"They say she has a temper. And a strong will and a stubborn heart."

Eavesdropping in the dark, I couldn't help but nod. All true. I wondered which servants or local lords had provided Dannette's information.

He laughed at her. "She sounds delightful."

"So you're really going to try to win her hand?"

"I really am."

I managed to choke back my squeal of excitement. At last! A man I could love, and a man who was already halfway enamored of *me*! A handsome, charming, talented man, blessed with a kind heart and a cheerful manner! How could he have been better? I was tempted to step forward and introduce myself, but the group of spectators that had absorbed me in the dark now began to shred apart, and I decided it was wiser to move on. My head was humming with elation; my heart was pattering with glee. After all, my father's competition to find my husband was turning out very well indeed.

* * *

I was thinking so blissfully about Darius that I was careless when I returned to the palace, with the result that I ran into Harwin within a minute of slipping in through a side door.

"There you are," he said in his measured voice, the syllables heavy with disapproval. "I should have guessed. Wandering through the contestants' camp, I suppose, picking out your favorites."

I gave a guilty start upon first hearing his voice, and for a moment I looked up at him like a small child waiting for a scold she knows she deserves. Unlike me, Harwin was properly dressed in formal evening clothes. The dull brown color of his jacket did not do much to lighten either his expression or his olive skin tones, though the garment was finely made and nicely showed off the width of his shoulders. I remembered that he had handily won his events in the joust. I was not used to thinking of him as being any kind of athlete, but he was big enough, and apparently dexterous enough, to handle himself with competence on the battlefield.

Then my natural insouciance reasserted itself. I tossed back my hair and dropped my hands instead of tightly clutching the cloak as if I wanted to hide inside it. "And what if I was?" I said breezily. "If I'm going to marry the man who wins my father's competition, shouldn't I learn about all of the contestants?"

"If that is really how you plan to choose a bridegroom, *I* will win the three competitions," he said.

His cool, blockish, unimaginative certainty inspired me with sudden rage, though I tried to tamp it down. "I have already said I will not marry you," I replied. "You have already been eliminated from the lists."

"Do you reserve the right to refuse any other contestant who might be successful?" he said with a little heat. "That clause was not in the proclamation that *I* heard."

I leaned forward, still angry. "I will *never* marry a man that I cannot stand," I said. "No matter how he is presented to me or what obstacles he has overcome."

Harwin's face smoothed out; almost, I would have said,

he was relieved. "I told your father this competition was ill-advised," he said. "I told him he could not possibly predict what kinds of rogues and ruffians might show up on his doorstep, prepared to go to any length to win a spectacular prize. There are plenty of villains who can wield a sword and solve a puzzle. Those are no criteria for deciding who will wed your daughter—and who will rule the kingdom after you." He gave me one long, sober inspection. "I do believe you have the courage to refuse any man who is not worthy of you."

I supposed that was a compliment in its heavy-handed way. "I wouldn't think my father plans to hold the wedding ceremony the very day the competition ends," I said. "No doubt I will get to know my prospective bridegroom during our engagement period. I'm not afraid of scandal—I'll break off the betrothal if I find he's not the man he seemed."

Harwin's eyes took on a sudden keenness. "Yes, that is a most excellent idea," he said. "Tell your father there must be an engagement long enough to enable you to assess the worth of your victorious suitor."

"Even if the victorious suitor is you?" I asked in a dulcet voice.

He just looked at me for a moment. "Yes," he said, at last. "I would hope you would use that time to get to know me. To learn things about me that perhaps you have not understood before."

"I cannot imagine what those things might be," I said. "I have known you my whole life."

"You have been acquainted with me your whole life," he corrected. "It is not the same thing."

I shrugged. I was tired of talking to Sir Harwin. "I will tell my father I want a betrothal period." Suddenly, for no good reason, I remembered Gisele's earlier advice to marry quickly before my father sired a son. I wondered if that had been her subtle hint that she was pregnant, though she could hardly know if she was carrying a boy. "Though I'm not sure I like the idea of a *long* engagement," I added.

"It is a splendid idea," Harwin said. "I will make the recommendation myself."

Now I scowled. "I don't know why you think you have anything to say about my engagement or my wedding or my *life*."

"I have everything to say," he responded, his voice cool again. "I'm the man who's going to marry you."

I made a strangled sound deep in my throat and spun on my heel, not even answering him. Within a few steps, I had turned the corner and slipped up the servants' stairwell, on my way back to my own room. If Harwin had any more ridiculously grave pronouncements to make, I didn't hear them.

I was not going to marry Harwin. I was going to marry Darius the magician, if he turned out to be as delightful as he seemed—and if he didn't, I wouldn't marry him or any other man who had flocked to my father's house with the hope of winning my hand. I was not a prize to be bestowed, won, or bartered.

I was a princess, and a rather difficult young woman. I knew how to get my own way.

2

THE DASHING SUITOR

I had not attended the joust that whittled my suitors from more than fifty to about two dozen, because I had never enjoyed the sight of violence. But my father insisted I be on hand for the competition that would judge the contestants' courage, whatever this test entailed. So the following morning I joined all the other spectators gathering before a makeshift ring that had been set up just outside the walls that surrounded the palace. A dais had been erected in the most favorable spot to overlook the grounds; this was where the royal party would sit. More rudimentary stands had been built to accommodate everyone else and to enclose a space that resembled a small arena. Overnight, this arena had acquired chest-high walls and an overarching lattice canopy—it had, in effect, been turned into a very large cage.

I sat on the dais, awaiting my father and the rest of his

guests, and surveyed the arena with misgiving. Would such a cage be used for keeping dangerous creatures *in* or not allowing terrified contestants *out*?

It was not long before the stands filled up with several hundred people of all ranks—servants, tradesmen, merchants, and nobles—including a few of my unsuccessful suitors from the previous round. The day was sunny and warm, except for a persistent chilly breeze, and the mood of the crowd was mostly cheerful. I was half excited and half fearful, since my father was an unpredictable and not very nice man, and what he dreamed up to test someone's bravery might be highly unpleasant to watch.

At last my father arrived on the scene, trailed by Gisele, a handful of guests, and five or six servants bearing food, drink, cushions, and other comforts. The audience cheered and applauded when he made his appearance—less because they were happy to see their king, I thought, and more because his arrival indicated that the entertainment would soon be under way.

There was a little fuss and confusion as he and his companions mounted the dais and disposed themselves in the waiting chairs. Like me, my father had dark hair and blue eyes, but I had a larger and more solid frame than he did; he often wore bright colors and a lot of jewelry to make up for the fact that he was not particularly tall. Today he was dressed in dark green with gold trim, and he wore a gold circlet on his head. I noted without any enthusiasm that his guests were Sir Neville and his daughter Mellicia, a pretty but rather silly blond girl close to my own age. Like Harwin's father, Sir Neville was a longtime ally of the crown and often at the palace. More than once it had occurred to me that Mellicia would make a perfect bride for Harwin. Perhaps, once I was betrothed to Darius, I would suggest her to Harwin as a substitute wife.

I had taken the seat at the very end of the row of chairs, knowing that my father would sit in the middle. I was not surprised to see Neville and Mellicia given the seats of honor on either side of him, and I was not surprised—but not particularly happy about it—when Gisele strolled down to take the chair next to mine.

"Your father asked me to look after you while he entertains his company," she said by way of greeting.

"I don't need looking after," I said.

"Good," she said, settling in. "Then I should have an easy day of it."

I glanced into the arena, where several of my father's grooms and trainers had slipped inside the cage and stationed themselves along the perimeter. Their hands were full of staffs and chains and other simple weapons, and my uneasiness increased. "Do you have any idea what he's planning for this competition?" I asked.

"Only a rather dreadful suspicion," she said. "I'm hoping I'm wrong."

Which was not reassuring in the least.

Almost on the words, a stream of men entered the arena from the left side and milled around inside the cage, waiting. I was surprised to find them all barefoot and stripped to the waist, except for a loosely knotted collar each wore around his neck. None of them bore weapons. Whatever they were to face, it seemed, they would have to fend off armed with very little except their personal courage.

I searched the crowd, looking for Darius. There. He stood perfectly still to one side of the cage, gazing around with curiosity. He had pulled his fair curls back from his face with a leather cord, which gave him the brisk air of someone prepared to do business. He did not appear particularly nervous.

Most of the other men, I thought, had started to show some apprehension. They glanced up at the latticework ceiling of their prison; they casually leaned against the half walls as if testing how easily they could be breached. One or two paused to confer with each other, casting quick glances over their shoulders in case a monster had been released while they were engaged in conversation.

I was not looking for him, but I spotted Harwin anyway. Like Darius, he was standing almost motionless, but his eyes moved as he studied his competitors, his jailors, and his terrain. I saw his features set as he came to some kind of conclusion. I guessed that he had a pretty strong inkling of what trial lay in store, and he did not like it. While I watched him, he turned his eyes toward the dais and gave my father one long, narrow-eyed appraisal.

Then, before I could look away, he turned his attention to me. For a moment we stared at each other through the wide bars of the makeshift cage. Then he dropped his eyes and offered me a deep bow, ridiculously inappropriate considering his attire and his situation. I turned my face aside before he could straighten up and try to meet my eyes again.

I was just in time to see my father rise to his feet, his arms outstretched. Despite his lack of height, he had a certain forceful charisma; all eyes invariably turned his way when he moved or spoke. “Let the second phase of the competition begin!” he called and dropped his arms.

Over the renewed cheering of the crowd, I heard a chilling sound.

“Oh, no,” I said and looked at Gisele with horror in my eyes.

Her own eyes were fixed on the field. “Oh, yes,” she said.

A large enclosed cart had been maneuvered toward the entrance to the grand cage, and now its rear door was opened. From the wagon into the arena streamed about fifty of my father’s fighting dogs, barking and baying and baring their teeth.

It was suddenly clear why all the contestants had scarves knotted around their necks. Each scarf had been drenched with some kind of bait-scent; each pair of dogs had been primed to hunt for one of those scents.

Within seconds, each of my luckless suitors was under attack by two of the fiercest fighting dogs in the kingdom.

The action was so sudden, so brutal, and so unchoreographed that it was almost impossible to tell what was going on. At first, I was not even able to find Harwin or Darius among the whirling, slashing, howling maelstrom of bodies, both canine and human. Almost instantly, there was blood. Almost instantly, shrieks of real terror and pain. A flurry of motion on the far edge of the circle brought my attention to one desperate battle, where a man had slipped to the ground, his arms flailing. One dog had his calf in a death grip and shook his head so hard the man was scrubbed back and forth along the grass. The second dog leapt in, closing its jaws over the man's throat.

"No!" I shrieked, leaping to my feet as if I would jump from the stage and fling myself into the arena to offer aid. Gisele shot up beside me, clasping my arm to hold me in place. I shook her off, but stayed where I was, my eyes riveted to the action.

Two of the handlers had waded into the fray, using their sticks and choke collars and practiced commands to call off the attack. One of them tossed the dogs reward meat and shepherded them out of the arena; they frisked at his heels, pleased that they had pleased him. The other knelt on the bloodied ground by the fallen contestant, putting his hands up to the fighter's throat.

Another man stumbled into my line of vision, blocking my view. He had one dog fastened to his left wrist, another gnawing at his right ankle, but he was still on his feet. His face was contorted into what looked like a hysterical scream. He tripped over something on the ground and almost came to his knees—a fatal mistake—but righted himself just in time. The dog worrying his wrist opened its jaws, crouched, and sprang for the man's throat.

I turned away.

Gisele stood beside me, her dark eyes fixed unwaveringly on the scene before us. There was no expression at all on her face, unless stony stillness could be interpreted as an expression. My eyes went past her to where my father sat. He and Neville had their heads together as they watched the fighting and tracked individual contests. Mellicia had slumped back in her ornate chair and lifted a fan to shield her eyes from the gruesome scene, but I noticed that she had lowered the pretty confection of paper and lace just enough to see the action.

"What a despicable man my father is," I breathed.

Gisele nodded without glancing at me. "Yes," was all she said. We both sank into our chairs again.

I forced my attention back to the arena. I was sickened at the thought that these men were being gravely injured—some could even *die*—all because they wanted the chance to marry me. This whole violent nightmare was in some sense my fault, and I owed them the courtesy of watching them display their courage.

I had looked away for only a few moments, but even in that short time, the field had thinned out considerably. Some of the contestants had fled, dogs harrying their retreat, for maybe a dozen scratched, shocked, bloodied men stood shivering outside the arena. Some had fallen and been hauled outside to be tended by palace servants. Maybe ten remained in the arena, still engaged in combat. Still proving their valor.

One was Darius. With the arena now more than half empty, he was easy to pick out and, amazingly, he appeared to be completely unharmed. The bare skin of his chest was untouched, and his trousers were not even muddied. He stood calmly, his hands before him, palms out as if pressing against an invisible wall. Before him, the two dogs assigned to him crouched and snarled. One was a mottled brown, the other a matted gold, and both of them looked ferocious enough to kill a man. But they were having no luck with Darius. They growled and leapt and snapped at his feet, but they were unable to close their teeth over any part of his flesh.

Magic, I thought, with a great uprush of relief. *He's protecting himself with magic.* I was impressed by his fearlessness, his ability to keep his wits about him in such mayhem. He must have called up a wall of protection the instant the animals were loosed. One of the dogs leapt again, aiming for Darius's throat, and then fell back to the ground, whimpering, after encountering some hidden obstacle.

"That's magnificent," I murmured. "That's bravery."

I felt Gisele glance at me, determine what I was watching, and then shake her head. "No," she said, and pointed. "*That* is."

I followed the direction of her hand and I gasped.

Harwin was still standing, but it was clear he'd been involved in a vicious fight. His left arm was dripping with blood, and his bare chest was marked with dirt, blood, and one long, ugly scratch from shoulder to waist. His pants were filthy and his feet so muddy that at first I thought he was wearing shoes. I supposed he must have vanquished his own attackers, because no creatures snarled at his heels or circled his body, looking for an opening. I thought I saw, in the frenetic shadows of the arena, a few lifeless animal forms—stunned, I hoped, not dead, for I hated the idea that my father's dogs might be killed simply for obeying their training.

But even victorious in his own contest, Harwin wasn't heading for an exit. Some scream or cry had caused him to whirl around in time to see an exhausted young man being dragged to the ground by a pair of sleek attackers, one black, one brown. Harwin didn't hesitate. He charged over and fell on the brown dog from behind, forcing its lower jaw open and down toward its chest. I couldn't tell if he was using his bare hands or some weapon he had appropriated from a watching guard. The young man scrambled to his feet, the black dog still clinging grimly to his thigh. With a tremendous effort, Harwin flung the brown dog against one of the half walls, where it landed with a pained yelp, scrabbled, and lay still. Harwin snatched up something that had fallen to the ground—yes, one of the heavy wooden rods that the guards had carried—and began beating the black dog on its nose and eyes. It loosed its hold and charged at Harwin, but he fended it off while the younger man stumbled toward the exit, coughing and sobbing. Backing away, but never lifting his eyes from the dog's face, Harwin moved slowly toward the arena wall, then felt his way to the nearest door.

I thought he would turn and dash out, but he didn't. He merely kept his back to the wall and his weapon upraised until one of the handlers slipped a collar over the dog's head. Then I figured out what Harwin had obviously realized—no one who *left* the arena could be considered a winner in this round. He had to stay until every other contestant defeated his dogs or fled in humiliation.

I took a long, long breath and assessed the situation again. Darius was still unharmed and unmarked, standing in the center of the arena. Three other contestants appeared to have survived their encounters. One was the big, stupid man who looked so likely to win any event that required force. I didn't even want to think what might have happened to the poor animals assigned to attack *him*. Two others were strangers, both so covered in blood and grime that I couldn't tell much about their physical appearance.

Five. Five men still left to vie for my hand. I surveyed the carnage and thought bleakly that I was not worth this kind of effort.

Gisele spoke up, her voice low and controlled but full of rage. "I hate your father's dogs," she said.

I shook my head. "I'm *afraid* of them, but they break my heart," I said. "They're only doing what they've been taught to do."

Now she looked at me. Her eyes matched her voice. "Then maybe I just hate your father."

I was too weary to be shocked. "Half the lords in the kingdom keep fighting dogs, and those who don't own such animals come to watch the fights."

"Then maybe I just hate all men," she said.

Remembering that I didn't like Gisele, I gave a mocking laugh. "And yet *you're* the one who's been insisting I get married as quick as can be."

"I encouraged you to choose a groom carefully," she said. She swept a hand toward the arena, which was emptying out as the dog groomers took away the last of the animals and other servants escorted the five final contestants back to the palace. "Surely you could see that there was *one* among those suitors who was worthy of you."

"Yes!" I said. "I was amazed by Darius!"

"Who's Darius?" she asked sharply.

"The blond man. The one who kept the dogs at bay through magic. He was not harmed, but neither were they."

"Magic," she repeated. "That's a dangerous sort of toy."

I tossed my head. People still talked about the wizard my

grandfather had kept as part of his household, a powerful and unscrupulous man who had sometimes used sorcery to enforce the king's less popular decrees. There had been some suspicion that my grandmother's first husband had not died a natural death, freeing the lovely young widow to accept the king's offer of marriage. But most of the magicians in Kallenore had relatively limited and benign power, and they were generally welcomed wherever they traveled. The ones I had encountered had been rare, itinerant, and cheerful. Well, wouldn't you be cheerful if you possessed the power to heal people or change objects or create illusions? I think *I* would be.

I think I would be happy if I had any kind of power at all, whether or not it was magical.

"Maybe magic is just the toy I need," I said.

"Listen, Olivia," she said. "I know you dislike me. But you should believe what I say. Your father plans to marry you off with all speed, and he won't be overnice in his requirements. *Please* make it possible for him to choose a generous man, a thoughtful man, a man who will care for you."

I sneered. "And were those the qualities *you* were looking for when you chose to marry the king?"

"I didn't choose," she said evenly.

I turned away with a flounce. The others were already climbing from the dais, my father solicitously holding Mellicia's hand to guide her down the temporary steps. "I hardly think, no matter who I marry, I shall fare worse than you," I said. Just to be contrary, I didn't bother with the stairs at all. Instead I dropped to the floor, flattened my hand against the wood, and vaulted down to land lightly in the grass. I was sure any spectators got a nice flash of my ankles and underskirts, but I didn't care.

I barely heard Gisele's reply. "But don't you wish you could do better?"

* * *

After the intensity of the middle round, the third trial my would-be suitors faced couldn't help but be anticlimactic. It was not even interesting to watch. My father had hired three of the most famous scholars of the kingdom to create a long list of questions about mathematics, history, and the natural sciences, and a series of these tests were administered the next day. Whoever had the lowest score on the first exam was eliminated first. Whoever scored most poorly on the second test was eliminated next. And so on. Each suitor was quizzed separately in a sequestered room, attended by a scholar and two witnesses. Those of us who cared about the outcome hovered anxiously in the hallways, watching as the scholars emerged to compare scores.

I was relieved, but not surprised, when the large brutish man was the first to fail. He burst out of the room where he had been questioned, slammed the door behind him, shoved aside the folks who clustered in the corridor, and stomped on down the hall. I was glad to see him go, but still nervous. Who would be the next contestant eliminated? Surely Darius was clever enough to pass this final test—if not honestly, then artfully, by bedazzling his judges into believing his answers were correct. I sighed in monstrous relief when the next two fallen contestants proved to be strangers. Only belatedly did it occur to me that Harwin was not among the losers, either.

The crowd in the hall had grown to sizable proportions by the time we were down to the last two suitors. By late afternoon, even my father had stopped by to see how the competition was progressing. Neville and Mellicia trailed after him.

"How many are left?" he asked Gisele. The queen had waited with me all day, not that I had wanted her company.

"Two," she replied. "I believe we will have results soon."

My father looked intrigued. "Well, then, perhaps I shall linger a few minutes," he said. His eyes sought me out and he gave me his wolf's grin. "So that I can learn who shall have the honor of wedding my beloved daughter."

Coming close enough to put his arm around my shoulders, he whispered in a voice loud enough for everyone to hear, "So you'll be married soon, won't you? My little girl! A wife before the end of the day. Maybe a mother before the year is out."

He squeezed me so tightly that words I hadn't planned to say came tumbling out of my mouth. "But, Father, I do not want to rush so hastily into marriage with any man," I said breathlessly. "Especially if he's a stranger. May I have an engagement period to get to know my groom?"

His face grew stormy. "What's this? An engagement period?"

"Marry her off right away, that's my advice," Sir Neville boomed out.

My father uncoiled his arm and practically shoved me aside. "What a troublesome girl you are!" he exclaimed. "First you won't marry the man of my choosing, and *now* you turn all nervous and shy. There's no dealing with you at all!"

I had stumbled a little when he pushed me, but now I straightened myself and smoothed down my skirts. I had not forgotten, if he had, that a couple dozen people were crowded into the hallway, avidly watching this entire scene. After spending a lifetime balking at my father's orders, I was very good at outmaneuvering him, especially if I had an audience.

"I do not think I have been so unreasonable, Father," I said, my voice low and hurt. I half turned to make sure old Sir Norbert could catch every word. Norbert was a fat, choleric, irascible old bore, but he was powerful, and he had always been my father's most outspoken critic. "All I'm asking for is time to accustom myself to my new life."

"An excellent notion," Norbert said in his loud, raspy voice. "My own daughter's betrothal period was six months, and she needed every day."

My father's eyes were icy. "You may have a month, if you require it," he said through gritted teeth.

I wasn't sure if that would be enough time, but I had no attention left to spare for quarreling. The doors to the final two exam rooms were opening—in minutes I would know who had won the right to marry me. My heart started pounding so hard it was actually painful to breathe. The two scholars whispered together, both of them growing slightly heated, and then whispered some more.

"Well?" my father demanded. "Who has passed all my tests and proved himself worthy of my daughter's hand?"

One of the scholars cleared his throat. He looked to be a

hundred and eighty years old, all crepy white skin and wispy white hair. I had to think he had forgotten at least half of the facts he had ever managed to learn. "My liege," he said. "There is no clear winner. Both men have answered all of our questions correctly."

There was a slight murmur of approval from the onlookers, a few desultory rounds of applause. My father scowled. "Well, she cannot marry *two* men," he said. "Ask another question."

"We have asked them all," said the second scholar, whom I belatedly realized was a woman. She was as fragile as a creature made out of dried leaves and corn husks, a notion reinforced by her papery skin and overall brownness of coloring.

My father's expression became even more thunderous. "Then think up another one!" he shouted.

Norbert pushed himself forward. "You say there are only two suitors left?" he said. "Let them stand before the princess so she can choose which one she will wed."

"Yes!" I exclaimed. The generally approving reaction of the crowd drowned out Gisele's gasp of, "No! My liege! You can't!"

My father was nodding vigorously. "Very well," he said. "Bring them both to the throne room in half an hour. We will see Olivia engaged before the day is out."

* * *

What do you wear to the announcement of your own betrothal? When you have only thirty minutes to prepare, you don the nicest gown you own that matches the accessories you're already wearing. My maids stuffed me into a dark yellow dress with lace foaming over the décolletage and quickly brushed and repinned my hair. The topaz necklace and eardrops stayed in place, and soon I was hurrying back down the long hallways to the throne room.

As you'd expect, it was a large domed chamber made gloomier than necessary by imposing carved pillars, lugubrious murals, and a complete lack of windows, so all the lighting had to be supplied by candles and oil lamps. When I arrived, my father and Gisele were already seated on the great carved, painted, and bejeweled chairs that were set up on a low stage in the center of the chamber. About two hundred other people were milling about the room, restless and excited. I wove between them on my way to the dais, then climbed up to take my place in the more delicate chair situated at my father's right hand.

"Let the contestants be brought forward!" my father commanded.

The crowd parted and the two scholars led Darius and Harwin deep into the room. Darius and I stared at each other, each drinking in details. In this much better lighting, he was much better-looking. His blond curls had been freshly washed and combed; he was wearing a silky blue shirt over black trousers and boots, and he looked young and hopeful and sparkly with possibility. I know men aren't *sparkly*, but he was, somehow. He seemed to be on the verge of breaking into laughter or bursting into song or flinging up his hands to call forth rainbows.

I hoped that, this close up, I looked as good to him as he did to me.

Harwin, by contrast, was much the worse for yesterday's

escapades and today's deep cogitation. The first thing I noticed was that he walked awkwardly, employing a cane and favoring his left foot. I had not seen him fend off the first set of attack dogs yesterday; clearly one of them had chewed on his leg or ankle. As he got closer, I saw that his face was almost haggard, perhaps with pain, perhaps with accumulated weariness. His eyes were fixed on my face, and his expression was dismal.

Only three people in the room knew whom I would choose, and two of them weren't at all happy about it. I saw Gisele lean forward and bend in my direction, but I would not look at her. I kept my gaze on the approaching men and tried to maintain a serious expression.

Harwin and Darius halted in front of the thrones and executed deep bows. "Well done, both of you!" my father declared. "Each of you has demonstrated his strength, his valor, and his wit—each has proved himself worthy of my daughter. Yet only one of you can marry the princess. Now is the time for her to choose which of you she will call husband."

My father rose to his feet and gestured for me to follow suit. Gisele and I both stood up. "Introduce yourselves," my father said grandly and pointed at Harwin. "First you."

Harwin stepped closer to the stage, his gaze still leveled on me. "I am Sir Harwin Brenley, twenty-eight years old, a man of property and my father's sole heir. If you choose me as your husband, I will treat you gently, love you fondly, share all my material goods with you, and consider myself a fortunate man."

A soft sigh ran through the room, produced, no doubt, by the women in attendance. I blinked at Harwin, for that was certainly the most romantic string of sentences I had ever heard him put together. But it was still Harwin staring back up at me, tall, brown, steady, dull. I didn't know how to answer him, so I merely nodded, thanked him, and turned my attention to Darius.

The magician stepped forward and dropped into a bow so low that his curls brushed the floor. When he straightened, he was holding a bouquet of enormous white blossoms that gave off a rich and heady scent.

"I am Darius Kent, son of a landowner and also my father's heir. I am possessed of a sunny temperament, a wealth of fantastical stories, and the ability to do small magics. If you marry me, your life will be filled with laughter and decorated with enchantments, and both of those serve to lighten even the dourest days." He flung the flowers into the air and they were transformed into white butterflies that danced and fluttered around my head before winging their way up into the painted dome. I clapped my hands together like a child, and all the women in the audience cooed and applauded along with me.

My father turned toward me. "Daughter, can you choose between them?"

"Darius," I said with what might have been unbecoming haste. "The magician. I will marry Darius Kent."

The reaction from the crowd was so loud that I couldn't hear what my father or Gisele might have said in response. But Darius flung his head back and laughed, then spread his arms wide in invitation. "Come to me, then!" he called, and I didn't even hesitate before jumping off the stage into his arms. He caught me deftly and twirled me around until I was as dizzy as one of those butterflies.

"We shall plan the wedding immediately!" My father's declaration rose above the excited chatter of the crowd. "Everyone shall be invited!"

That caused the noise to intensify even more, but somehow Gisele's cool voice cut across the clamor. "Not for another month," my stepmother said. "You promised Olivia her period of betrothal."

Still in Darius's arms, my feet ten inches off the ground, my eyes locked on the smiling face of my chosen fiancé, I desperately wished I had not negotiated such a concession from my father. But before I could recant, Norbert's loud voice came from somewhere among the watchers.

"The lad must take the princess to meet *his* family," the old lord said. "It would be unseemly for her to marry him without such an introduction."

"I shall take you to meet my grandmother," Darius said. Although everyone in the hall could hear him, he seemed to be speaking only to me. "Will you like that?"

"Indeed, I think I will like anything you have to show me," I replied breathlessly.

"Excellent," my father said. "You can leave in the morning."

I was delighted at the notion of wandering off in Darius's company, so I was greatly displeased when Gisele's voice once again made itself heard above the din. "She cannot travel alone through the kingdom with a man she has just met," the queen said coldly. "The possibilities abound for misfortunes and errors in judgment."

"She is to marry him," my father said. "There could be no scandal attached to any of their intimacies."

The very word made me blush and suddenly wish Darius would put me on my feet. As if he could read my mind, he set me down gently, but kept my hand in his, and planted a light kiss on my knuckles.

"I think you are too sanguine," Gisele said. "There must be a chaperone."

There was a movement in the crowd behind us, and a young woman stepped up beside me. I remembered her from the fire-lit circle two nights ago. "I will guarantee the groom's good behavior," she said. "I am Dannette Kent, and he is my brother. I will travel with the princess on this journey."

My father spread his hands. "There! All problems solved!" he said. "Let us retreat to the dining hall for a grand meal to commemorate this occasion."

3

THE MAGICAL JOURNEY

My betrothed and his sister and I set out the very next morning, waving good-bye to the servants and friends who had gathered in the courtyard to see me off. My father was not among them. I had elected to travel without a maid, since, at dinner the night before, Darius had made some offhand comment about how tiresome it was to always be waiting for women to primp and beautify themselves.

"Especially when they are already beautiful," he had added, smiling at me.

I had also considerably cut down on the amount of luggage I packed, though even so he had seemed astonished at the number of trunks and boxes I had brought to his campsite. Dannette had merely grinned. "Good thing there's room in the wagon," she said.

I had not realized until that very moment that an ordinary

farm wagon, and not a luxurious carriage, would be our method of transportation. It was relatively large and well built, with a raised tarp over the bed to shelter all of our possessions, but it was still a wagon. The bench up front was only long enough to hold the driver and one passenger, so someone would have to sit in back among the crates and bundles. When we first started out, Dannette volunteered to take that less desirable spot, and so I sat beside Darius and watched as the countryside unrolled around us.

Which it did very slowly. It turned out that traveling in a heavily loaded wagon behind two horses could not be compared to traveling in a specially built coach pulled by a team. The road seemed rougher than I remembered, and much longer, though the lightly wooded countryside offered a pretty enough colorful autumn landscape. By nightfall we had made it no farther than a crossroads town that I had never bothered to stop at before because it was too close to the palace grounds.

"This looks like as good a place as any to break for the night," Darius said, and Dannette agreed. I thought glumly if I turned my head and squinted hard enough, I might be able to glimpse the turrets of the palace behind me.

But what did I care how much ground we covered in a day? I had no particular eagerness to make our destination; I just wanted the chance to enjoy the company of my fiancé. In the wagon, it had not been so easy to talk to him as you might suppose, for we spent more of our energy surviving the jouncing than making conversation, and half the time Dannette took the reins while Darius sat in the back. I hesitated to admit it, but our first day of travel had teetered between boring and uncomfortable, and though I was resolved not to complain, I was glad to finally pull off the road.

But I was shocked when we checked into a modest inn and Darius requested only a single chamber. "*One* room?" I hissed to Dannette while Darius paid the fee. "For all three of us?"

She seemed surprised. "By the time we make it to my grandmother's and back to the palace, we might be on the road ten days or more. We can hardly afford two or three rooms a night."

"We cannot?" I said blankly.

I thought she was trying to hide a grin. "Well, Darius and I cannot. If you have brought lavish funds with you, I suppose you could reserve your own accommodations."

I stared at her. I hadn't brought any money. I never did. Bills were always paid by footmen and servants. The proprietors this close to the palace would surely recognize my face, but once we made it another fifty miles down the road, would anyone believe me when I claimed to be Princess Olivia? Would they sell me goods on credit and send the bills to my father? Would he pay them?

"No, no," I said faintly. "I will share the room with you and Darius. We are supposed to be getting acquainted, after all."

Now her grin was definitely visible. "Nothing like a journey to find out everything you need to know about someone," she said cheerfully.

After this, I was not as surprised as I might have been to find we were dining in the taproom, and not a private parlor. Still, Darius's charming smile—and perhaps a little extra magical persuasion—secured us our own table in the corner where we didn't have to share trenchers with laborers, families, and local shopkeepers.

"To my bride!" Darius toasted me with his beer while we waited for food to arrive.

I'd never had beer before, my father considering it common, and I wrinkled my nose after the first sip. "I don't like that so much," I said. "It's bitter."

Darius took a few hearty swallows. "Once you accustom yourself to the taste, you find that you like it quite well," he said. "Plus it gives you a very pleasant"—he swirled his fingers over his blond curls—"feeling in your head."

Dannette laughed. "It takes a little longer to get drunk on beer than wine," she interpreted. "But the effects are very similar. I would go slowly, if I were you."

I tried another sip. Hard to imagine coming to like *this*. "How many more days to your grandmother's house?" I asked.

Darius shrugged. "Four? Five? I rarely go straight there—or anywhere—so I'm not sure how long any journey lasts."

"Where do you live when you're not traveling?" I said.

Darius laughed. "I'm always traveling."

My eyes widened. "You don't have a home? *Anywhere?*"

"Well, technically my grandmother's house is mine, since the estate was my father's and now belongs to me," Darius said. "But I consider the wagon my true home. Everything I need I bring with me wherever I go."

I looked at Dannette. "What about you?" I demanded.

She considered. I had the feeling she was trying to decide

exactly how much of a particular story to tell me. "I would just as soon find a place and stay," she finally said. "But the last place I lived eventually became unbearable. Which is why I have chosen to travel with Darius for a while. I'll settle down when I find a situation that appeals to me."

My eyes were big again. "What made your last situation unbearable?"

Darius leaned forward. "Scandals," he whispered theatrically. "Accusations in the dead of night. Secrets."

I sat back in my chair, staring at Dannette. Who, after all, *was* this woman? When it came down to it, who was Darius? What did I know about either of them, really, except that they were attractive and friendly and eager to make the king's daughter one of their family?

She laughed ruefully and put a comforting hand on my arm. "Don't let him tease you, Olivia. It is true that there was some turmoil attached to my last situation, but it was all personal and confined to a very few people. We are quite respectable." She glanced at Darius and back at me, her face amused. This was a woman who found the world around her to be endlessly entertaining, and it was hard not to relax in her smiling presence. "And my brother has developed the most ridiculous infatuation for you. I have never seen him like this with any girl."

Now he was the one who was blushing and bashful. "It's true," he said. "I saw you the day before the joust. You had just come back from a ride, and your hair was all wild and your face was flushed. And when the groom helped you out of the saddle, you kissed your horse on the nose. I was never so charmed!"

I laughed. "Oh, that was Bumblebee, my favorite mount!" I said. I had spent some time during today's tedious journey wishing I were riding Bumblebee instead of sitting in the wagon. Of course, then I would not have had the opportunity to get to know Darius along the way.

"I got the impression you did not enjoy the second trial that your father set up for your suitors," Darius went on. "I suppose a girl who kisses horses doesn't like to see dogs being beaten down by men."

"I know that these particular dogs are bred to fight, but no, I do not enjoy watching them. I never attend when my father holds matches on the palace grounds."

He smiled at me. His eyes were a misty gray, full of secrets and promises. "Then I am glad I was able to hold them off with magic instead of brute force," he said.

I smiled back, a little shy but sincere. "It was one of the things I liked a great deal about *you*," I said. "You don't seem to be a cruel man."

"Lord, I would hope I was never cruel!" he exclaimed in dismay.

Dannette was laughing. "Darius has many faults, as I'm sure you'll discover, but he's simply never unkind," she said. "He forgets things, sometimes on purpose—"

"Hey!"

"He dawdles, he develops a sudden passionate interest in the most *boring* topics, which he then expects you to appreciate, he refuses to be cowed by your anger and is always convinced he can wheedle his way back into your good graces—"

"I always can."

"He is happy to share his time, his campfire, and his food with anyone who stumbles across his path, and he has never been on time for a single appointment he's ever made. But he's not unkind."

None of these traits sounded particularly bad to me, and I beamed at my happy-go-lucky betrothed. "I'm sure we will get along famously," I said.

* * *

I was a tiny bit less certain of that sometime after midnight. We had settled into our rather small room, going to elaborate lengths to make sure we each had a semblance of privacy as we washed up and changed into sleeping clothes. Danette and I shared the only bed, which was narrower and much lumpier than the bed I had all to myself at home, while Darius claimed to be entirely comfortable on the floor. He must have been; he instantly fell asleep.

And began snoring.

It was not a great gusty snoring such as Sir Norbert inflicts on us when he's fallen asleep during some long dinner or council meeting. The sounds were gentle and muffled, but they did not *stop*, and I was quite unused to having to listen to anyone even *breathe*. Meanwhile, Dannette was restless. She tossed and turned and murmured short, agitated phrases before subsiding again. It was a little surprising that someone who seemed so cheerful in her waking hours would betray such distress in her unguarded sleep.

Well, obviously Dannette would not be sharing our room once Darius and I were married, and I supposed I would eventually get used to the snoring.

I finally fell asleep, but morning came too soon, and Darius's jovial manner was a little grating to me in my groggy state. Nonetheless, I endeavored to be pleasant company as we dressed, packed, and headed downstairs to eat a quick meal before taking off again.

Harwin was awaiting us in the taproom.

I saw him first, and I came to a dead stop. Darius actually stumbled into me; Dannette, who tended to pay more attention to things, managed to halt in plenty of time. From the corner of my eye, I could see her grinning again. "What are *you* doing here?" I demanded.

Harwin rose to his impressive height. His face and voice very grave, he said, "I, too, passed all your father's tests. I, too, am eligible to be your bridegroom. So I, too, am going to take this opportunity to travel beside you and allow you to get to know me better."

Darius was nodding and smiling. He stepped forward to shake Harwin's hand. "That sounds reasonable," he said. "Have you ordered breakfast yet?"

Harwin looked surprised at the easy welcome, while I was incensed. "Darius!" I hissed. "He is your *rival*! You should be angry that he would try to usurp your position and steal my affections!"

Now Darius was the one to show surprise. "Well, if your affections can be stolen that easily, we won't have a happy marriage anyway," he said. "Besides, he's right. He did pass the tests. He should have a chance to win your hand."

"He had a chance and I *refused* him. You should order him to leave this minute."

"I won't," Harwin said instantly. "If I can't join your party, I'll just follow you."

"See?" Darius said. "We may as well let him travel with us. We can't stop him from coming along behind."

"Well, of course we can! *You* can! Put a spell on him! Make him forget he saw us here—make him believe there's something urgent awaiting him back home. Do *something*."

Darius rubbed the back of his hand against his cheek and looked apologetic. "I don't really do those kinds of spells," he said.

Dannette touched me on the arm. Now she was openly smiling. "I forgot to mention one of Darius's other faults," she said. "He never does what you tell him to."

I stared at her helplessly. "But—we can't have Harwin traveling with us! I mean, how very odd! Not to mention I don't want him coming along!"

She moved past me to sit down at the table where Harwin had been waiting. "Nonetheless, I think he's coming with us," she said. "So let's all have breakfast and then be on our way."

* * *

I fumed throughout the meal, refusing to speak to any of them, not that any of them seemed to care. Harwin sat very stiffly, eating his meal with his usual formal manners. Dannette made some effort to draw him out, asking him about his estates and his family, to the point where I almost wanted to make a comment about how *she* should marry him if she found his assets so desirable. Darius chatted amiably, not seeming to notice that Harwin's replies were as terse as civility would allow.

Once the dreadful meal was over, we were finally on our way through more of the gently rolling countryside, all green melting into gold. I sat beside Darius on the seat of the wagon, while Dannette settled in back. Harwin, who had undertaken the journey on a very fine bay gelding, didn't seem certain about the best way to proceed. At times he ranged ahead of us, but not too far, and he always came back to make sure we hadn't tried to elude him by turning off on some minor road. At times he rode beside the wagon and attempted to talk with me, but I gave him only the briefest and most unencouraging replies. I could tell that, like me, he was finding our slow pace to be maddening—but, like me, he was more interested in the actual trip than the destination, so he managed to keep his impatience in check.

I was a having a harder time maintaining a good-natured attitude, though I doggedly pursued my goal of getting to know Darius. *Tell me about some of your adventures. When did you realize you had magical ability? What is your favorite kind of spell?* He answered readily enough, but he was too preoccupied with the horses to go into great detail, so his stories were sketchy and a little flat. I tried to think of amusing anecdotes about my own life to share with him, but even to myself my tales of hunts and balls and celebrations sounded shallow and vain. Was it possible I was such a useless, uninformed creature that I couldn't even come up with an hour's worth of decent conversation?

When we stopped for lunch at a small-town inn, Harwin made a point of sitting next to me and trying to draw me out, but I just sat at the table and brooded. If I was going to be a successful queen, not to mention an interesting wife, I would need to widen my experiences and broaden my mind.

I wasn't entirely sure how a person went about doing that, but I supposed that traveling around the kingdom was not a bad place to start.

Shortly after we set out again after lunch, it started to rain.

"Shouldn't we pull over somewhere?" I asked Darius.

He squinted at the sky and shook his head. "Looks like it'll continue on like this for a few hours, so no point in trying to wait it out."

"We could stop at an inn somewhere," I suggested.

"Oh, I think we can make another ten miles or so today," he said.

"But I'm getting wet!"

"Climb in back with Dannette," he said. "If there's room."

I swallowed a growl of exasperation and, when it was clear Darius was not going to stop the wagon for this maneuver, clambered over the bench with the barest minimum of grace. The back of the wagon was a welter of boxes and bags and pillows and *things*—black kettles and dried plants and glass globes and loose shoes and walking sticks and what appeared to be a large collection of desiccated insects. The heavy tarp overhead, loosely stretched over curved wooden ribs, somewhat kept the rain at bay, but even as I pitched to my knees and felt around for an open space to sit, I could feel a few drops of rainwater seep through and fall into my hair.

Dannette was scrunched down toward the back of the wagon, near enough to the half-open back flap to be able to read by weak sunlight. "There's a little space there between the table and the black trunk," she said helpfully, pointing. "You have to put your feet up on the bag of goose feathers, though."

I situated myself with a little difficulty, eventually deciding to sit on the goose feathers to protect myself from the jostling of the ride, even more pronounced back here than up on the bench. "It's raining," I said unnecessarily. "Darius doesn't want to stop."

"Yes," she said absently. "That's fairly typical."

"I don't think I like traveling in the rain," I added.

She laughed. "I find it's just not worth fussing about."

I sighed. I usually found everything to be worth fussing about. I squirmed in my spot, found a pillow to wedge behind my head, and finally leaned back against a crate of unidentifiable items that chimed together in time with the jouncing. It wasn't more than another ten minutes before I fell asleep.

* * *

The cessation of motion woke me and I guessed we had stopped for the night. The rain had ended, but the air had that cold, sodden feeling that reminded you how very unpleasant wet weather could be. Climbing out through the back of the wagon, I found myself standing in the cluttered yard of an inn appreciably bigger than the one we'd patronized the night before. I allowed myself to hope it would have more amenities and better food.

Once grooms had come for our horses, our whole group filtered inside. I noticed that Harwin was limping, but I turned my head away without asking him why. Dannette was the first to arrive at the proprietor's desk, and I heard her ask for two rooms.

Two! I thought with excitement, before realizing that Harwin could easily afford his own and I still would be sharing a space with the others.

The innkeeper, a very tall, very thin man with lank gray hair and overlarge spectacles, looked down at her over the rims and shook his head. "We only have one room left," he said. "A great number of people were caught in the rain earlier today and checked in instead of traveling on."

Dannette glanced over her shoulder, her eyebrow raised in a silent question. Darius shrugged. "I don't mind four to a room," he said.

Harwin appeared shocked. "Four! You don't mean that *you* plan to sleep in the same room as the princess!"

Darius shrugged again. "I did last night."

Harwin was even more shocked, so much so all he could do was stare at Darius. Dannette touched him lightly on the arm. "I played chaperone and lay beside Olivia in the bed, while my brother curled up on the floor," she said. "You need not worry. I take my responsibilities seriously."

Harwin had recovered the power of speech. "Well, you will not share a room with the princess while *I* travel with you. You and I shall sleep in the stables in your own wagon."

"There's not much room in the wagon," Dannette began, but Darius spoke over her.

"*You* may sleep there if you like, but *I* will sleep in the bedchamber. I see no reason to camp in a barn when there's a room available."

"I cannot allow you to compromise Olivia's virtue in such a fashion."

Darius shrugged, took the key from the hand of the *very* curious innkeeper, and settled his bag over his shoulder. "Well, you can stand guard over me in the room, or you can bed down in the stables, whatever you choose," he said. "I'm going to wash my face and then come down for dinner."

Trying not to smirk, I followed him up the stairs, Dannette at my heels. I was not surprised, upon looking over my shoulder, to see Harwin reluctantly following. He was still favoring his left leg.

The room we had been assigned was more spacious than the one we'd had the night before, and featured a small settee in addition to a fairly sizable bed. Harwin was obviously too tall to fit on the settee, so Darius claimed it, but then Darius went to some trouble to gather blankets and pillows to fashion a bed for Harwin on the floor.

"No doubt you're tired enough to fall right to sleep," Darius said.

"No doubt," was Harwin's cool reply. "Let us repair to the taproom for dinner."

He hobbled toward the door and Dannette said, "What's wrong with your foot?"

Hand on the knob, Harwin gave her a wintry look. "I have a small cut."

She came closer to him. "Not walking that way, you don't. You have a deep wound, I'm guessing, and it's gotten worse during a day of travel."

I suddenly remembered. "Oh! You were bitten during the dog trial!" I exclaimed. "Harwin, you idiot, did you not have someone take a look at your hurts?"

He looked both embarrassed to have roused our concern and irritated at being called an idiot. "I cleaned all the bites myself before setting out," he said. "I'm fine."

Dannette pointed toward a stiff-backed chair that was set before a graceful table, as if inviting travelers to pause and write out correspondence. "Sit down," she said with such authority that Harwin stopped protesting and dropped into the chair. "Take off both your boots and roll up the ends of your trousers."

Not that I wanted to, but I was seeing in my mind the last few moments of Harwin's competition against the dogs. "He should take off his shirt, too," I said. "I know he got hurt on his arms and his chest as well."

"I am not disrobing in front of all of you," Harwin said shortly.

"Olivia will look the other way," Dannette said and knelt on the floor in front of Harwin.

I did not, in fact, look the other way, but watched in some fascination as Harwin slowly removed everything except his trousers. I heard a low whistle from Darius as he settled on the floor beside his sister.

"That's a nasty piece of work," he observed, touching Harwin's left foot. I couldn't see too well past the screen of their bodies, but I thought it looked swollen and red. Perhaps there was a little pus oozing out along the anklebone. "It must feel like your flesh is on fire."

"It's a little painful," Harwin acknowledged.

Dannette sat back on her heels and looked at her brother. "Do what you can, then I'll put on salve and bandages."

"No," Harwin said sharply, jerking his foot away and tucking it under the chair. "I don't want his magic. I don't want his *help*."

Dannette came to her feet. "Don't be an idiot," she said calmly, using my word again and making Harwin glare. "You don't like my brother, but you have no reason to distrust him. And don't say you don't want to be beholden to him," she added, raising her voice when he tried to interrupt, "because that's just stupid. Let him heal you. Or let your foot fester, and succumb to gangrene, and require amputation. That will certainly improve your lot and make your next bride easier to woo."

As if he couldn't help himself, Harwin looked directly at me. His face was so wretched that I actually felt pity for him. "Don't be silly," I said softly. "Accept his help. Maybe you'll be able to save his life a couple of days from now, and then you can feel better about it."

That made Dannette laugh, and even Harwin's face relaxed into what was almost a smile. He offered his foot to Darius again, who took hold of it in a businesslike fashion and began pressing his fingers along the toes and heel. Now Harwin's expression was one of wonderment.

"That already feels much better," he said. "What did you do?"

Darius laughed and kept manipulating different sections of the foot. "Magic," he said. "My greatest strengths are in altering the basic structure of things. So I can turn a butterfly into a bird, for instance. Or I can change a broken bone to a whole one and an infected patch of skin to a well one."

"It is a most useful skill," Harwin said stiffly. "I thank you for using your talents on me."

"I always enjoy the chance to put my magic to use," Darius said. "It's like swordplay. If you don't practice your skills, you lose them."

Dannette had gone to rummage in her bag, and now she returned with a small bottle and a roll of gauze. She bent over Harwin's naked chest, examining slash and bite marks on his arms and torso. She touched two of them and shook her head. "You should have had these taken care of before you left the palace," she scolded.

"I was in a hurry," Harwin said. He was looking at me again.

I sniffed and tossed my hair. "I suppose you told my father you were coming after me," I said. "Maybe he even suggested it."

"I had no conversation with him at all," he replied.

He didn't say anything more, but I could read his tone. Harwin had never openly criticized my father, but more than once I had been convinced that he had a low opinion of how my father ruled his kingdom. I knew Harwin had hated the idea of the competition, but I figured that was just because he had so little chance of winning, or so I'd thought. Now I wondered if he had just believed it to be a callous and random way to select a husband for a princess.

Considering who might have won, I had to agree.

Darius stood up and ran his hands lightly over the wounds on Harwin's upper body, while Dannette spread salve on his foot and wrapped it in a winding layer of gauze. Harwin flexed his toes.

"Thank you," he said, smiling down at Dannette. "You have a most gentle touch."

She patted his knee and came to her feet. "There. Now we don't have to worry about you dying before you can challenge my brother for Olivia's hand."

He actually laughed. "It is kind of you both to preserve me for such a future."

"You deserve to have your life saved, since you saved another man's life two days ago," Dannette said. At his inquiring expression, she went on. "During the trial against the fighting dogs. A man had gone down and you went to his aid, even though he was a rival."

"You saw that?" Harwin asked, gazing up at her. "I didn't realize the actions inside the arena were that plain to spectators outside it."

She glanced briefly at her brother. "I had reason to be paying close attention. I thought you showed honor—and bravery."

Harwin shrugged. "Hard to exhibit either quality in a competition that possessed neither."

"Well, I observed you, and I was impressed," Dannette said softly.

He bowed his head and made no other answer. I shifted uncomfortably where I sat. I had seen his act of courage as well, but it seemed awkward and insincere to add my own praises. *Oh, yes, now that you mention it, that was a very noble thing to do.* It was very annoying to have to feel bad about not being nice enough to Harwin.

"Well, that's as much as I can do for you," Darius said, stepping back. "How do you feel?"

Harwin rolled his shoulders experimentally, and the muscles on his chest briefly stood out in relief. "Extraordinarily improved," he said, standing up. I noticed that Darius looked quite short next to him—although Harwin looked even plainer next to Darius. "You must let me buy dinner for your sister and yourself as part of my thanks." He glanced at me with a touch of humor. "I will still wait eagerly for my chance to save your life in turn, but perhaps the meal will serve as a stopgap measure of gratitude."

"Excellent," Darius said. "I'm starving. Let's eat."

4

THE WICKED STEPMOTHER

The meal was more convivial than I would have expected, for either the act of kindness itself or the sheer relief at being out of pain had served to make Harwin more outgoing than usual. He asked Darius and Dannette where they had traveled and was particularly interested in their expeditions to cities outside Kallenore's borders. It turned out—I had not known this—that Harwin and his father had pursued commercial ventures in a few neighboring nations but without receiving as much return as they'd hoped, so he was keen to hear their opinion of other markets. Darius didn't seem to have paid much attention to the possibilities of trade and profit, but Dannette had formed strong opinions, which she was happy to share. I listened, bemused, as she talked about the diamond mines in Liston, the spice routes through Newmirot, and the drought in lower Amlertay that had left the countrymen eager to trade for seed and other staples.

"I do not think I would have learned half so much if I had passed twice as long in any of those places," I said in an undervoice to Darius.

He was finishing up his second beer, and I held out my glass to silently ask for a refill. I still didn't like the taste, but I didn't find it quite so unpleasant, and I did enjoy the way it softened the harder edges of the day. "No, everything that she says comes as quite a surprise to me," he said airily. "Now, what *I* noticed while we were in Newmirot was how the women wore their hair, with ribbons braided into it right around their faces. It was so colorful and lovely."

I felt a moment's flash of stupid jealousy. "And I suppose all the women in Newmirot were very pretty?" I said.

He smiled and tipped his glass against mine. "All women are pretty in their way," he said, "but you are the most beautiful of all."

I laughed, but even that was not enough to earn me more than a glance from Harwin. He didn't seem to care that I was getting along so well with my fiancé; he just returned his attention to Dannette to ask a question about coin denominations in Amlertay. I took another few large swallows of my beer.

* * *

As I had expected, sharing a bedroom with Harwin was even stranger than sharing one with Darius and Dannette. I was always aware that he was on the other side of the room, even though he did not snore, as Darius did, or thrash about, as Dannette continued to do. Merely, I could sense him lying there, disapproving of us all. Well, I would not let Harwin's presence oppress my spirits. The beer had made me too sleepy to fret for long, anyway, so I closed my eyes and drifted into dreaming.

I woke up once, abruptly, when Dannette uttered an urgent cry of warning. I jerked upright, unable to see anything in the utter darkness. I heard a stir on the other side of the room—Harwin, surely, since Darius's gentle snores went on uninterrupted.

"What's wrong?" he asked sharply. I could see a shadow move through the blackness. "Olivia? Was that you?"

"Not me. Dannette," I replied softly. I could tell by the way she curled in upon herself that she was still sleeping.

"What's wrong with her?"

"I think she has nightmares. This happened last night, too."

Now his shadow was beside the bed. I could smell the soap he had used to wash his face and the herbs from Dannette's salve. "Should we wake her?"

"I think it will just start again when she goes back to sleep."

I waited for him to say something like, *It's intolerable that you should have your slumbers interrupted in such a way.* But, from what I could tell by staring at his silhouette in the darkness, he was merely looking down at Dannette's restless form. Perhaps his face, if I'd been able to see it, would have been creased with compassion or concern.

"What gives her nightmares?" he asked.

Scandals. Accusations in the dead of night. Secrets. "I don't know."

He hesitated a moment. I didn't need to see his face to be able to imagine his expression: serious, considering, truthful. "I like both of them better than I thought I would," he said at last. "But they are still strangers about whom you know almost nothing. It was reckless of your father to send you off with them in such a scrambling fashion."

"Well, you're here now," I said flippantly. "You can make sure they don't harm me or lead me astray."

"Indeed," he said, "that is exactly what I mean to do."

* * *

In the morning I felt absolutely dreadful. My head was pounding and my stomach clamped down when I so much as *thought* about breakfast. For some reason, this seemed to amuse Darius and Dannette. "Too much beer the night before makes the dawn a grievous chore," Darius chanted. I gave him a heavy look of condemnation from eyes that felt scratchy and hot. His stupid little verse didn't even make sense.

"I don't think I can move," I said, still sprawled on the bed after the other three had washed and dressed. "Let's stay here another day."

"You'll feel just as bad lying here as you will sitting in the wagon, so you may as well travel on," Darius said, with rather less sympathy than I'd hoped for. "Come on. Dannette will help you get dressed while Harwin and I go down and order a meal."

I allowed Dannette to cajole me into a loose-fitting gown, and then she combed out my hair and put it in a simple braid. I was horrified at my image in the mirror, my face pale, my eyes shot with red. "I'm ruined!" I cried.

Dannette laughed. "You'll be fine later today and show no ill effects at all by tomorrow," she said. "That's because you're twenty-one. If you drink a pitcher of beer every night until you turn fifty, well, that's another story."

I met her eyes in the mirror. *She* looked perfectly rested and cheerful as always. She'd put her own ginger blond hair back in a bun, a careless style that looked good on her since it accentuated her high cheekbones. This morning she had added small gold earrings to her ensemble, or maybe I saw them only because her hair was pulled back. I wondered if she was trying to improve her appearance in subtle ways to attract Harwin's attention.

"Why do you cry out in the middle of the night?" I asked abruptly.

"Do I?" she said. "I'm sorry. Does it keep you awake?"

"Yes, and it kept Harwin awake last night, too," I said, watching her closely.

She turned away from the mirror. "I'm sorry," she said again. "I will try to muffle my sounds."

I stood up and turned to watch her as she put the last of her clothes in her bag. "But *why* are you so upset? What are you dreaming about?"

She merely continued to fold her skirt, carefully lining up the pleats. "Things I cannot remember in the morning," she said.

Clearly, she was going to give me no better answer. I made a little snort of irritation, hoisted my own bag over my shoulder, spared a moment to be vexed that neither Darius nor Harwin had thought to carry it downstairs for me, and left the room. Dannette came behind me, no longer smiling.

"Let's throw our things in the wagon before sitting down to breakfast," she suggested, so I followed her out into the innyard.

The wagon was already in place and a groom was leading the horses up to be hitched. Ours was not the only vehicle in the yard; I saw half a dozen gigs and carts lined up, waiting for their owners to down a hasty breakfast. My attention was caught by a particularly fine black carriage pulled by a matched team. I had a moment of intense longing. Oh, if only I could travel in *that*, how much more tolerable this expedition would be!

When I was married to Darius and I became queen of Kallenore, I might journey around the kingdom from time to time watching him practice magic if it made him happy, but I was *not* traveling in a cart and I was not sleeping four to a room, listening to people breathe and snore and chatter in their sleep.

Well, of course I would hear *Darius* breathe. And snore.

"Hungry?" Dannette asked.

"Not really," I said, "but let's eat and move on."

We stepped into the crowded taproom, trying to avoid the three women and one boy threading their way through the packed tables as they delivered trays of eggs and sausage. My stomach clenched as it had this morning, but this time I thought the response might signal hunger, not nausea. I looked around for Darius and Harwin, and finally spotted them sitting at the end of a long common table. I was a little surprised to see Harwin speaking intensely to a woman sitting next to him, for he was not the type to strike up conversations with people he did not know.

I was astonished when I realized the woman was Gisele.

I marched through the taproom without bothering to get out of the way of the scurrying servers. "What are *you* doing here?" I cried, standing behind Darius and pointing at Gisele.

She touched a coarse napkin to her mouth and gave me a limpid look. "Having breakfast," she said.

Dannette slipped into one of the two empty seats next to Darius. "You're the queen, aren't you? I saw you sitting by the king in the throne room."

"I'm married to the king, yes," Gisele replied with some bitterness.

"What are you *doing* here? Why are you *following* me?" I demanded.

Darius smiled at me over his shoulder. "Sit down and eat something," he said. "The oatmeal is very good if your stomach is queasy."

"Why should her stomach be queasy?" Gisele wanted to know.

"Too much beer last night," Dannette said, helping herself to one of the platters handed to her by a woman sitting toward the middle of the table. "Olivia, do you want any of this? It looks like apple fritters."

"Yes—I suppose," I said, flopping into the seat next to her

and still staring resentfully at Gisele. "You haven't answered me."

Harwin spoke up. "She says your father decided that Dannette would not be a sufficient chaperone. He did not know that I had come after you as well, or perhaps he would not have been so worried."

Gisele gave him a quick, droll look. "Exactly so."

I tried a bite of the fritters. They were excellent. When the woman to my right handed me a steaming bowl of oatmeal, I ladled out a lavish portion and passed the bowl to Dannette. "My father never worries about me," I said.

Gisele shrugged. I noticed that her clothes were very neat but not at all fancy, and her hairstyle was almost as plain as Dannette's. She looked as tired as I felt, but her eyes were not as puffy. "Perhaps now that you are about to be married, he is realizing how much he will miss you."

She was obviously lying. I narrowed my eyes and took a big mouthful of oatmeal. It had been seasoned with honey and raisins and tasted delicious. "So you plan to travel with us for the next week or two?" I asked slowly.

She nodded. "I know you do not like the notion, but—"

"Oh, we're happy to have you with us," Darius said. He sounded sincere; after two days in his company, I was pretty certain he was. "But I'm not sure how much more room there is in the wagon."

"And she brought a maid with her," Harwin said. He glanced at me as if to say, *And if you truly cared about your reputation, you would have brought a maid as well.*

"Well, it'll be a tight fit, but if one sits up front and three ride in back—"

"I have my own coach. And a coachman," Gisele interposed. "All I require is that you allow me to join your caravan."

I stopped with another spoonful of oatmeal on the way to my mouth. "The coach," I breathed. "It's yours. Oh, Gisele, I want to ride with *you*!"

* * *

"Tell me again how sitting inside the coach with me is helping you become better acquainted with your bridegroom," Gisele said twenty minutes later.

We were on our way again, a much augmented party from the one I'd started out with a couple of days ago. The coach, with its team of high-spirited horses, led the wagon by an appreciable distance. Harwin had cantered ahead of us but I was sure he would circle back soon to check on our progress. Gisele's maid was sitting outside with the coachman, probably flirting madly. Dannette rode with her brother. Everyone was happy.

"*You* tell *me* the real reason you came after me in this ridiculous fashion," I said. "I know it wasn't because my father asked you to."

There was a flare of malice in her eyes. "Oh, but he did," she said. "I could tell how pleased he was when he came up with the idea. Ever since Neville arrived, he's been trying to get me out of the way."

I was bewildered. "What does Neville have to do with it?"

"Nothing. His daughter Mellicia? Everything. Your father

is infatuated with that simpering, stupid, *soulless* girl. He wants to court her while I am not on hand to watch."

"But—what—I mean, you're his *wife*. I suppose he could take her as his mistress, but—"

"I am a wife who has failed to produce the son he is determined to have," Gisele said softly. "I will not be his wife much longer, I guarantee it."

I simply stared at her.

She met my gaze briefly, then looked out the window. The prospect was not particularly inviting. The treelined hills of the past two days had flattened into grasslands that supported grazing livestock, though the occasional stand of elm and oak shuddered in a brisk wind. The sky was scudding over with clouds, and the air had that damp, overburdened feel that promised a storm.

"So!" she said brightly. "If he's going to marry again, he needs to review the likely candidates. Naturally, she must be young enough to be fertile, and beautiful enough to catch his fancy. And by now he's realized that he doesn't like clever women—or, at least, he doesn't like *me*, and I'm clever—so vapidity has become an important attribute—"

It took me this long to find my voice. "Is he going to *divorce* you?"

She turned to look at me again. I had never seen her face so sad. Then again, I had never paid much attention to the emotions on Gisele's face. "I *hope* he is going to divorce me," she said.

"Why, if he wants to marry again, what else could he . . ."

My voice trailed off. "Surely you're not suggesting . . . I mean, I know he is not an admirable man, but . . ."

She looked out the window once more. "I have been wondering if I should take a ship to Newmirot," she said. "Dannette was describing it over breakfast. Surely your father would be so glad to be rid of me that he would just allow me to disappear, don't you think? And declare me dead, rather than killing me outright."

"*Gisele!* You can't be serious!"

"I'm quite serious. I should like to see Newmirot."

I reached across the open space between us and shook her by the shoulder. "You don't truly believe my father would have you murdered," I said. "Merely so he could marry again."

She met my eyes for one long, sober stare. "I don't know," she said at last. "Perhaps he wouldn't."

But perhaps he would.

I released her, took a deep breath, and leaned back against the cushions. I was on the seat facing backward, which I normally despised, but today I was so happy to be traveling in relative luxury that I didn't mind at all. "Can you go to your father?" I asked. "Would he take you in if you told him you were afraid for your life?"

She made an inelegant sound. "No."

"Do you have other relatives who would give you sanctuary?"

"A brother who is so much like my father that he could not be trusted. No one else."

"Do you have money? How long can you afford to travel

like this?" I gestured at the interior of the coach, with its silk-covered walls and leather-bound seats.

"Your father is footing the bill for this particular trip," she said. "The coach is his and I have his vouchers for any inn I patronize while I am with you. I believe he expects Neville and Mellicia to stay with him two weeks. After that—" She shrugged. "I have some money. I have all my jewels. I might be able to find work in Newmirot. They have quite a textile industry there, and I'm a good seamstress. I'll get by."

"I might be able to send you money," I said. "My allowance is generous enough."

"That's kind of you," she replied. "But don't forget what I said before."

I had to think a moment. She had warned me to be safely married before my father managed to get himself a son. At the time, I had scoffed at her, and I still had no proof that anything she said was true, and yet . . .

And yet I believed her. My father *was* the kind of man who would get rid of an inconvenience in the most efficient way possible. I remembered the piebald stallion that had been my father's favorite ride until the horse took a tumble that nearly snapped his right leg. The groom had thought the horse might be succored and saved, and certainly would be able to hobble around well enough to serve at stud, but my father had ordered the stallion destroyed. "If I can't ride him, I don't want him," he'd said. "He's of no use to me now." A wife who could not bear him a son was of no use to him.

Was a daughter of any use to him?

Particularly if he had a son?

"So you're not going back to the palace," I said.

"That's my plan."

I leaned forward, rested my elbow on my knee, and cupped my chin in my hand. After three years of trying to pretend Gisele did not exist, I found myself suddenly wanting to be her champion. I did not stop to puzzle over why it did not seem strange. "I wonder," I said. "Perhaps you can meet with an accident on the road. Harwin and I can bring back the sad news that you died while we were traveling."

Gisele looked amused—and a little intrigued. "But wouldn't you be expected to return with my corpse in tow?"

"Not if you—fell off a cliff and drowned, and the water carried you away," I said, improvising quickly. "Not if you were mauled by wolves and *eaten*."

"Oh, yes, do have me devoured by wild creatures."

"We could bring back your bloody clothes as proof," I said. "And maybe your wedding ring—with the finger still in it. Someone else's finger, of course, but no one else will know that."

"Where will you find such a thing?" She was trying not to laugh.

I waved a hand. "I don't know. Maybe we'll come across a fresh grave while we're traveling. Maybe Darius will manufacture one for us. He can change things from one shape to another, you know."

"Yes, so I had heard. Perhaps he will not like to use his magic in such a fashion, however."

"Oh, if he thinks you're being abused, he'll be happy to oblige. He's very softhearted."

She studied me a moment. "And perhaps Harwin will not like to lie to your father."

"He will if I ask him to," I said confidently.

"Well! You are quite fortunate in the men who attend you," she said. "How will you choose between them?"

Now I scowled at her, my sudden amity evaporating. "I have already chosen."

"So you have," she said and settled back against the cushions. She closed her eyes, as if she was too weary to keep them open any longer, and in a few moments, she was either asleep or pretending to be.

I looked out the window and watched the autumn trees shake off their red and yellow leaves as if they were dogs shaking off water. I saw the clouds overhead grow angrier and closer to the ground, reminding me of furious taskmasters bending down to berate a clumsy servant. I wondered if anything Gisele had told me was a lie.

I wondered how I could bear it if everything was true.

5

THE DREADFUL SECRET

We arrived in a prosperous little town just around sunset and followed Harwin to the inn he had recommended, having patronized it with his father. By this time, it had been raining steadily for two hours, and both Harwin and Darius were thoroughly soaked. So was the coachman, I imagined, but Gisele's maid had taken refuge inside the coach the minute the first drops started falling, and I had invited Dannette to join us as well. The four of us passed a rather pleasant afternoon playing cards with a dog-eared deck the maid had in her bag. She was a freckle-faced and friendly girl who didn't seem to understand her place, but I was too lazy to try to stare her down and Dannette wasn't the type to enforce class distinctions. I spent a few moments wondering how much we would have to bribe her to lie about Gisele's death before I realized that such a step wouldn't be necessary. This was a servant Gisele had brought with her when she married; this was a servant loyal to the queen. No doubt she would accompany Gisele as she set off for Newmirot or Amlertay. I felt a little better knowing Gisele would not be completely alone.

"I cannot tell you how grateful I am that you joined us when you did!" Dannette said to Gisele as we prepared to disembark in the courtyard of a *very* fancy inn, four stories high and faced with white marble. I started to glow with happiness just thinking about the luxuries awaiting us inside. "How lovely to sit in your coach on such an ugly day."

"I am glad that someone appreciates me," Gisele returned with a smile.

"Even *I* appreciate you today," I said, climbing out after the two of them. The maid clambered down behind me.

"Then I must call the journey a success," Gisele said.

I grinned at her and hurried in. Darius was still outside with the wagon, but Harwin had arrived ahead of us, and I could see he had already dealt with the proprietor. He stood near the front desk, a cluster of keys in his hand, and let water drip from his overcoat to the floor. Oh, *surely* in such a large hotel we would not all have to cram together in one room!

"The inn is quite full but I have bespoken three rooms," he said, pushing his wet hair from his eyes. "There are bunks in the servants' quarters for the coachman and the maid."

Dannette was glancing at the heavy tapestries on the wall, the brightly woven rug on the floor. "The place looks a little dear for Darius and me," she said quietly.

"I have paid for one room, and the queen's vouchers will cover the other two," Harwin replied, smiling down at her. "You will have a room to yourself for a change."

I mentally populated the remaining two rooms and instantly frowned. "Wait—you and Darius will share quarters, of course, but I should not have to sleep with Gisele," I said.

"And here I thought you had started to hate me a little less," Gisele remarked.

"It's just that—I can't *sleep* with other people in the room. I would so much like privacy, just for a night."

Harwin's frown was as heavy as mine. "Yet one of them must act as chaperone so that no one takes advantage of you in the night. If you do not want your stepmother, then Dannette must stay with you."

"Oh, let her have the room to herself," Dannette said. "You don't need to worry about Darius accosting her in the middle of the night, but even if he *did* have such plans, you'll be there to thwart him."

"Yes, Harwin, please, let me have the room."

Dannette laughed and patted me on the shoulder. "You don't have to plead with him. We'll just apportion the chambers as we like. He can hardly force us to rearrange to his taste unless he wants to bodily carry us from bed to bed."

Gisele and I both laughed at that, though Harwin looked embarrassed. "I am merely trying to make sure the princess is treated with the utmost care," he said.

Now Dannette patted him on the arm in the same friendly fashion. "And maybe you'll find that Olivia likes you better if you don't always make such a fuss," she said.

Darius swept through the front door, totally drenched and unrelentingly cheerful. His boots left wet footprints all the way down the hall. "Isn't this fit for royalty!" he exclaimed. "I've never stayed at a place so elegant! I like traveling with the queen."

"Harwin chose it," Gisele said with a laugh. "Not I."

Darius rubbed his hands together to warm them. "Then I like traveling with Harwin! Who's hungry? I imagine the dinner here must be outstanding."

* * *

The meal was excellent—and Harwin paid for everyone's dinner, not even bothering to use Gisele's vouchers. I know, because I saw him do it. My room was splendid, heavenly, regal, *private*, and I even took a real bath in a hammered tin tub. I tumbled into bed and lay in the middle of the mattress, stretching my arms and legs as wide as they would go. I had peeked inside the other two rooms, so I knew that Gisele and Dannette had to share a bed, but Darius and Harwin each had his own. I imagined this would be the best night of sleep any of us had managed so far.

The morning brought sunshine and clear skies and all of us smiling at one another around the breakfast table. "I want to ride with Darius today," I said, for Gisele had been right yesterday. Sitting in the coach with her was not doing much to acquaint me with my betrothed. "Dannette, you can ride with Gisele. It's much more comfortable than the back of the wagon."

"I'm happy to do so, unless the queen prefers solitude."

"The queen prefers any company that is good-natured," Gisele retorted.

"Then Dannette is the one you want," Darius said with a nod. "There's not a mean bone in her body."

Scandals. Accusations in the dead of night. They must not have been crafted from cruelty, then. "Then we're all satisfied," I said. "Let's go."

Harwin was not satisfied, I could tell by his expression, but soon enough we were on our way. As before, Harwin took the lead on his bay gelding, followed by the carriage, followed by the wagon. After yesterday's extraordinarily comfortable coach ride, travel in the wagon was even more torturous, but I was determined not to complain.

"How much farther to your grandmother's house?" I asked as we set out.

"About a day and a half."

"Have you sent her a note? Is she expecting us?"

He laughed. "She knows that I might drop in on her at any time, so in some sense she is always expecting me, but she will be quite astonished to see *you*."

I smiled. "She didn't think you would marry a princess?"

He rubbed the back of his hand along his jaw. "She didn't think I would ever marry," he said. "I have never been particularly interested in the notion."

"Oh, with your blond curls and your handsome face, you must have had girls falling for you wherever you went," I teased.

He laughed. "I didn't say I wasn't interested in *women*,"

he corrected. "It's all the things that belong to *marriage* that haven't appealed to me."

I was a little deflated at that. "What don't you like about it?" I said.

"I'm not very good at staying in one place," he explained. "Even after a couple of nights, I'm itching to move on. The wagon broke down once just as I was leaving a small town, and it took a week to get it fixed. By that third day, I felt like I'd been shackled in a dungeon for a year. No sunlight, no fresh air. It was an awful time."

"But, Darius," I said. "Once I'm queen, I'll need to stay at the palace, conferring with councilors and—well—ruling the kingdom."

"Yes, but not *all* the time," he said eagerly. "Wouldn't your subjects like it if you traveled around the country, meeting them in the towns and villages where they live?" He fluttered a hand over his shoulder. "We'd travel in something much finer than *this*, of course. We'd have a carriage like your stepmother's, and we could travel for weeks."

I thought it sounded both exhausting and impractical, but I didn't like to say so outright. Surely once we were married, Darius would see that he would have to give up parts of his old life. He would see how many responsibilities he must assume once he was king. "Well—that does sound delightful. I'm sure I would enjoy getting to know my subjects that way," I said, and was rewarded with Darius's blinding smile. "Perhaps we can take a honeymoon trip all around the kingdom," I added. "People will line up in every small town to greet us—"

But he was shaking his head. "No, no, for our honeymoon we should go to Liston and tour the diamond mines," he said. "You can pick the very stone you want from the bones of the land itself, and I'll chip it out for you and polish it by hand."

I yielded to a moment's worth of romance at the picture, but then— "Isn't Liston very far away?" I asked.

"Two thousand miles," he said with a nod. "Depending on the weather through Amlertay, the journey could take six months each way."

"But I can't be gone for a year!"

He looked surprised. "Why not?"

"I have to be ready to rule if something should happen to my father!"

"He looks pretty healthy to me."

"Even so! He could fall off a horse—or be felled by an assassin—or devoured by wolves—"

"Wolves? At the palace? His fighting dogs, maybe, but not wolves."

Perhaps I was too enamored of the idea of someone getting eaten by wild animals. "The point isn't *how* he might die. The point is that if something happens to him, I must be available. We must stay within the kingdom for our honeymoon, I'm afraid."

He was silent for a moment, something so rare for Darius that I feared he was angry. I was relieved when, finally speaking, he sounded disappointed instead. "Maybe I should go to Liston by myself one last time before we get married."

Now I was bewildered. "But that would mean we wouldn't be able to marry for at least a year. And I wouldn't see you that whole time."

He nodded. "I know. But I can't bear the thought that I'll never see Liston again."

"Surely you will," I said, having no real idea how to answer that. "Surely we will work it all out."

At that I, too, lapsed into silence. We watched the road ahead of us, lost in our own thoughts, and I imagined we were thinking about two very different futures.

* * *

By noon, the autumn sun was warm enough to make us forget we'd ever been chilly, all of us were hungry, some of us were cranky, and one of Darius's horses had thrown a shoe. Fortunately, we had arrived at a good-sized town with a central square that offered everything we needed at that exact moment: a blacksmith, a butcher shop, and a chance to switch passengers around. There was even a modest fountain in the center of town where Dannette declared she was going to sit so she could splash her face and cool her feet.

"How very common," Gisele said with a laugh.

Dannette had already perched on the edge of the basin and trailed her fingers in the water. She laughed back. "I never pretended to be quality," she replied.

We had left Darius, the coachman, and all the vehicles at the blacksmith's shop. Harwin was eyeing the butcher's storefront, where a sign promised fresh meat, smoked meat, and meat pies. "I will undertake to purchase our luncheon if you ladies would like to stay here," he said, glancing down at Dannette. He added, "Amusing yourselves."

I had spotted lengths of fabric and ribbon in another

storefront. "Ooh, let's go look at pretty things," I said to Gisele, tugging her in that direction. "I don't have any money, so you'll have to buy me anything I like."

She followed willingly enough, her maid at her heels, but said, "I thought you were worried about my finances?"

"Oh. That's right. Well, we'll just look at things and feel sad that we can't purchase them."

The shop was small and crowded, with bolts of fabric piled up in no discernible fashion and knots of ribbon covering the walls like the most chaotic and jubilant pattern of wallpaper. Women that I assumed to be the shopkeeper and her daughters darted among the seven or eight customers who were probably the high-ranking gentry of this county. Gisele and I looked bedraggled enough that I was glad we were both plainly dressed; I wouldn't have wanted anyone to recognize me at this juncture. But, aside from giving us speculative glances because we were clearly strangers, no one seemed to notice us.

I strolled between aisles, rubbing the velvet between my fingers and letting the silk pour through my hands like falling water. "Look at this blue," I said to Gisele as I unwrapped a few inches of a cobalt-colored wool. "Wouldn't I like a cape made of this!"

She had been right behind me up till this point, but somehow I had lost her attention. "Olivia," she said, staring out the window. "Someone's approached Dannette, and she looks afraid."

That brought me right across the shop so I, too, could peer outside and see that two men had accosted Dannette. It was clear she had made good her promise to cool off in the fountain, because the front of her dress was spattered with water and her shoes lay on the ground. One of the men had hold of her shoulder, the other was leaning down and shouting in her face, and Gisele was right: She looked afraid.

"Where's her brother?" I demanded as I charged for the door.

Gisele grabbed my arm. "You can't endanger yourself—Olivia, you are too valuable to go brawling—"

I gave her one incredulous look, broke free, and raced outside. Behind me I heard the rising murmur of women's excited voices, and the sound of Gisele's footsteps as she followed. "Get Darius!" I called over my shoulder.

But that wasn't necessary.

I didn't see where he came from, but suddenly Harwin was on the scene, crashing into the interlopers and sending one cartwheeling to the ground. Gisele caught me from behind and held me in place, while her maid grabbed one of my arms. Nonetheless, we were close enough to hear the other man's oath as he whirled around to confront his assailant. Harwin already had a sword drawn and a look of menace on his face. He appeared to have shoved Dannette into the fountain to get her out of the way, for she was splashing around in the water, dripping from head to toe.

"Step away! Leave this young woman in peace!" Harwin thundered.

"You wouldn't be defending her if you knew what kind of soiled goods she was!" shouted the man who had been knocked to the ground. Unfortunately, he was now on his feet.

"I would defend any woman, no matter how debased, from someone as contemptible as you," Harwin snarled in reply.

I had to admit, that surprised me a little. That he would say such a thing, and about a woman he scarcely knew—and that his size, posture, and attitude indicated he would be able to make good his boast.

"Would you?" sneered the other man, and then he leaned in to hiss some kind of accusation in Harwin's ear. I noticed that Dannette, floundering about with her wet skirts, suddenly grew very still.

Whatever he said didn't impress Harwin unduly. With his free hand, he shoved the man hard in the chest, knocking him into his unsavory companion. "Leave her in peace," he said. "*Now*, unless you truly want to contest her virtue against my sword."

The two men growled a few more insults but slouched away, glancing back over their shoulders twice. Half turned to watch them leave, Harwin extended his free hand to Dannette to help her out of the fountain. I shook off my captors and ran over to Harwin just as Darius came racing up from the stables. In a moment, we were all huddled together around Dannette, and Darius was stripping off his jacket to put it around her shivering shoulders. Only then did I realize that we had gathered a small audience of townspeople, standing in the corners of the square and peering out from the surrounding storefronts. All of my companions ignored them, so I did, too.

"What happened? Who were those men?" Darius demanded.

Dannette gave him one despairing look. It was an unfamiliar expression to see on a face that was usually so merry. "They were from Borside," she said.

It was a town toward the western edge of the kingdom. I supposed it couldn't be far from where we were now.

"They recognized me," she went on in a halting voice, "and they said things—"

Darius looked around in swift fury. "Where did they go? I'll turn them both into toads."

"No!" she cried, and grabbed his arm. "Harwin was here to defend me, and I don't want to cause any more uproar. Let's just go."

His arm still in Danette's grip, Darius gave Harwin a stiff little bow. "If there was ever a debt between us, it is canceled now," he said with unwonted formality. "Thank you for coming to my sister's aid."

Harwin shrugged. "Any man would have done the same. This erases no imbalance between us."

"To me it does," Darius said.

"Let us discuss who owes whom at some later date in more privacy," Gisele interposed. "Come. Let's gather all our conveyances and go."

Darius was unwilling to be separated from Dannette, and I did not want to intrude on her unhappiness, so we completely redistributed ourselves. We swathed Dannette in a cloak and bundled her into the coach, Darius beside her. Harwin parceled out the meat pies he had just bought for all of us, then took the reins of the wagon. Gisele rode Harwin's horse.

I sat beside Harwin, getting to know the wrong potential bridegroom.

But I didn't mind because I was dying to ask him a few questions.

"How do you know how to drive a wagon?" were the first words out of my mouth.

He was negotiating around a narrow turn, the last little kink in the road before we were able to leave this benighted town behind, but he had attention to spare to cast me a sardonic look. "Why wouldn't I be able to? It's no harder than driving a team, and you know I keep my own stables."

"Well—but—I never thought about it," I said.

"Imagine how surprised I am," he said dryly.

I bounced a little on the hard seat. "What did those men say to you?" I demanded. "Did they tell you whatever Dannette's dreadful secret is?"

"I suppose."

"What is it? Tell me."

He gave me another look, this one considering and troubled. "I'm not sure it's my place to repeat it."

"Are you going to make me ask her?"

He thought it over and then, in a voice completely devoid of emotion, he said, "It seems that when she lived in Borside, Dannette was found in a compromising situation—with another woman. There was a scandal because the girl was the daughter of a prominent local lord. Apparently this was not the first time Dannette had been known to take women as intimate companions."

It took me a moment to comprehend exactly what he meant with his delicate phrasing. Then I said, "So? She prefers women. Who cares?"

I could tell I had surprised him, but I didn't know why. "You seem singularly free of shock," he said. "You live a life so sheltered that I would have thought you would find the concept hard to grasp and perhaps revolting."

I shrugged. "My father's apothecary and her assistant have been sharing quarters since I was born," I said. "And there are days I like them better than anyone else at the palace. But I don't see why anyone would care—me or you or those men who assaulted Dannette or *anybody.*"

"No," Harwin said, clucking to the horses to encourage them to improve their speed, if only a little, "neither do I."

"I would have thought *you* would be even more conventional than *I* am," I said. "And yet, you don't seem offended."

He considered a moment. I had always found it irritating that he often paused to think over his replies, but now I found myself respecting his unwillingness to give an easy or incomplete answer. "I have seen too much damage caused by individuals who were certain that theirs were the only ideas with merit," he said at last. "It has engendered in me a passionate desire to extend tolerance to anyone who does not seem to be harming anyone else by his or her actions. I am not always quick to adopt new or unfamiliar behaviors—but I am slow to condemn them."

I sat back against the bench. "But that's admirable!" I exclaimed. "Why do you say it so apologetically?"

I thought I caught the faintest trace of humor on his face. "Perhaps because you dislike so many of my opinions that I always feel apologetic when I am talking to you."

I felt a hot blush spread over my face. "No—not that—well—I think perhaps I have not always extended tolerance to *you,*" I said in a rush.

"You think me dull and lumpish, and you think that being married to me would seem like a lifetime sentence in prison," he said calmly.

"No!" I exclaimed, feeling even worse. Because of course he was exactly right—except it didn't seem quite so true as it once had. "It's just that—perhaps I am silly and shallow, as Gisele has said—"

"But you're twenty-one and you think life should offer a little excitement and romance," he said, nodding as if that was a perfectly legitimate expectation. "And I do not seem to embody those traits."

I didn't know how to answer that, so I unwrapped my meat pie and took the first bite. Neither of us made the obvious remark. *Darius embodies both those traits, and quite beautifully, too.*

"Well," Harwin said, clucking at the horses one more time, "perhaps this trip will give you as much excitement and romance as you can handle, and then you might assess how much of it you really want in your life."

I thought he was probably right on both counts.

* * *

We didn't stop again until nearly nightfall, when Gisele circled back for us on Harwin's horse. We had long ago lost sight of the faster carriage, but Gisele had moved between the two vehicles a couple of times during the afternoon. By the pleased expression on her face, I could tell she relished the freedom of riding in the open air.

"Darius has found an inn for the night. It's not very big, so there might not be three open bedrooms—but he's reserved a private dining room," she told us. The chill afternoon wind had whipped color into her face and she looked very pretty. I wondered how my father could prefer Mellicia to Gisele. "I think he doesn't want to expose Dannette to any more chance travelers who might recognize her."

Harwin glanced around. We were in farm country now, and no mistake. Stretching in every direction for limitless miles were flat, brown fields filled with the dying clutter of harvested crops. "Might there be many people here who know her?"

Gisele nodded. "His grandmother's house is half a day's ride away, he says."

"I thought he couldn't afford a private dining room," I piped up.

Gisele looked genuinely amused. "I think he's found a way to pay for it."

Indeed, twenty minutes later, after we'd found the quaint little inn, turned our horses over to the grooms, and strolled inside, we found Darius in the taproom performing tricks. He turned one man's hound into a tomcat and then changed it back. He passed his fingers over a woman's dull gray hair and made it a vibrant gold, not neglecting to make her eyebrows match. He waved his hand over the back wall of the taproom, and it ran with vivid autumn colors, cranberry, then ochre, then frosted pumpkin. The patrons were murmuring their delight, while the proprietor stood behind his bar, nodding and smiling. It certainly looked like a performance that merited some remuneration in return.

"The servants are already settled in the kitchen, but we're down this way," Gisele said, leading us through a narrow hallway to a small, smoky room. The ceilings were low and the paneling was so dark as to create an air of foreboding, but the prospect of a private meal among the five of us made the room seem welcoming and warm. Dannette was pacing between the table and the far wall, a matter of about six steps, and she turned jerkily to face us as we stepped through the door.

Afraid of what Harwin might think of her, afraid of how much he had told me, afraid of how she might be judged.

I crossed the room to kiss her on the cheek. Then I took hold of both her shoulders and held her at arm's length to inspect her. The look on her face was one of profound relief, and she couldn't quite keep the tears from spilling over.

"You should have told me," I said. "All this time I was thinking how you might make the perfect wife for Harwin, and now I have to abandon those excellent plans."

She laughed a little too long at such a feeble joke, and it was clear she was still feeling shaky. She accepted Gisele's hug with melting gratitude, but continued to watch me over the queen's shoulder. "I don't know that I trust your judgment in matters of the heart so much that I would let you pick someone out for me," she said, attempting to tease in return.

"She is singularly blind to both good and bad qualities in other people," Harwin agreed. "But now and then she allows her natural intelligence to assert itself, so I don't quite despair of her."

I gave him a mock scowl, though I thought his assessment was fairly accurate. "I'm hungry," was all I said. "I hope Darius ordered food before he went off to astonish the masses with magic."

"I believe he did," Dannette said, wiping her eyes and attempting to restore herself to her usual state of sunny serenity. Just then the servants' door opened, and two scrawny young housemaids stepped in, bearing platters. "And here it is."

There was the usual jumble of scraping chairs and bumping bodies as the servants set the table and we found our seats. Gisele asked Harwin something about driving the wagon and he answered, while Dannette began pouring water into all our glasses.

And the whole time, I sat there determinedly keeping a smile on my face, while I felt as though my stomach had been opened up by a rough hand and scraped out with a jagged blade.

How could I feel so relieved at the notion that there was no chance Dannette might fall in love with Harwin?

* * *

Oddly, that mediocre dinner in the cramped room of a slightly run-down roadside inn was the most delightful evening I had spent with this group of travelers so far. I couldn't exactly tell why. Maybe it was because Dannette was so grateful to be relieved of the burden of her secret among people who did not think it was such a shameful thing. Maybe it was because surviving a threat brings you closer to anyone with whom you've shared it. Maybe it was because Darius was in high spirits, or I was, or Gisele was, for the three of us laughed a great deal, while the other two smiled at us benignly.

Maybe it was because, for no real reason that I understood, I suddenly had an overwhelming sense that each person in this room was in some way a dearest friend. Even Harwin. Even Gisele.

I didn't even mind that there were only two rooms available to the five of us. I made Gisele and Dannette share the bed while I piled pillows and blankets on the floor. A hard night's rest, but at least there was no thrashing bedmate to contend with.

Dannette's nightmares did wake me up once, sometime in the dead of night. It took me a moment to remember where I was and why I lay on such an uncomfortable bed. While I was working it out, I heard Gisele's voice, soft and comforting in the dark. *Everything is all right. You're safe here. You're with friends.*

And since that was true for me as well, I instantly fell back to sleep.

6

THE WISE OLD GRANDMOTHER

A half day's easy travel brought us to the house where Darius and Dannette had grown up, and where their grandmother still lived. It was a sturdy, well-built country manor of warm gray stone, with a flower garden out front, a small orchard to the left, a few outbuildings arrayed in back, and enough rambling bulk to make me guess there were about twenty rooms inside.

We were met at the door by two footmen and an aging butler, but we had barely crowded into the hall before the lady of the house swept up to greet us. She was thin and tall and dressed in the height of fashion, with artfully styled dark blond hair and a smile that made her look like her grandchildren.

"Darius," she said, putting her hands on either side of his face and inspecting him with great pleasure. "You look well."

"As do you," he replied. He kissed her cheek, put an arm

around her shoulder, and turned her to face the rest of us. "I've brought company, as you can see—and very exalted company, at that."

It seemed that it was only with some reluctance that she brought herself to look away from him. Though she extended her smile to us, I had the sense she wasn't interested in anyone except Darius. "Welcome," she said. "I am Arantha Kent. You must be the princess and the queen."

"How did you know?" Darius exclaimed. "I had thought to astonish you!"

Arantha made very correct curtsies to me and to Gisele, but she eyed me as if I were a horse she might buy and she wasn't sure I was up to her weight. "The news has spread throughout the kingdom about the king's competition for his daughter's hand," she said a little absently. She reached out a hand to rearrange the way my hair fell across my forehead. Frowning a little, she moved it back. "When the winner was described as a blond young man with a knack for magic, I knew it must be you."

"I hope you did not find the news overwhelming," Gisele said kindly. "Sometimes people are awed at the idea of marrying into a royal family."

But Arantha shook her head. Now she pursed her lips as she considered my gown, muddied and travel-stained. "I always believed Darius was destined for great things," she said. "I could hardly have hoped for better."

I heard a muffled laugh behind me, which was when I realized Dannette hadn't uttered a word since we walked in. Nor had her grandmother even bothered to acknowledge Dannette's presence with so much as a wave. Even now, Arantha didn't glance in her granddaughter's direction when she said, "I'll have the servants show you to your rooms. You must be starving. Luncheon will be on the table in an hour."

* * *

In contrast to the companionable dinner the night before, the first meal in Arantha Kent's house was formal, awkward, and just plain *odd*, although the food was superb. In defiance of traditional protocol, Arantha had seated Darius to her left and let the rest of us choose our own seats. Dannette had taken the place at the foot of the table—more to distance herself from her grandmother, I thought, than to stake her claim to some position in the family. Gisele had pulled up a chair between Darius and Dannette; I sat across from Gisele and next to Harwin.

Arantha spoke to no one but Darius for the entire meal.

They discussed matters pertaining to the property itself—crops and taxes and a drainage problem in the lower acres—but that took up very little of their conversation. Mostly Darius filled her in on his recent adventures, which required a great deal of laughing and gesturing. She hung on his every word, rarely even noticing what she might be putting in her mouth. She was not a demonstrative woman, but the glow on her face as she watched him speak left no doubt that Darius was the center of her world.

And Dannette did not even have a place in it.

After about thirty minutes of keeping near silence, Gisele and Dannette and I began speaking to one another in low tones. "Does she dislike you because of your choices in life or because of your gender?" Gisele asked.

Dannette shrugged. "I'm not even sure she dislikes me. When Darius is not present, we have very civil conversations. She's never indicated that I wouldn't be welcome to make this place my home if I had nowhere else to go." She smiled mischievously. "Of course, that might be because Darius has made it plain that I would always be welcome here, and she would never do anything counter to Darius's wishes."

Harwin scooted his chair down to join our discussion, since it was clear otherwise he had no hope of conversation at all. "She seems to have done an admirable job of running the estate, but I wonder what she expects to happen to it once she passes on," he said in his serious way. "Since—from what I've observed of your brother—he does not seem ready to settle down and farm."

Gisele gave me one quick glance, hard to interpret. "And he will soon be living in the palace with Olivia," she said.

Harwin's look was even harder to interpret. "Of course," he said.

Dannette shrugged again. "She is certain Darius will choose the right course, so she does not worry," she said.

"*You* could take over on your brother's behalf," Harwin suggested. "You possess great intelligence and a steadiness of purpose that seems to exceed your brother's." When all three of us giggled, he added hastily, "I meant no disrespect to Darius."

"It has occurred to me," Dannette admitted. "I am not sure it has occurred to Darius. And I do not believe the thought has crossed my grandmother's mind."

Servants brought in a new course, which ended that topic,

and we did not get back to it for the rest of the meal. Gisele and Dannette had fallen into a discussion about clothing, so I took pity on Harwin and asked him a few desultory questions about his family estates, which I knew he was very proud of. I can't say I was excited to learn about his successes with a new breed of pigs, but I was impressed by the depth of knowledge he had about every aspect of the land that one day would be his.

I didn't know half so much about my *own* inheritance, the entire kingdom that would one day be mine if Gisele never bore my father a son.

Or if Mellicia never did.

I swallowed and glanced at Gisele. Since that first conversation in the coach, we had never again discussed the danger she was in. I turned to Harwin and asked in an abrupt undervoice, "Do you like Gisele?"

He watched me a moment with narrowed eyes as if trying to discern the question that lay under the question. "I do," he said at last. "We have similar sober natures, and I have from time to time served as her confidante."

Then he might know the answer to the next question. "Do you think my father wants her dead?"

He took even longer to answer this time. His eyes went briefly to Gisele and then back to me. "I think your father feels she has failed him in the singular duty for which he selected her."

"She hasn't given him a son."

"Precisely."

"She thinks he wants to get rid of her so he can marry Sir Neville's daughter and *she'll* have a son."

His face didn't change; this was not a new idea to him. "I'm not certain your father's ruthlessness is so extreme," he said. "But possibly it is."

I took a deep breath. I had always disliked my father, but my reasons had been purely selfish. He was careless of *me.* Unkind to *me.* Uninterested in *my* wishes and desires. It hadn't occurred to me to notice how cruel he might be to others, and to despise him for it. "He's a bad father and obviously a bad husband," I said. "Is he a bad king as well?"

"He could have been better, he could have been worse," Harwin replied quietly. "He elevated favorites and seized lands from families that had held them for generations, but many kings do that. Ten years ago, he promoted skirmishes along the southern borders in a fruitless bid for territory, but it caused him to strengthen the army, and that might not be an entirely bad thing. Some of his taxes have been excessive. Some of his trade decisions have been disastrous. He has been open to bribes. He has been unfaithful to both of his queens. He has been an indifferent king, I suppose, but he has been a wretched man."

"You hate him," I said.

Harwin looked at me a long time. "He's only done one thing that I've ever completely approved of," he said.

He didn't specify, but I had no doubt what he meant. *He produced you as his daughter.* I felt my cheeks heat up, and I quickly turned my attention back to my plate of food. But I have to admit I was smiling.

* * *

Arantha and Darius disappeared after lunch, no doubt so she could show him estate accounts or rent rolls or other receipts. Dannette invited us to a small sitting room, where we all collapsed on a pair of dilapidated sofas. Warm afternoon sunlight poured in from the tall windows and made us all cheerful. It was the first time we'd relaxed since we'd walked into the house.

"This was always my favorite room," Dannette said. "Probably because I usually had it to myself. My grandmother was always in her office, and Darius was rarely even on the property."

"Where were your parents?" Gisele asked.

"They died when we were quite young. Darius remembers them better than I do, and he says they were very like the two of us—my father was improvident, kind, and full of magic, while my mother was practical, lighthearted, and curious."

"My sympathies, then, that you missed the opportunity to get to know them," Harwin said.

She smiled at him. "It is hard to regret something you never had," she said. "And we managed well enough without them."

I remembered my own mother quite clearly. When I was a child, she had seemed like a fairy princess, beautiful and glittering and magical. And, like a fairy princess, impossible to get close to, impossible to touch. I don't imagine I spent more than an hour a week with her for the whole of my existence. But I cried and cried after her funeral. I had been looking forward to the day I grew old enough for her to take notice of me. I had been so sure that once I was ten, or fifteen, or twenty-five, she would be interested in me, would find me fascinating and delightful. But I had not grown up fast enough. She had died before she could love me.

My father had married Gisele six months later.

I caught Harwin's quick look and knew he was remembering my tears at the funeral. He had tried so hard to comfort me, but I would not let him take my hand, or distract me with a story about a new litter of puppies, or even talk to me at all.

I wondered if it was too late to tell him how much I appreciated his effort.

Darius poked his head inside the door before any of us had replied to Dannette. "Oh, good, I was sure you would be here," he said, crossing the room to flop down beside his sister.

"Free so soon?" she teased. "I was sure we wouldn't see you again until tomorrow—if then."

"There was a crisis in the kitchen, and you know she doesn't like me to worry over small domestic trifles," he said with a grin. "So I made my escape."

"Is it always like that?" Gisele asked. "You so favored, Dannette so ignored?"

Dannette laughed but Darius looked embarrassed. "Yes," he said. "I don't know how to change her. Apparently she was the same way with my aunts. While my father lived, they were invisible. I think the situation was even worse because my father was the youngest of four, and she had wanted a boy for so long."

Gisele and I exchanged swift glances, and she spoke up in a quiet voice. "I believe a lot of people pin so many of their hopes on their sons that they have no energy or interest left for their daughters."

"Perhaps there would not be such emotional inequity if there were economic parity," Harwin said.

Dannette smiled at him. "I love to hear you speak, but I often have no idea what you're trying to say."

Gisele stirred. "I think he means that if women were allowed to inherit more property, parents would find it just as easy to love their daughters. But if they know their property most likely will fall into other hands if they only produce daughters, it is hard to feel much affection for a girl."

"Which makes me think that if I ever have children, I'm going to *try* to have a girl," I said, so fiercely that the rest of them laughed. "Well, I am."

"I would want a daughter also, if I were ever to have children—but—well—I'm not so sure—" Dannette began, and then floundered a little. This earned another laugh from the assembled group.

"I am *supposed* to be having a son," Gisele said with some astringency, "but so far I have not been fortunate enough to conceive at all."

She didn't say it like she was sorry for herself, but nevertheless I felt a certain amorphous dread in response to her words. If she bore a son, I was cut out of the succession. If she failed to bear a boy . . . she might well be dead.

Dannette nudged Darius with her foot. She had slipped off her shoes, and her toes were long and elegant. "What about you? Do you hope for boys or girls?"

Darius looked surprised. "Oh, I never thought much about it," he said. "I'm not sure I would be a good father. I might be very careless. It's probably better if I don't bother with children at all."

Gisele's voice was carefully neutral. "Of course, when you're living at the palace, there will be many servants on hand to care for your children, no matter how many you produce."

"Living at the palace?" Darius repeated, and then actually blushed. "Oh, right, right! Then, I say, why not have dozens? Boys *and* girls."

"Perhaps not dozens," I said. "If I am to bear them all."

Darius looked, for a moment, even more abashed, and then he offered me a smile of breathtaking sweetness. "Then we will have just as many as you desire," he said, reaching out to take my hand.

I wondered if I was the only one in the room who realized, at that moment, that Darius would never be my husband—or if I was the only one who had not realized it until right now.

Gisele made sure the silence did not become awkward. "And you?" she asked Harwin. "Have you given any thought to your own progeny?"

"I have," he said in his serious way. "I am certain I would welcome any child born to me and a wife I love. And if I am privileged enough to have a daughter, I will fight to give her the same advantages any son of mine might have, and I will not allow her to be placed in any situation that stifled or abused her."

"Now, there's the kind of man I wish my own father was," Gisele said with a sigh. "Or my own husband."

I had to admit, I was thinking the same thing.

Dannette poked Darius with her foot again. "So how long must we stay here to appease our grandmother?" she asked. "A day? A week? A month?"

He looked as if he hadn't given the matter a moment's

thought. "Must we stay? Don't you think we could leave in the morning?"

All of us cried out against that—not because we had any particular desire to linger, but because none of us, even Dannette, could bear the idea of depriving Arantha so soon of the joy of Darius's company.

"A week, then, I suppose," Darius said glumly. I wondered if it was the thought of staying put here, or merely of staying put, that made him despondent.

"And then what?" Harwin asked. "Would you travel on to visit nearby sights and cities? Or would you return straightaway to the palace and begin planning your nuptials?"

There was a small blank space of silence, and then, almost in unison, Darius and I said, "Travel on."

"We are not far from the coast," Dannette said to me. "If you've never seen the ocean, you will find some magnificent views."

"I would like to make my way to a harbor town," Gisele said. From the matching looks Harwin and Dannette wore, I knew both of them realized why Gisele was interested in such a destination.

But Darius hadn't noticed. He said, "My grandmother asked if we were planning to visit Kannerly, since we're so close."

Harwin and Gisele exchanged significant glances. "No," Gisele said tightly.

"What's Kannerly?" Dannette asked.

I was frowning. "One of my father's properties," I said. "He goes there three or four times a year."

Dannette looked at me. "But you've never been?" When I

shook my head, she transferred her thoughtful gaze to Gisele's face. "I wonder why."

"If you're to inherit the estate, shouldn't you at least know what it looks like?" Darius said.

"I don't think Olivia would find it a very—welcoming—place," Gisele said. She was still staring at Harwin, who wore an unreadable expression.

"She'll have to visit it sometime," he said.

If they were going to be all mysterious, I had better find out what secrets lay at the heart of Kannerly. "I say we should go there now," I said firmly. "Just as soon as we can get clear of here."

Gisele wrenched her gaze from Harwin and said, "Olivia, I truly do not think you will enjoy the journey."

"A princess has many duties she does not enjoy," I said loftily. "But that does not mean she should shy away from them. We'll go to Kannerly when we travel on."

7

THE CURSED DESTINATION

As it happened, we did not stay a full week at Arantha's house. All of us were restless by the end of the second day, and Darius himself was like a caged hunting cat who had been deprived of too many meals. I enjoyed the chance to sleep in private, bathe in luxury, and spend the days in idleness, but soon enough even I was longing to be on my way. So four days after we arrived, we packed our bags, bid our hostess farewell, and set out again.

Another day and a half of travel took us to Kannerly, where my life changed.

It was a smallish property, accessed off a narrow road devoid of any ornamental planting or fencing. In fact, the ground on either side of the drive was tangled with unkempt vegetation—low shrubs, tall weeds, and the occasional oak standing surprised and doleful on the overgrown land.

The manor house itself was squat and narrow, built of yellow stone that had molded over to black along the foundation. It was smaller than some of the outbuildings that fanned out behind it—what looked like a couple of enormous stables, constructed of weathered wood, and a few storage sheds. I saw three circular arenas, heavily fenced, and a huge pile of mounded debris. Something was giving off an unpleasant smell, heavy and meaty and foul, but I could catch only the occasional whiff as the wind shifted—and as we grew closer.

From some distance out we could catch the ceaseless cacophony of many dogs.

I happened to be riding in the wagon with Darius for this leg of the journey. I looked at him with a questioning expression that in no way mirrored the trepidation that had coiled in my stomach. I could not have said what, exactly, but something at Kannerly was very wrong.

Darius was looking about him with a small frown weighing down his cheerful features. "Strange sort of place," he said in a hesitant voice. "It feels—off—somehow, doesn't it?"

"It does," I agreed. "I don't like it."

Harwin had circled back and now wheeled his rangy bay up beside the wagon. "There will be guards at the entrance," he said. "I assume they'll recognize your stepmother."

"Harwin," I started, but he spurred forward to say something to Gisele through the coach's open window.

Another few minutes brought us to the gate, where four soldiers lounged, looking bored, though they all came to attention to inspect us. Gisele poked her head out and said in a colorless voice, "I have brought Princess Olivia and some companions to spend a day at Kannerly. We will travel on in the morning."

The guard who seemed to be in charge studied her face for a moment, then glanced at me. Unimpressed, he waved us toward the gate. "Pull on through," he said.

A footman and a butler awaited us on the exceedingly modest front porch, and two grooms raced up to take charge of the horses. The footman helped Gisele and Dannette out of the carriage, while the butler bowed to the queen.

"Majesty," he said with an inflection of surprise.

"An unexpected detour on an unexpected trip," Gisele said lightly. "Grayson, this is Princess Olivia, who has never had the honor of touring Kannerly. We will require five rooms for a night, dinner, and breakfast. We do not plan to stay past the morning meal."

"Very good, majesty," Grayson replied.

Just inside the door was a woman who looked less like a housekeeper and more like a tavern waitress, young and full-figured and sullen. She recognized Gisele, because she dropped an unwilling curtsy, but she neither knew nor cared who the rest of us were. In silence, we followed her through the house, which was clean enough, though not nearly to the proud standards of the palace. It was also rather bare—no portraits or tapestries on the walls, no rugs to soften the hard stone floors. I peered into a few rooms as we passed and saw nothing but dark leather furniture and heavy, blockish cabinets and tables.

The property seemed more like a hunting lodge than a family estate. The sort of place men would go without their womenfolk.

"Cozy," I heard Dannette murmur to Gisele, who smothered a laugh.

The bedroom I was assigned was utilitarian and chilly. I took advantage of the amenities and then stepped over to the window, hoping for a scenic view. But nothing so pretty awaited me, since my room looked out over one of the monstrous barns and an attached arena.

Through the still, sunny, autumn air, I caught again the sound of barking. A little more distinct from this vantage point, so that I could almost make out layers of sounds. High, fast yips of excitement or distress; low growls of warning; an occasional howl that made my skin prickle all the way down my spine. How many dogs *were* there at Kannerly? And why were they so agitated?

I intended to wait for Gisele and the others to get settled, so we could tour the grounds together, but curiosity and that growing uneasiness in my stomach shoved me out of my room. The housekeeper was nowhere to be seen, so I found my own way down the stairs and out the front door. The footman held it open for me, but made no attempt to stop me.

I supposed I could wander around Kannerly on my own and find out what made it so mysterious.

I hiked directly toward the nearest barn. With every step I took, the noise of the dogs grew louder and the stench from the mound of debris grew stronger. Other odors were also mixed in, the smells of dung and urine and wet fur, all of them so intense that I pulled a handkerchief out of a pocket and held it over my nose to ease my breathing. As I got closer, I could hear the sound of men calling to one another over the whining and baying of the dogs. Although no one had told me *not* to investigate the property, I instinctively shrank back against a side wall of the barn, not wanting to be seen. I waited until their voices faded away as they headed toward one of the other buildings, and then I looked around for an unobtrusive entrance. A small side door had been left conveniently ajar, so I kept in the shadows and slipped inside the barn.

For a moment I couldn't understand what I was seeing.

Partly that was because the lighting was poor, provided by a couple of murky skylights and a handful of oil lamps. Partly because the scene itself made no sense.

There were cages. Dozens of cages—crates—stacked on top of one another. Each one held a dog that barked and howled and whined and scraped its paws at the flooring as if trying to dig its way free. Some dogs were quite big—too big for their quarters—others were so small, and so thin, they looked as if they might squeeze out between the slats. They were all mangy and matted, covered with dried mud and what took me a few minutes to realize was old blood. Most of them sported a variety of half-healed wounds; more than one had had an ear partially torn off, or a nose slashed, or an eye clawed out. Several were missing limbs. There might have been more horrors, but I couldn't look long enough to find them. I pressed myself back against the wall, squeezing my eyes shut and still holding the handkerchief to my nose.

These were fighting dogs.

Kannerly was where my father bred and trained them.

The arenas must be where the handlers introduced them to the sport, after the animals had been beaten, starved, or whipped into a frenzy so they would attack on command.

My eyes still closed, I frowned. But the creatures in here were too thin and scrappy to last for long against the dogs in my father's kennels back home. I called up a memory of the last time I had seen those beasts in action—when they had been loosed on Harwin and Darius and my other suitors. All those animals were well kept, well muscled, well fed.

The ones here must be bait dogs—prey for the fighters no doubt kept in much better condition in the *other* barn. Once an animal was relegated to a cage in *this* building, its life expectancy must be very short. Which no doubt explained the odor of rot and decay seeping from the large mound at the back of the property.

I barely made it out the side door before I fell to my knees and vomited. And then all the mixed, dreadful smells of the property overcame me, and I vomited again. And again, and again, until there was nothing left in my stomach but bile.

When I pushed myself to my feet and turned to stumble back toward the house, I saw Harwin running across the lawn in my direction. He must have spotted me from the house and instantly come after me.

Which meant he had known exactly what I would discover when I went roaming through Kannerly.

I could not talk to him—I could not speak to anyone—I could hardly think. How could such cruelty exist in the world? I turned blindly away from the barn, away from the house, and blundered on in a random direction, hoping my path didn't take me past some fresh abomination. I had gone maybe twenty steps before Harwin caught up with me and took my arm.

"Olivia," he said, his voice both wretched and compassionate. "Olivia, please wait—"

I shook my arm free and then turned both of my hands into fists and beat at his chest. "You *knew*!" I sobbed, for it turned out I was weeping. "You brought me here and you *knew* what I would find! How *could* you? How could such a place *be*? How could you *bring* me here and let me *find* it—"

"Shh—shh—let me explain—I would never have let you out of my sight if I had realized you would start exploring—Olivia, *hush* a moment, be still—"

"I *can't* be still, I can't stop crying, and everything is too horrible, and it's all your fault," I wailed. I dropped to my knees and began crying even harder.

Harwin bent over, scooped me up, and, heedless of my flailing fists, carried me a good hundred yards before settling down on a narrow bench that appeared to be situated for no good reason in the middle of a desolate acre of lawn. From one of his pockets he pulled out a rather shriveled orange and handed it to me.

"Here. Peel that and eat a slice. You lost your lunch back there and your mouth must feel horrid. And don't say a word," he added, raising his voice when I began ranting again, "while you listen to what I say."

My hands were shaking so much I couldn't make the first gouge in the tough skin of the fruit. Harwin took it from me, teased back a small section, and returned it. My hands grew sticky with juice as I continued to work away at the rind. When

I crammed the first two sections in my mouth, I couldn't remember anything that had ever tasted so good.

"Your father brought Gisele here the day after they were married," Harwin said. "Told her to pick out a dog that she could call hers, and then proceeded to fight it in a few rounds, all of which it won. Her own father keeps a pack of fighting dogs, so she'd known how to choose a good one. She knew if she selected a weak animal, and it was killed in the first round, her marriage would be unbearable, because it was clear your father thought this particular exercise represented something about power. She said she cried herself to sleep every night they spent at Kannerly on that first visit, and then she never let herself cry again."

"How can someone do such awful things?" I burst out. "Because he's the king? Because he has money and power and he can always get his way?"

"There are people with much fewer resources who are just as brutal as your father," Harwin answered. "What makes a man enjoy someone else's pain? What makes him feast on violence? The answer is, I do not know. It is not just kings who are cruel. All sorts of people are unfair, unkind, or truly evil."

"You're not," I said.

He bowed his head. "I try not to be," he said.

"You don't own fighting dogs."

He shook his head.

"And you don't shout terrible names at people in the town square," I said, remembering the scene with Dannette at the fountain.

He half smiled. "And I don't beat my horses or starve my servants or kick beggars in the streets," he said humorously. "The list of my virtues is truly long."

"I mean it," I insisted. "You're a good man."

"I hope so," he said, serious again. And then, as if he added the words reluctantly, "And so is Darius. I find him—more frivolous than I might like, but I also find him completely devoid of malice. I think you might have chosen him for reasons other than his good heart, but I have discovered that it is the most impressive thing about him."

I didn't want to talk about Darius. I ate another section of the orange, then shut my eyes, but that just caused my mind to re-create the nightmarish scene in the barn. We were still close enough to hear the incessant howls and whimpers of the dogs, though the smell was not so strong here. I sighed and leaned my head back against the nearest support. That happened to be Harwin's arm, still wrapped around my shoulders.

"Why did you let me come to this dreadful place?" I whispered. "Why didn't you tell me no when I insisted?"

He was quiet a moment. "It's not my place to tell you yes or no," he said at last. "I will always offer you my counsel, but I will never tell you what to do." There was another pause before he went on, his voice even slower. "And, in this case, my counsel would have tallied with your inclination. If you are to be queen, you must know everything your country holds. You must know what your father has promoted and what his subjects have embraced. If you become queen, Kannerly will fall into your hands. What will you do then with this possession?"

"Tear it down," I said instantly. "Burn it to the ground."

"And the other estates that train such dogs?" he said. "And the men and women who profit from such activities?"

I opened my eyes and glared at him, but found I had no easy answer. If I indeed became queen, I would instantly outlaw the practice of raising fighting dogs. Of that I had no doubt. But folk who had run what formerly had been a legal enterprise would suddenly be without an income. What would my responsibility be to them? "I don't know," I snapped. "I'll figure something out."

A somber smile broke through the habitual gravity of his face. "Yes," he said, "I have faith that you will."

A sense of puzzlement settled over me; I felt my brows draw down in a frown. "I don't know why," I said.

"Why what?"

"Why you would have faith in me. I've never done anything particularly memorable."

His smile grew by the tiniest margin. "Oh, there I must disagree. You have managed—with great creativity and boundless stubbornness—to thwart your father at almost every turn for your entire life. He wanted you to be charming and empty-headed, but instead you became sharp-tongued and opinionated. He wanted you to be meek and biddable, but you would not make friends where he wished you to or court the nobles he asked you to. He wanted you to marry *me*, and we all know how that turned out. You have won every battle of wills with your father, and he is not an easy man to withstand. I imagine you will accomplish almost anything you set out to do, no matter how difficult. It will be an entertaining saga to watch."

Everything he said just made my frown blacker. "I sound like a terribly disagreeable person!" I exclaimed, sitting up straighter. I would have pulled myself away from him altogether except his hold tightened enough to keep me in place—and I did not try very hard to slip away. "Nothing to recommend me but a contrary disposition!"

"Yet fifty men showed up to strive for the honor when your father invited them to compete for your hand," he reminded me.

"They wanted to marry me because I'm a princess," I said glumly. "Perhaps one day to be queen." I risked one sidelong look at his face. "That's why *you* wanted to marry me, no doubt. A throne makes even a shrew seem attractive."

"I would have wanted to marry you if you were a beggar's daughter fighting for survival," he said quietly. "I will want to marry you if Gisele is right and your father manages to sire a son by some new bride. I am moved by your indomitable spirit, I am awed by your determination, and I am impressed by your intelligence."

He reached up his free hand to brush a stray lock of hair from my face. "And I remember always the lonely child you were, growing up in that unfriendly palace," he went on. "The expression on your face, when your mother would walk into a room—the hope you would show—the smile you would produce. And the look of abandonment you would wear when she turned aside without noticing you. I never saw anyone so willing to be loved and so surrounded by people who were not capable of such an emotion. I thought, '*I* will love her, if she will let me.'" He gave me a smile of such tenderness that for a moment I couldn't catch my breath. "All these years later, and that's still how I feel."

I wondered why he didn't kiss me, and then I thought perhaps it was not quite so pleasant to be kissing someone who had just been throwing up, no matter how many oranges she had eaten since then. I didn't have the right words to respond to his extraordinary speech, but I had to say something. "I don't think I will be marrying Darius after all," I said, speaking airily to cover my slight dizziness. "I feel rather bad about that, except I'm not so sure Darius wants to marry me, either."

"I think Darius likes you very much," Harwin said. "But I also think Darius would be relieved to learn he's not expected to take up the crown and scepter after all. He is not—shall we say—a man who flourishes in a lifestyle bound by conventions."

That made me laugh, but I tried to assume a thoughtful expression. "Still. I agreed to marry the man who proved his strength, valor, and intelligence by winning my father's three contests. I can hardly break my word now."

"May I remind you that I also succeeded at each one of those contests and that I am therefore a perfectly eligible bridegroom?" Harwin said. "I do not like to boast about myself, but I, too, am strong, courageous, and wise. You will be breaking no compact if you marry me instead."

"Well," I said. "I will think about it."

I expected him to come back with some kind of gallant reply—I mean, think of it! Harwin was actually *flirting*!—but suddenly I felt his muscles grow tense and I sensed that I had lost all his attention. I slewed around to see what he was staring at and saw a line of soldiers trotting in through the front gate.

Royal soldiers. Eight of them. Sporting my father's livery. The leader wore a closed, purposeful look, and all of them were armed as if for combat.

"Why are they here?" I asked in a fearful voice.

Harwin came swiftly to his feet, almost dumping me on the ground, though he kept a hand clamped around my arm to help me find my balance. "Gisele," he said.

We both took off running for the house.

* * *

The parlor was a scene of madness.

Soldiers milled in the cramped hallway outside the room, half of them with their swords drawn, three of them shouting. The slatternly housekeeper was shrieking and sobbing, but no one paid attention to her until one of the guards shoved her unceremoniously down the corridor, where she fell to her knees. Two of the soldiers were beating at the door to the parlor, as if trying to break down a heavy panel of wood, but there was nothing there except a block of shimmering, translucent air. Through this scrim I could spot bodies roiling inside the room—Darius, Dannette, Gisele, her maid, even the coachman—all of them holding makeshift weapons, all of them poised for battle.

Darius's weapon appeared to be the magic in his hands, with which he had created a shield across the open doorway, and none of the soldiers could breach it with their blades or their fists.

Behind me, I felt Harwin gather his strength as if to join

the fray. But he hadn't been wearing a sword when he came after me and I didn't know if he carried a dagger and I did *not* want him plowing through the mass of irate soldiers with only his rage to defend him. I drew a deep breath and demanded in my iciest voice, "*What* is going *on* here? Answer me, in the name of the king!"

That caused a big swell and commotion as the soldiers spun around to face me and my friends began shouting to me through the ensorcelled doorway. I held up a hand for silence and glared at the whole group.

"Quiet!" I shouted. "One of you—give me some answers! Why are you here?"

One of the guards pushed to the forefront—a man I knew, more's the luck. His name was Mackoby, and he had been at the palace since I was born. A bleak, hard, but honest man. "Princess Olivia," he said, his voice raspy. "Your father has sent troops out across the land, looking for the queen. We got word that she arrived at Kannerly this afternoon." He gestured toward the doorway. "And you see we have found her."

I kept both my expression and my tone glacial. "And why are you so interested in Gisele's whereabouts?"

"She has practiced treason and must be brought to justice," Mackoby said.

"I did *not*!" Gisele retorted furiously. "What treason? What is the charge?"

I didn't look at her. "The queen asks a legitimate question," I said. "What is her exact offense?"

Mackoby stood to stiff attention. "It was not my place to

know that," he said. "But she knew she did wrong, because she stole jewels and money from the palace and she ran away."

"I stole nothing! I only took what was mine!"

I was thinking very fast. Everything depended on the soldiers' orders. Gisele was convinced my father meant to kill her. It would be simpler to do that several hundred miles from the palace walls with very few witnesses. But a public condemnation might earn my father sympathy for an execution, once he manufactured evidence of Gisele's crime. That was the question. Did he want her back at the palace alive or dead?

"Those are serious accusations," I said. "What is my father's plan for the queen once she is back in his custody?"

"Olivia!" Gisele cried, but I continued to ignore her. I could not make it appear as though I were her ally, or I would lose any leverage I had with the soldiers.

"He spoke of a trial to produce proof of her wrongdoing," Mackoby said.

I gave him my sternest look, one of the regal stares I have cultivated over the years. "If I allow you to take her now, will you swear that she will come to no harm in your custody?"

Mackoby looked insulted. "Princess! My orders are to return her to the palace with all speed. During our journey, I will defend her with my life."

I pretended to deliberate. Behind me, I felt Harwin standing mutely, a strong, supportive presence. *He* certainly would understand that I was playing a role. *He* certainly would know that I was straining my wits to think of a way to save Gisele, not betray her. But those others inside the enchanted parlor—oh,

I could tell they were all shocked and horrified by my sudden treachery.

"I will allow you to take her," I said, "but I insist on accompanying you. All of us will come," I added. "My betrothed and all my companions." I let everyone in the hallway determine who they thought my betrothed might be. I was fairly certain not everyone guessed correctly.

Mackoby spoke stiffly. "We cannot breach the door. Magic blocks our way."

"Darius will remove his spell," I said, "once he is convinced the queen will suffer no harm at your hands."

"I swear it," Mackoby said, "and I offer surety for my men."

I finally faced the parlor again, letting my gaze rest on each occupant in turn, trying to convey a silent message first to Gisele, then to Darius, then Dannette. I don't know; maybe Harwin, behind me, was adding his own unspoken reassurance. But Gisele's face smoothed out, and she nodded infinitesimally, and Darius let the golden screen evaporate. Mackoby stepped across the threshold and took the queen's arm in a firm hold.

"We leave as soon as you are all ready to travel," he said.

"We need no more than a few minutes," I said.

So, as it happened, I did not spend even a single night at Kannerly. Not that I minded. I had learned everything I needed to know in the few short hours I had been on its tainted acres.

8

THE CRUEL FATHER

We made the journey back to the palace in half the time our outbound trip had taken. Mackoby had conjured a second carriage and a handsome team of horses from the Kannerly stables, so I traveled in comfort, if you discounted the high level of anxiety. Even Darius had been outfitted with another pair of horses, so that the wagon kept up with the rest of the party. Not that I was allowed to speak to Darius, or Dannette, or Gisele, or even Harwin. Mackoby didn't trust me, and in order to keep us from plotting Gisele's escape, he kept me segregated from everyone in my party.

Except Gisele's maid. Who ever notices the servants? She came to me every morning to help me dress and carried messages from me to Gisele and the others. We formulated a hasty and desperate plan, but none of us had any idea if it would work.

We arrived at the palace close to midnight on our third day of travel. I was kept locked inside my own carriage until Gisele had been escorted inside under heavy guard. When I tumbled out the door, I looked around wildly. Dannette and Darius were being ushered inside—by servants, not soldiers, so they were probably safe—and Harwin, still on horseback, was being crowded back toward the courtyard exit.

"Don't leave me!" I called in a sudden panic.

He pulled on the reins to bring his horse around. "If they make me go, I will be back in the morning!" he shouted.

We had no more time to speak, for footmen were on either side of me, urging me toward the door. The minute I stepped inside, I let all pretense of cooperation fall away. "Take me to my father," I said in my haughty-princess voice.

The steward, who had overseen this whole debarkation, said smoothly, "Princess, the hour is late, and the king is no doubt sleeping."

"The king has no doubt been wakened with the news that his queen has been returned," I said coldly. "Take. Me. To. Him."

The steward hesitated a moment, then bowed. "Highness," he said, and led the way.

My father was indeed awake, wearing a gaudy purple dressing gown, drinking a glass of wine, and conferring with Sir Neville. The minute I stepped into the room, I asked a single bald question. "What are your plans for Gisele?"

He rose to his feet and eyed me with disfavor. I was reminded of the fact that he was a rather small man. Not nearly as tall as Harwin, for instance, and I myself was almost exactly his height. "I see you are back from your trip with your betrothed," he said. "I trust you have grown well enough acquainted to consent to a hasty wedding."

"Yes, I feel certain I will want to marry soon," I said. "What are your plans for Gisele?"

"Why would you care?" he said. "You have never had any interest in her fate before."

"I am always interested in the affairs of the kingdom, Father," I said in an edged voice. "The soldiers said she will be tried for treason. I would like to see how such a trial is carried out."

Sir Neville spoke up in his gruff voice. "Your father will convene three trusted lords to sit in while he reads off evidence of her crimes. If we agree that she has committed the acts she has been charged with, she will be convicted and punished."

"Traitors are executed," I said.

My father nodded. "They are. And she will be, if she is found guilty."

So it was true. Gisele had not lied. He planned to kill her and then marry Sir Neville's stupid, scheming daughter. It was not a surprise, but somehow the news caught me like a blow.

What good sense I had always shown by hating my father.

"I want to watch the trial," I said.

My father looked annoyed, but shrugged impatiently. "Fine. We will meet in the morning. Sir Norbert and Sir Milton have agreed to be ready at such short notice."

"I will bring my betrothed with me," I said. "And his sister."

My father flung his hands in the air. "Shall you invite the cooks and the grooms as well?"

"It'll be like a damned fair," Neville snorted.

I made a show of hesitating, and then I said in an uncertain tone, "We all traveled with her for the past week, you know. She said some things—they might be useful to you—all of us heard her."

Now my father's eyes sharpened. "Did she, the little bitch? Then, yes, you may bring them both, if they are willing to testify."

I was not feeling civil enough to curtsy, but I did nod my head in acknowledgment. I could only imagine how unkempt my hair looked, how ratty and wrinkled my clothing. But I fancied I still managed to make the nod look stately. "We will join you in the morning."

* * *

Smoky oil lamps and sputtering candelabra provided suitably gloomy lighting in the throne room the next day as we gathered for Gisele's trial. My father sat on his engraved chair while Norbert, Neville, and Harwin's father, Sir Milton, settled in more ordinary chairs beside him. Sir Milton was a big man, as brown as his son, and even more serious and less inclined to idle conversation. It was no surprise that he was frowning.

Gisele stood meekly before the four of them, plainly dressed, head bowed, silent; a heavily armed soldier was in place beside her. Darius, Dannette, Harwin, and I had been relegated to uncomfortable benches at a slight angle to the dais. My father hadn't seemed to notice that I'd augmented my party by one. No one else was present, though two more soldiers watched the door.

It was clear my father wanted to get through this charade as quickly as possible. "Gisele, queen of Kallenore, you have been charged with crimes against the throne," he rattled off. "If you are found guilty of them, you will be put to death."

"I would hear the list of my sins, majesty," Gisele said quietly.

My father consulted a piece of paper. "You stole jewelry cases filled with three diamond necklaces, a complete set of emeralds, a complete set of rubies, and a total of fifteen rings. You also ransacked the royal safe for three bags of gold and a bag of silver. In addition, you took a royal seal with which you could forge my orders. How do you plead?"

I came to my feet. "Guilty," I said.

My father sent me an irascible look. "You—what? Sit down, Olivia. I'm speaking to the queen."

"Gisele did not take the jewels and coins," I said, looking at my feet and mumbling a little. "*I* did. I've never traveled from the palace without your protection before, and I was afraid. I thought if I had money, I could buy my way out of any trouble."

The look on my father's face was indescribable. Norbert said in a fair voice, "Well, she makes a good point. Money *will* make almost any problem go away."

Neville peered at me in some uneasiness. "So you're saying—*you* took the goods? Not the queen?"

"I swear it."

Sir Milton was frowning again. "Then that accusation must be struck."

My father looked ready to burst into flames, he was so

angry. "There are other charges," he bit out. He rustled the paper again. "You sent messages to the envoy from Amlertay and arranged to meet with him to share secrets about Kallenore defenses. You sent similar messages to the envoy from Newmirot."

Still on my feet, I turned to give Darius a wide, wondering stare. "Darius," I breathed. "You told me you were talking to those men about trade goods. Not *state secrets*."

A very satisfying tumult ensued. Darius leapt up and cried, "We *were* discussing trade! Nothing more!" while Norbert and Neville and Milton all talked at once, very loudly. It took my father's roar of "*Silence*! All of you!" before the room subsided into anything like quiet.

"It appears she is not guilty of this crime, either," Norbert said, his round, red face puffing up with disapproval. "If she has done nothing truly heinous, I do not think—"

"Perhaps this will strike you as a significant enough betrayal," my father snarled. "While she traveled with my daughter, she took a lover into her bed. Two innkeepers will testify they saw a second person entering and leaving her room. She sought to bear a bastard to the throne—to make a cuckold of the king and disinherit his true daughter."

"That's very bad," Neville said eagerly.

It was—extremely bad. Harwin had been the one who guessed what the first two charges would be, so we had crafted defenses that might be far-fetched, but difficult to disprove. But it had not occurred to any of us that Gisele would be cited for infidelity, a crime that had sent more than one queen to her death before this.

"Yes," Harwin's father intoned, "that is a serious and treasonable offense."

Norbert added, "A grievous accusation."

"And completely untrue."

Everyone turned to gape at the person who had just spoken. Dannette, rising gracefully to her feet to stand between her brother and me. She continued. "It was *I* they saw coming and going from the queen's chambers, for we indeed shared a bed upon the journey. You may ask my brother—my grandmother—anyone who is acquainted with me. Everyone knows that all my lovers have been women. The queen is only my latest paramour."

Now everyone was staring. My father looked flummoxed, but Neville and Norbert appeared to be intrigued, in a nasty, lascivious way. Even Gisele had turned to give Dannette a sidelong look over her shoulder—and I swear the queen was wearing a small, private smile.

It occurred to me with a sort of blank shock that this might be the only defense of the day that was actually true.

Harwin's father gave a dry chuckle. "Well, Reginald, if that's your queen's lover, you might not like it, but there's no chance she'll be bearing any bastard child," he said. "It doesn't look to me like any of these charges are going to stick."

My father's face was suffused with fury, and beside him Neville looked nearly as angry. Both of them saw their carefully laid plans going awry. "I am not satisfied by the refutations," my father ground out. "I do not believe the queen was blameless, particularly in the matter of treating with foreign nations. I suspect some collusion with—with that scoundrel my daughter has decided to marry." He leaned forward on his throne, his eyes narrowed to evil slits. "And if you *have* shared secrets with spies," he said, "it is *you* who will be charged with treason and *you* who will be put to death."

Darius looked alarmed. "Majesty! I beg you! Shall I bring you proof of my innocence? In my bags—back in my room—there are contracts, deeds of sale, descriptions of the most common wares. Let me go fetch them—"

He made as if to dash for the door, but Harwin caught him by the collar of his jacket and hauled him roughly back. "I knew you could not be trusted to marry the princess," Harwin growled. "I knew you were a charlatan and an opportunist. I would be *glad* to see you hanged for treason."

My father's rage was starting to subside as he saw a chance of salvaging this disastrous morning. He even managed a very unpleasant smile. "Yes, and you will be hanged," he said silkily, "if you do not recant your testimony."

Harwin jerked on Darius's coat, practically choking him. "Throw yourself at the king's feet and plead for your life, you commoner," he said contemptuously. He dragged Darius up to the stage, while Darius continued to bleat that he was innocent, he was blameless, he had intended the king no harm—

His smile growing, my father leaned down and took Darius's chin in his hand. "Now tell me," he purred. "Who exactly was meeting with the representatives of Amlertay and Newmirot? Was it you? Or was it the queen?"

Darius lifted both hands in an unthinking gesture of lèse-majesté, and wrapped them around the king's wrist. "My liege—"

"Who deserves punishment?" my father whispered.

Darius whispered back, "You do."

And when the brief gold flash of sorcery evaporated, Darius was holding on to the forepaw of a small, furry black dog.

There were screams. Shouts. Swords drawn, doors thrown open. Soldiers rushed in; servants dashed up and down the hallways. The little black dog snapped and howled and scurried from one end of the dais to the other, snapping some more. He was a nasty little cur, his teeth bared in a permanent snarl; if Darius had been close enough to bite, no doubt the dog would have chomped hard on the magician's arm.

But Darius had used more of that magic to whisk himself out the door, and he was nowhere to be found.

We were left with an exonerated queen, a trio of flabbergasted councilors, and one elated princess.

And her betrothed.

Epilogue

THE HAPPY ENDING

There were any number of loose ends to tie up, of course.

Milton and Norbert instantly had soldiers grab hold of Dannette, who showed no disposition to flee. Indeed, she offered to hold herself hostage to her brother's eventual return.

"I will happily stay at the palace until my brother realizes the enormity of his crime," she said. "I will be his living collateral."

Perhaps only I noticed the smile that passed between her and Gisele as Dannette made this generous offer.

Harwin immediately displayed his practical nature. "We must find fitting accommodations for the king as long as he is in this incarnation," he said as he and the councilors gathered to discuss a plan of action. "For surely the kennels will not do."

"Won't they?" I murmured, loud enough for only him to hear.

"And then we must proceed with a provisional installation of the princess," Harwin added. "She must govern the kingdom until her father is restored to his proper state."

"I will assume my duties with a heavy heart," I said, "but indeed, I must assume them before the day is out."

Neville still looked stunned at the turn of events that had dashed all his hopes, but Norbert and Milton appeared quite willing to see me on the throne, at least for the time being.

"But who will the princess marry now?" Norbert said with a frown. "That fellow won the competition!"

"I will have to make do with the only other man who passed the tests my father devised so carefully to ensure my happiness," I said soulfully. "Sir Harwin will be my husband. Very soon."

Harwin's father did not look in the least displeased. "Not a bad day's work, then," he said, earning a glare from Neville and a smile from Norbert.

"Not a bad day at all," Norbert echoed.

I didn't say so aloud, but I heartily agreed.

* * *

I was very busy, of course, in the intervening hours, but after lunch I did have time to slip away to the gardens, where Darius was awaiting me by prearrangement. Laughing, I ran up and flung myself into his arms.

"You were brilliant!" I exclaimed. "Magnificent! I cannot believe we were able to pull it off!"

He swung me around in one full circle, then set me on my feet. "And Gisele is safe?" he asked urgently. "And Dannette?"

"The councilors have apologized to Gisele and she is totally restored to her former position," I said. "I have noted very solemnly that I will rely on her for guidance in the days ahead, and she has replied solemnly in turn that she will do anything she can to aid me. Dannette expressed great chagrin to learn her brother is such a rogue and she has offered to do whatever it takes to make up for your crime. I believe Norbert plans to have her confined to the palace, at least for the time being, but she seems to be quite pleased at her sentence."

"Dannette never did like roving as much as I did," Darius replied. "A settled home and a familiar hearth constitute her idea of bliss, whereas I find the very notion of staying in one place for more than a day or two—" He shivered and did not complete his sentence.

"The very notion sounds like death to you," I said calmly. "Which is why I cannot marry you, much as I adore you."

He peered at me anxiously. "I cannot marry anyone," he admitted. "But I feel dreadful about it. I know I have let you down."

"I'm going to marry Harwin," I said. "The thought makes me quite happy, actually."

Now he looked relieved. "He's a very good fellow," he said. "No one I would rather see you with! But it seems a little unfair. I won the competitions, after all, but I don't get to marry the princess. I never even got a chance to kiss her."

I tilted my face up. "There's one last opportunity."

He didn't need to be invited twice, and he laid a most enthusiastic kiss upon my mouth. "Oh, now," he said, lifting his head and giving me a devilish smile, "I liked that so much I might want to stay another day."

I laughed and pushed him in the chest. "No, you must go before someone finds you. But you must come back, you know—in disguise, perhaps, but as often as you can bear it."

"I will," he promised. "And whenever I return, you will have to let me know if it is time to change your father back to a man."

"Well, I will," I said, "but I don't think that day will come soon."

He kissed me again, touched a finger to my cheek, and spun away into a golden sparkle. When my eyes cleared, he was gone, and not even his shadow remained.

I sighed a moment, remembering his blond curls, his happy air, his good heart. And then I shook my head and remembered my *true* fiancé, with his steady soul, his deep affection, and a very good heart of his own.

We would be married soon—by week's end, if I had my way, and I always did. But before then, there was so much else to take care of! I must settle my father in his new quarters, make sure Dannette was comfortably situated, confer with Gisele, meet with my advisors, and write a proclamation for my subjects. And there would be much to do *after* the wedding as well—learning about trades and tariffs, outlawing the ownership of fighting dogs, changing the laws of inheritance, and generally becoming the very best monarch I could be. Oh, and doing everything in my power to secure a lifetime of happiness—for me and for everyone I cared about.

And if I didn't achieve that final goal, it damn well wouldn't be for lack of trying.